DARK VALENTINE

A DARK VISTA ROMANCE

Visit us at www.boldstrokesbooks.com

What Reviewers Say About The Author

"Fulton has rescued the romance from formulaic complacency by asking universal questions about friendship and love, intimacy and lust. The answers reflect both depth and maturity; this is the romance novel grown up a bit. Girl gets girl is always popular; more inspirational is when the girl gets to know herself."—*The Lesbian Review of Books*

"Fulton takes an age old formula for love and plants it in modern surroundings. The writing is smart and quick, and she portrays innocence with loving, irresistible humor. She delivers flesh-warming, flush-inducing seduction and pages of slippery, richly textured sex. Her knack for depicting current social dilemmas also makes her a compelling contemporary author."—*The Lesbian Review of Books*

"Fulton has penned another wonderfully readable, erotically-charged book...fun, and well worth your time."—*Lambda Book Report*

"Fulton tells a dark and disturbing tale of friendship and betrayal, of love lost before it has a chance to begin. That may sound rather hackneyed but her use of these themes is anything but trite. The writing is outstanding...Fulton creates characters that live on in the memory and in the heart...An extraordinary novel. I could not put it down and days later, I'm still thinking about it."—*Bay Area Reporter*

"Perhaps needless to say, the paths the friendships take are fraught with, among other things, lust, unrequited love, infidelity and dishonesty. Good intentions are trampled in the pursuit of passion. Problems, both past and present, shape the relationships the women share...The writing is sharp...a realistic account of contemporary urban lesbian life."—*Melbourne Star Observer*

"The ending left me grinning to myself for hours and wishing for an immediately available sequel...One of the best writers on the roster...Her books are always entertaining and often thought provoking."—*Dimensions*

"I'm not sure why I found the book so completely erotic. The author knows how to tease and how to deliver."—*Lesbiana*

"One of those books that is hard to put down until you finish it... Whether you're in the perfect relationship or still looking for it, you'll enjoy this story."—*MegaScene*

By the Author

ROMANCES as Jennifer Fulton

Moon Island Series

Passion Bay

Saving Grace

The Sacred Shore

A Guarded Heart

Dark Vista Series

Dark Dreamer

Dark Valentine

Others

True Love

Greener Than Grass

More Than Paradise

CONTEMPORARY FICTION as Grace Lennox

Chance

MYSTERIES as Rose Beecham

Amanda Valentine Series

Introducing Amanda Valentine

Second Guess

Fair Play

Jude Devine Series

Grave Silence

Sleep of Reason

DARK VALENTINE

A DARK VISTA ROMANCE

by

Jennifer Fulton

2007

CREDITS
EDITOR: SHELLEY THRASHER
PRODUCTION DESIGN: STACIA SEAMAN
COVER DESIGN BY SHERI (GRAPHICARTIST2020@HOTMAIL.COM)

Acknowledgments

I worked on this novel with the love and support of the women who make my life make sense: Fel, Sophie, Wyn—my mother, and JD. My daughter Sophie also carried out research and gave useful feedback as I worked.

Shelley Thrasher edited with her usual sensitivity, for which I am very thankful. Sheri has designed another wonderful cover. She always manages to turn any lame idea I might suggest into a concept that much more accurately reflects the story.

Radclyffe's friendship and mentoring make a qualitative difference to my work, and for that I am in her debt.

Dedication

For Karen, brave and darling friend.

CHAPTER ONE

The survival instinct eclipsed all. Perception. Reason. Despair.

Rhianna Lamb knew the feeling. Dangling a cocktail napkin into her wine, she collected the insect flailing in the ruby liquid and lifted it to safety. As she gently shook the napkin beneath the table, she felt someone behind her.

In a throaty bass, a woman asked, "If I tell you I'm drowning, will you save me, too?"

Rhianna looked up and met bold, dark eyes the color of wet shale. They were a little creased in the corners, like the owner's mouth, and just as shamelessly sensuous. The face did not belong to the woman she'd expected to meet here.

"Well, that would depend," she responded.

A sigh. "That's cold."

"It's a harsh world." Rhianna could easily expand on that topic, but she was not sitting here wearing a slutty dress and dangerously high heels to have a deep and meaningful dialogue.

She stole a look at the clock above the bar. Her date was an hour late. Louise was supposed to be driving over from Los Angeles that afternoon. Maybe she'd been held up along the way. Rhianna had tried her cell-phone number several times, but all she got was voice mail. She supposed she should have known better than to plan a face-to-face with someone she'd met online. Anything could go wrong, and obviously had. She and Louise—if that was even her name—had exchanged pics three weeks ago and had spoken on the phone several times, planning this meeting. If Louise had cold feet, why not say so? How rude to simply not show up.

Rhianna let her gaze travel slowly over the stranger who had unknowingly taken her place. She had already decided not to have unrealistic expectations about her date. She would have settled for a seven out of ten, maybe even a five with decent manners and clean fingernails. But the woman standing at her table was fantasy material. A ten, and then some.

Rhianna glanced at the hands held loosely at her sides. No nervous fidgeting. They were streamlined and beautiful, the nails short and perfectly manicured.

"I have other pickup lines if you would like to hear them," the woman offered.

"Well, since I've been stood up," Rhianna smiled at her, "why not?"

The stranger promptly pulled the two spare chairs out from the table, asking, "May I?"

"Be my guest," Rhianna invited.

The woman pushed one chair into a gap at a next table before occupying the other. "How to score. The second rule—discourage rivals."

Rhianna laughed. "You got rid of the extra chair to stop anyone else from joining us?"

"Absolutely. And my proof...ball cap and attitude at nine o'clock?" She indicated an athletic brunette with her back propped against the bar counter. "I think she got the message."

Rhianna had noticed the woman at the bar just before the insect episode. She'd felt someone watching her but had paid her prickling nerves no mind. She hadn't come this far to be undone by her own paranoia. "Okay, if the second rule is to scuttle the competition, what's the first rule?"

Without batting an eye, the stranger said, "She who hesitates masturbates. I'm Jules, by the way." She stretched out her hand.

First names only. Good idea. Rhianna took the hand. As her cool palm connected with warm, firm flesh, she offered the name she'd been using for the past six months. "I'm Kate."

"That's my mother's name."

"It must be a sign," Rhianna said with a dry edge.

"Spoken like a true cynic. How about this—I buy you a drink without a bug in it, and you tell me why you're as romantically disenchanted as I am?"

Rhianna grinned. She had no plans to go down that track. Keeping their conversation strictly superficial, she teased, "What will you disclose in exchange?"

Jules smiled lazily and her eyes dropped to Rhianna's breasts, earning a taut response from her nipples. "My room number."

"Very smooth." Rhianna's belly took a nosedive and she realized she no longer gave a damn what had happened to her online hookup.

Jules moved her chair a little closer, and Rhianna caught the scent of her. Subtle. Mildly spicy with a trace of something mouth-watering, like rich chocolate. "When I'm hitting on a woman who could have anyone," Jules said, "I try harder."

Was such determined banter the norm in this type of situation? Rhianna did not usually meet women in bars, so she had no idea. Even attending the occasional lesbian fundraiser, she had never encountered anyone who could flirt as slickly as this woman. She decided Jules had probably done speed dating.

Trying to sound more lighthearted than she felt, she replied, "I take it the third rule involves paying insincere compliments."

"On the contrary." In earnest deadpan, Jules said, "My most brazen flattery is reserved for women who rescue fruit flies from their wine. Everyone else just gets a comment about their great shoes."

Rhianna burst out laughing, surprised to find herself charmed by this unsubtle pickup technique. "I have to tell you, the drinks aren't that good here. No one should have to die for one, not even an insect."

Warm indulgence flooded Jules's expression. "You sound like a Jain, although I guess you wouldn't be sitting here imbibing alcohol if you were."

"I'm impressed. Most people have never heard of the Jain."

Jules gave a self-effacing shrug. "I knew the comparative religion studies would pay off one day."

This was how it was done, Rhianna thought, no pretense that anyone was going to exchange a life history or even talk about their pets. Some amusing verbal sparring, then sex. They both knew what they were negotiating, and Jules was clearly at ease with the transaction. Rhianna wondered if she had any idea that she was flirting with a woman who was faking it. Probably not. The trashy dress had turned out to be a good investment, making up for her lack of natural charisma.

Rhianna had left the more elegant clothes she owned back home in her closet for this trip. In her last job as a fashion buyer, she had accumulated a wardrobe of carefully chosen high-end garments that were more subtle than sexy. None of them had seemed appropriate for the occasion she was planning when she set out for Palm Springs.

Striving to send the right signals and not to allow her body language to betray her, she tilted her head back just enough to emphasize her breasts. Then she slid a finger slowly around the neckline of her dress as if to loosen it a little, a laughable idea for a bodice so skimpy she might as well be wearing lingerie.

"Tell me honestly," Jules said. "Is there a line you *haven't* heard tonight?"

"Actually, I've been sitting here for more than an hour and you're the first woman who's talked to me."

"Seriously?" Jules glanced around the room with an expression of incredulous derision. "That's the best news I've heard all day."

"Brazen flattery again?"

"There's plenty more where that came from if you want to hang out with me. But first, are you taken?"

Rhianna hesitated. She hadn't been "taken" for almost a year, and hadn't wanted to be. "Not lately."

The stone-dark eyes glittered. "I would be honored to end that, er…dry patch for you. Interested?"

"Hmm…let me think about that." Rhianna hoped her stalling tactic sounded mischievous instead of dubious.

Her companion responded with a knowing smile. "Oh, don't be coy. You've been thinking about it ever since this afternoon. I saw you cruising me by the pool."

Rhianna stiffened in surprise. "You're staying at Casitas Laquita, too?"

"As luck would have it." Jules's stare burned so hot Rhianna's skin felt flushed. "Convenient, huh?"

The woman she'd seen lounging under a shade umbrella earlier in the day had been wearing dark glasses and a visor. Rhianna pictured Jules in a tankini. Yes, hers could definitely be the body that had made reading impossible. Rhianna had fantasized about stretching out alongside that body, letting skin slide against skin. She had even imagined a kiss. Now, incredibly, she was just inches away from the lips that could deliver on that daydream. She promptly froze with anxiety.

I need a stiff drink. Several, in fact. "I didn't recognize you fully dressed," she said unevenly.

"That's easily fixed."

Here it was, the offer she'd been waiting for; and here she was, stranded at the same impasse that made her turn back every time. Rhianna drained her wine and reached for the tumbler standing to one side. She gulped down some water and let an ice cube slide into her mouth to soothe the rough tension clamping her throat. No matter how hard she tried to move forward, sex stopped her in her tracks. That's why she was sitting here in this bar, feeling self-conscious in a dress any porn star would be proud of, with her flaxen hair cut short, dyed Titian red, and thinned so the ends were wispy.

She had come to Palm Springs with this exact scenario in mind, a hookup with a desirable stranger she would never have to see again. No-strings sex with someone who knew zero about her other than a few details exchanged online. The plan had seemed brilliant when she first hatched it, the perfect solution to her problem. It was time to reclaim her body and rid herself of the sense memories that haunted her. She would maintain complete control, dictating all the terms for the encounter so she would be touched only as she wanted to be touched. Now, thanks to good luck rather than good management, the perfect opportunity was sitting across the table from her. All she had to do was say yes, but paralysis had set in.

All of a sudden, her expectations seemed completely unrealistic. Only the most robotic person would patiently await a partner's cues and commands and behave like a toy. The woman hitting on her didn't seem the passive, obedient type. How was this ever going to work? Rhianna had thought it would be easier to sleep with a stranger than someone she knew. But without trust, how could there be physical intimacy? How could she explain what she needed?

Masking her unease with what she hoped was a playful, sexy look, she said, "You don't waste any time. What happened to verbal foreplay?"

"I can go there," Jules drawled, "if it's a prerequisite."

Rhianna's stomach hollowed, and her nipples scraped against the thin silk knit of her dress. "Then let's go there."

"An invitation to talk dirty…there is a God."

Pushing her empty wineglass aside, Rhianna said, "It's time to buy me that drink. Grey Goose, please. Make it a double."

Normally she didn't mix spirits and wine, but she thought something stronger would calm her nerves. She felt disoriented. It wasn't like her to have one-night stands; in fact, this would be her first. But the old rules no longer applied, and the woman she once was no longer existed. All she needed to do was switch off her mind and allow her body to react naturally. It was happening already, unless stress was to blame for her pounding heart and the heat in her cheeks.

She watched Jules saunter to the bar. The walk said it all. She was stunning and she knew it. Her look was plain. White tee, casual black pants, black loafers with the same matte finish as the belt at her waist. Her build was lithe, her movements graceful, her height a little taller than average. She was the only woman Rhianna had ever seen who could wear a ponytail without looking girly. Her hair was dead straight and just long enough to be clubbed back at her nape with a thin satin ribbon. The style flaunted a face that lodged insistently in memory, the lines cleanly sculptured, the nose and jaw strong, the eyes set deep.

She was handsome more than beautiful, Rhianna thought. Nothing was quite perfect. Her mouth was slightly uneven. A small scar bisected her left eyebrow, creating a slight quirk. Her cheekbones weren't prominent enough for classic beauty, and the planes below seemed muscular, not soft.

When she returned, she placed their drinks on the table and bent so that her mouth drifted by Rhianna's ear. "Like what you see?"

"Very much." Rhianna turned her head, but did not allow her lips to graze the cheek so close to her own. She felt Jules shiver.

"But you're going to make me work for it?"

Rhianna felt something soft on her cheek, and she realized Jules was blowing on it. Warm breath teased a path down her neck, making her body ache. She had not realized how desperately she missed touch. So much had been spoiled for her, so much taken away.

For the past nine months she had lived each day, one at a time, with an overwhelming sense of loss: Her peace of mind. Her job satisfaction. Her sense of herself as a full and functioning person. Her confidence as a woman and a lover. Her hopes and dreams. Everything. Werner Brigham had robbed her of the self she was, leaving a crippled ghost to inhabit her skin.

Physically she had changed too, so much that sometimes she almost failed to recognize herself as she walked by windows and applied lipstick in restroom mirrors. Stress made some people eat; Rhianna had lost her appetite instead. She had dropped over thirty pounds in the past year and every soft line seemed sharp now, her face angular, her jawline emphatic, her eyes bigger because everything else was smaller.

There were days when she wondered if she would ever feel fully alive again, if the woman she had been would ever return, or if this was it and she would have to reinvent herself. Rhianna stole a darting glance toward the exit. She could leave now and forget this whole crazy plan. It had been a big mistake to imagine she could pull this off. She stared down at the liquid swaying back and forth in her glass. A hand firmly closed over her own, arresting its trembling.

"What's wrong? Is it something I said?" Jules tightened her grip. The hand beneath hers felt small, she thought, and unexpectedly square, suggesting a practical nature.

A pair of bright, expressive eyes lifted to hers. They were not exactly green. Nor were they brown. They were dappled, like sunshine spilling across foliage. A delicate feathering of dark eyelashes screened them just enough to suggest shyness. There was something else in the wide-eyed stare, too. Distress.

Jules glanced around, almost expecting the looming figure of a jealous girlfriend, fists swinging. Before she could be certain of what she'd glimpsed, Kate's expression changed.

"I'm fine. I was just thinking…To be quite honest, I don't normally pick up women in bars."

Cold feet. Jules knew she should have bought that drink sooner. Keeping her tone light and noncommittal, she said, "Feel free to hone your technique on me."

Everyone had their sorrows and inadequacies, herself included. Jules could sense the woman opposite her retreating by the moment. In fact, she half-expected her to leap up and scuttle away into the shadows. She was as nervous and tightly coiled as a trapped animal, sitting rigidly in her chair as though chained to the table. She was probably planning her escape, rehearsing some lame excuse she would make as soon as she'd finished her vodka. Not exactly the willing sexual accomplice Jules had hoped for.

She stole a glance around the bar and concluded that Kate might be a shaky possibility, but she was the *only* possibility. The place was jammed with retired women out socializing with their friends, bisexuals hitting on each other while hubby looked on, and youngsters who probably lived at home with Mom and Dad. Jules had stopped sleeping with the early twenties when she was in high school.

She returned her attention to Kate and was struck anew by the perfection of her skin. Its tone was even and lightly tanned. The woman was deliciously touchable. Her chest and shoulders glowed like she'd had some sun recently. Her hair was shot with gold, shimmering in fine streaks through the copper. It was layered and chin-length, its slightly ragged cut calling attention to an unusual face, wide at the cheekbones and narrowing to a small chin. She had dimples when she smiled, and it was a great smile. Warm and real.

Jules had already been stopped dead by that smile several times today. The first of these occasions was still fresh in her mind. She'd just parked her car outside the peach walls of Casitas Laquita, and Kate had been standing a few feet away talking to one of the owners.

When the women went their separate ways, Kate smiled a farewell that transformed her face so completely, Jules could only stare in astonishment and wonder if she was seeing a movie star trying to keep a low profile.

The slender beauty from earlier in the day, wearing the loose linen shirt and rolled-hem shorts, was nothing like the sophisticate sitting opposite her now. Kate's clinging halter dress and stilettos were the last thing Jules would have picked out for her. The flesh-and-flash outfit and the woman wearing it had certainly gotten her attention as she walked in the door, no doubt the desired effect.

But Kate didn't seem comfortable in the kind of trophy-wife clothing Jules was used to seeing at South Beach when she partied with the team from the Miami office. Her body language and micro-expressions were at odds with her seductive appearance, and now that Jules was paying closer attention, she could read between those lines. The only reason a nice girl steps out wearing fuck-me clothes is to prove something. She ran through the obvious possibilities. Recently broken up and trying to get back in the game. Straight and in a lesbian bar on a dare, her friends waiting outside.

Jules sighed. It would be nice, for a change, if she could take something or someone at face value, if she were not trained to read the most subtle cues. Life would be so much simpler.

She watched Kate get serious with her vodka, draining the glass in a series of gulps. Her skin was flushed and her movements were losing their grace.

"Another?" Jules asked.

Kate looked slightly dazed. Her eyes dropped to her empty glass and registered surprise. "Oh, I finished it."

"You did." Jules waited for her to decide she'd had enough, but Kate gave a nonchalant shrug.

"Thanks, I will have another."

Jules was never comfortable sleeping with a woman who'd had too much to drink. But the night was wearing on and she wanted to get out of here, preferably with company. Resigning herself to being the designated driver, she returned to the bar.

Less than five minutes later Kate was downing the next double like it was water.

Jules said, "Whoa. You might want to slow down."

"I'm not drunk." Kate giggled. "Okay, maybe a little."

If she didn't want to carry this woman out, it was time to leave. "How about this?" Jules suggested. "Let's go back to Casitas, change into comfortable clothes, and have a nightcap by the pool."

"Yes, good idea." Kate fiddled awkwardly with her handbag. It fell on the floor, spilling half its contents beneath the table. "Oh, I'm sorry."

"No need to apologize." Jules shoveled everything back into the purse and returned it. Any minute the multiple vodkas would kick in and Kate would be non compos mentis. Jules wrote her room number on a cocktail napkin and slid it across the table. "This is where you can find me. See how you feel when we get back. If you want to call it a night, fine. If you don't, just dial the room. And the other thing…"

"Yes?"

"I'm not expecting anything. Do you understand?"

A wobbly smile. "Yes."

"Come on. Let's get out of here." Jules helped her up and escorted her toward the door, a guiding hand at the base of her spine. "I'll drive you. No argument."

Kate acquiesced without a word, and Jules let her hand drift slightly lower. The arch of her back was so very tempting, she had to exercise self-control not to caress it, not to slide her hand down to cup the rounded perfection of her butt. However, this was not the time to unsettle her quarry with a hasty move. Jules hadn't abandoned her plan to spend the night with this woman, but she detected an ambivalence in her that rang alarm bells. Even if Kate wanted to give the impression that she knew the score, Jules had a feeling she was out of her depth.

Women had all kinds of reasons for hooking up with strangers, and Kate's were none of Jules's business. But if they slept together, the experience needed to be good for both of them; otherwise, what was the point? She opened the passenger door and waited for Kate to get settled. The dress was hitched up over one tempting thigh and as Kate fumbled with the seat belt, Jules got an eyeful of breasts so beautiful she almost whined.

Whatever this winsome babe's reservations were, Jules hoped she would get over them and decide to call her. As they drove back to the inn, she had her doubts. Kate was obviously a nice woman. *Probably too nice.*

CHAPTER TWO

Bad stuff happened to women all the time and they didn't turn into neurotic wrecks who couldn't stand to be touched.

Get over it! Rhianna ordered herself. She was spending money she couldn't afford, staying at a lesbian inn hundreds of miles from Oatman, Arizona, the ghost town she now called "home." She had been stood up by the woman she had traveled to see, and when a highly attractive alternative had presented itself she'd chickened out. What was wrong with her? She'd promised herself that no matter what, she would go through with this.

Perched on the end of her bed, she studied the digital clock on her night table, trying to bring the numbers into focus. Her head swam and she felt fuzzy and sluggish. Twenty minutes had passed since she'd showered and changed. She had hoped she would start sobering up by now. Instead she felt alternately giggly and sad.

It was crazy to hide in her room, she knew that. If she waited any longer Jules would give up on her. There were other women staying here, some cute and obviously single. Maybe one of them was out by the pool now, just waiting to offer hot sex. Rhianna had a mental flash of two bodies writhing in passion. She was immediately despondent. Even if she took Jules up on her offer, she'd probably blown her chances already. Jules had stopped flirting with her before they left the bar, and had hardly spoken a word all the way back to Casitas.

Rhianna wasn't sure how she felt about seeing her opportunity evaporate. Relieved. Let down. Frustrated. A dull, distant anger shadowed her like a dark mist, swirling around the edges of her thoughts, reminding her that she had failed to beat this thing. She had set out on this journey with a plan that seemed workable, but she had sabotaged herself. The truth was, she had lost control over her life and was too weak to take it back again. How pathetic.

She wished she could magically become someone else, not just change her clothes and hair so she looked like someone else. There were confident, sexy women everywhere. She wanted to feel like them. That breed of woman would not be sitting here alone in her room, feeling sorry for herself. She would be having a good time.

Impulsively, Rhianna picked up the phone and dialed room 28. She almost dropped the receiver when Jules answered.

"It's me. Rhi—" She coughed to cover her blunder. For a split second her false name eluded her. Trembling, she told herself *Kate Kate Kate*. "I'm sorry I took so long. I needed a shower. I'm quite drunk."

"I know."

"Thank you for driving me back here."

"You're welcome."

Rhianna held her breath as the silence between them grew. Jules was making her do the work. It was almost funny how frightened she was for no reason at all. The thought made her choke back a laugh. What was the worst thing that could happen? One of those fumbly, awkward encounters no one wants to think about the next morning?

On a sharp exhalation, she blurted, "Can we just go to bed?"

The pause that followed was long enough to rattle her. "If that's what you want."

"It is." Rhianna defied the voices hammering in the back of her mind.

"Then come on over. My door's open."

"Where's your room?"

"Next to yours." The tone was one of patient amusement.

Rhianna stifled hysterical laughter. How did she not know that? "Okay. I'm coming."

She dropped the phone back into its stand with a clatter. Her heart felt too big for her chest, crushing the air from her lungs. Before she had time to talk herself out of her decision, she marched out the door in the straightest line she could manage and fled into the clement night.

You won't be sorry, she promised herself. *This is going to change everything.*

❖

The shorts, the thin cotton shirt. Jules discarded them next to the bed. Tonight's plaything was braless and her breasts were fuller than Jules had expected, small perfectly shaped globes. They were lightly tanned like the rest of her, the nipples a tawny hue. As Jules worked the panties down she noted sparse ash hair and concluded she was about to sleep with a blonde.

She had already guessed that the brilliant coppery hair came from a bottle. Kate's skin was not the buttermilk pale usually sported by natural redheads, and there wasn't a freckle on her, not even across her shoulders. Her eyebrows and lashes were very dark, almost black, another giveaway. They could be dyed, but nature also bestowed that combination on blondes sometimes. Not that it mattered. Jules wasn't one of those people who had a thing for a certain hair or skin tone. So long as there was some chemistry, her prospective pillow friends only had to be clean and speak in complete sentences.

She ran her hands slowly down the beautiful body that was hers to pleasure, appreciating its sleek musculature. She wanted to be more excited than she felt, but she sensed an unease in Kate that kept her own arousal in check. Unsure whether she was queasy from alcohol or genuinely apprehensive, Jules asked, "Are you sure about this?"

The reply was tactile. One hand drifted up beneath Jules's tee to cup her right breast, the other found her cheek. Kate stepped in closer and her lips moved slowly against Jules's, sending a hot shock of awareness through her. "Let's not talk."

All of a sudden Jules was anchored in the moment, caught up

in a skin-prickling thrill of anticipation. Her mouth flooded. Desire gnawed, deep in her gut. Her nipples grew raw, grating tensely against the cotton of her tee. Too much time had slipped by without a woman. It had been months, and her body was letting her know all too plainly that relief was overdue. She stripped quickly. Her heart raced, her temples pounded, her clit pulsed. Her hands shook as she explored Kate's warm, smooth curves.

She took complete control of the kiss, parting the soft lips sealed to her own and propelling Kate firmly back against the bed. As the kiss intensified, Kate arched against her, clasping her hands firmly behind Jules's neck. When Jules paused for air, Kate begged, "Don't stop," and ground seductively against her.

"I haven't even started," Jules said.

She kissed a path along the goose-bumped plane from throat to shoulder and sank her teeth in just below the serpentine throb of the jugular. Cradled in her hands, Kate's breasts felt increasingly heavy with arousal. Jules nudged a knee between her thighs and applied pressure until Kate responded in kind, bearing down, moving her hips, opening her legs wider.

Wetness spread where Jules's thigh worked the crushable seam of flesh. Her own responses started galloping. Quite suddenly, she was desperate for touch and intent on the buildup before release. She could feel her own moisture gathering, her clit straining in appeal. She moved her palms back and forth against Kate's nipples while her own ached for attention.

Urgently, she murmured in Kate's ear, "Touch me."

Their eyes met, their hearts pounded together through fragile bone and flesh. Kate's pupils flooded huge and black within a ring of green gold. Her face was hard to read. For several seconds, she studied Jules, then she dragged a single fingertip from her bottom lip to her sternum. There was a subtle alteration in her expression, a breath unevenly released. Her gaze seemed inward-looking, and for a fleeting instant Jules had a sense that just being present took all the emotional energy she had.

Before she could confirm her impression, Kate's eyes grew bright with avid concentration and she turned her attention to Jules's breasts, teasing her fingers over the sensitive skin. With perfect pressure, she flattened both hands over the nipples and toyed mercilessly with them. At the same time, her mouth wreaked havoc, sucking, kissing, and biting until Jules could hardly stay upright. She yelped softly as her nipples were clamped between Kate's fingers and tugged hard. Sweat broke across her forehead, and naked craving stole through her veins, making her limbs heavy with supplication.

"Does it hurt?"

Jules couldn't tell if the question was a tease or if Kate was really concerned. Her expression seemed glazed. Transfixed with lust, or just drunk and barely holding it together? Jules hoped she wouldn't pass out before they could both get off.

"It hurts good," she replied thickly.

Kate smiled and lowered her head to add yet another exquisite sensation to the mix. Her tongue roved from one nipple to the other, both still jutting between the fingers that compressed them. Jules groaned, captive suddenly to the need boiling up from deep in her core, seeking an answer in naked, hard coupling. She caught Kate's wrists, flung her hands aside, and toppled her roughly onto the bed. She had intended to indulge in a slow, languorous seduction, but it was too late. Her body had been condemned to solitary confinement for too long.

She moved over Kate, scissoring their legs and coming to rest where the pressure at her groin was most intense. Both breathing unevenly, they released small pants as they built a rhythm together. Kate splayed her legs wider and Jules bore down, sinking fast into a hot oblivion of desire.

She wanted to roll over and push Kate down between her own legs, but at the same time she loved being right here, climbing the razor's edge of arousal before the inevitable plummet to release. She wanted to stretch time, to wring every ounce of divine yearning from the moment, but she was always so driven, so hungry to reach the pinnacle. Past experience had taught her self-discipline and she called upon the art now, breaking her single-minded focus just enough to impose her will. Holding back was always worth it. When her tension finally shattered and she fell into orgasm, the plunge would be all the more profound.

Shifting her weight to one elbow, she zeroed in on the slippery gateway of flesh where Kate's body opened to hers. She drew her fingers slowly back and forth, her focus sharpened by adrenaline. A rush of awe stifled her breathing as she looked down to watch her fingers slowly vanish between the parted folds. Even if she had wanted to switch focus to her own clamoring body, she couldn't. She was too caught up in the wetness and beauty that were hers to enjoy.

Her fingers were gripped and drawn deeper. Kate's eyelids fluttered, and she stared up at Jules with a disturbing mix of intensity and cool distance. An uncertain silence stretched out between them. Was Kate a participant in this feverish ritual or an onlooker? Jules could not tell. She stilled her hand, aware of a disconnect.

Seeking a way to check in without destroying the mood, she murmured, "More?"

"Yes." Her accomplice seemed fully present again. "Don't stop."

Jules changed position, trailing kisses down Kate's belly, drawing upon her honeyed tang until all doubt was locked out and there was room only for sensation. Their bodies moved in synch and Jules finally felt attuned to the subtle cues she'd missed until now. Kate's fingers signaled her needs, sliding across Jules's scalp, playing a delicate staccato of stop and go. As her arousal climbed, her soft moans became guttural and the roll of her hips more pronounced.

Jules extended her tongue across the arch of flesh she'd already stroked rigid. Seeking out the tiny gleaming organ it sheltered, she gently sucked and pressured. Her steady, insistent caresses drew sharp little begging cries, and she moved down the bed so she could adjust the angle of her hand. Kate's body slithered against hers with unmistakable craving. She was close, so close. Shivering. Pink-faced. Her head thrown back like she had lost all track of time, place, and even the presence of another. She seemed far away in her own private universe, spellbound in her surrender.

Jules suppressed a selfish urge to speak her name and summon her into the present just because she wanted to feel joined on some level other than the purely physical. Intimacy, no matter how casual, was always more than a mere transaction of the flesh for her.

Something else had to exist when two people conspired to grant each other pleasure, if only a shared recognition that the sacred could be found in all physical union.

Eventually, Jules felt the muscles around her fingers compress, and a small quivering ripple augured the tremors to follow. Breathing hard, she surfaced from between Kate's legs, wanting to watch. She loved to see a woman come.

Kate needed no more stimulation. A hoarse, involuntary cry of release tore from her as spasms rocked her body. Eventually, leaving her fingers snugly sheathed, Jules slid her free arm beneath her panting companion and coaxed her into an embrace. They lay, in wordless aftermath, their bodies heaving together at first, then settling into satisfaction.

As her own deep, sweet pulses subsided, Rhianna allowed herself to sink onto Jules's chest, taking refuge in the warm press of flesh and bone. Peace stole over her and she drifted in a haze of serenity. Her breathing slowed. Lulled by the hypnotic thunder of Jules's heart, she felt incredibly safe for the first time in months. For a long while, they lay communing like two solitary travelers who found themselves stranded on the same lonely road.

Rhianna felt a small pang as Jules's hand eased free of its hot, wet cocoon. Holding her even closer, Jules said, "I can tell this was hard for you, and I'm not sure why. Is everything okay?"

Self-conscious, and surprised that this woman had picked up on her wavering emotions, Rhianna said, "It wasn't anything you did. You're a very good lover."

"So are you." Jules's mouth brushed her hair and her cheek. "And when you get your breath back, I'd like to take advantage of that."

Their lips met. Eyes closed, they kissed deeply.

"Will you do something for me?" Rhianna asked, then wished she had simply kept quiet. Did she really want to put into words the fantasy that preyed on her mind? What would Jules think of her?

"Talk to me," Jules whispered. "Tell me what you want."

"Can I tie you up?" Rhianna prepared herself for dismay and shock, but there was only the briefest hesitation.

"Do you want me to resist?"

"No. I just want to…" Rhianna thought, *Be serious.* A complete stranger could not be expected to consent to some kind of bondage scenario. She was puzzled by the urge to act out this fantasy. Normally, she was vanilla in her desires. Embarrassed, she said, "It doesn't matter. Forget I even asked."

But Jules was smiling. "Don't try to make sense of a fantasy. I'm cool with being tied up, and if something doesn't feel right, I'll tell you I've had enough. And that's when we stop. Okay?"

She was making it irresistibly easy. "Really?"

"So long as you don't leave me naked and hog-tied for housekeeping to find in the morning."

Rhianna giggled. She wasn't sure if her reaction was from nerves, discomfort, or excitement.

"I'll even help," Jules said matter-of-factly. She detached herself and got out of bed. A few seconds later she returned with some nylon stockings.

"Do you wear those?" Rhianna asked.

"Sometimes. For work. Think they'll do the job?" She looped one untidily around her wrist. All the while her gaze devoured Rhianna, a predatory glint calling into question who was really in control.

Rhianna sat up and took the stockings from her. "Lie down on the bed," she said. "On your back. Spread your legs."

Many hours later as Rhianna located her clothing, Jules asked, "Where do you live?"

"Near Vegas."

"I'm based in L.A. but I work for a national firm. They send me all over."

Although she sensed Jules intended the disclosure as an opening, Rhianna didn't ask about her job. She didn't want to start down that getting-to-know-each-other track. They were done, and in a few hours' time she would be driving back to Oatman, "mission accomplished."

She glanced toward the windows they'd opened during the

night, when the hot tangle of the sheets was too much. The chill of the desert morning made her shiver, and she pulled on her panties and shorts, then looked around for her bra and realized she hadn't worn one. Her breasts felt full and her nipples incredibly tender. She was sore, too. Every time she took a step her panties teased her still-swollen sex, and she could feel the imprint of Jules's hands and mouth all over her body, smoldering reminders of the night before.

The sensations unsettled her. She had expected to wake up this morning with her sense of self at least partially restored. She had thought she would fully "own" her body once more, that she would feel inviolate and in complete control. Instead, she was aware of an unwelcome connectedness to the woman languidly watching her from the bed. Unable to separate memory from craving, Rhianna averted her eyes, feeling exposed.

"I'd like to see you again." As if taking agreement for granted, Jules continued, "I was thinking we could come back here since it's pretty convenient for both of us. Once a month, maybe, for a long weekend. I could probably make that happen."

"I'm not looking for anything ongoing," Rhianna said.

Jules elbowed her way up the bed until she was sitting back against the pillows. She was even more striking in the watery light of early morning. A little crumpled, her mouth slightly swollen and her eyes bedroom-heavy. She ran a hand over her hair, and Rhianna couldn't help but recall the feel of those blue-black strands gliding silkily between her fingers the night before.

"I'm not asking you to marry me," Jules said. "But I thought we were pretty good together."

"I thought so, too," Rhianna conceded. "And I appreciate the offer."

"But this is good-bye?"

"It is."

Jules seemed confused, then her eyes hardened with a flash of comprehension. "You have someone?"

Rhianna supposed she could just take the easy way out and let this woman believe she had cheated on a partner. But the idea was somehow unpalatable. "No, I don't. And to be quite honest, I prefer to keep it that way."

"I understand. Look, I don't have time for commitment either, so we're on the same page. And life's short. Why not enjoy?"

"I'm sure there are plenty of women who'd be thrilled to take you up on an offer like that," Rhianna said.

Jules studied her closely as if she found her responses puzzling. "Frankly, picking up women in bars is getting old."

"Then maybe you ought to bite the bullet and get a regular girlfriend."

"Is that an offer?" The arrogant charm of the night before was still in evidence, but it was tempered with a softness that surprised Rhianna and complicated her feelings.

She made a show of looking around for her room key. She felt awkward for all kinds of reasons, and she needed to terminate this conversation. The idea of seeing Jules again was far too tempting. Already she was rationalizing the possibility, thinking like a crazy woman. They could meet for another long weekend and get to know each other better. Maybe she could even invite Jules to Oatman sometime when the Mosses were away.

"You're very determined," she said.

"So I'm told."

"And not used to a woman saying no?"

Jules laughed. "I don't run into it too often."

Rhianna slid her feet into the sandals she'd left near the bedroom door. "Well, don't take it personally."

Jules crossed the room to stand in front of her, tempting in a white tee and nothing else. She slid an arm around Rhianna's waist and gave her a long, hard look. Then she kissed her like she mattered. "So, it's good-bye."

Rhianna leaned into her embrace, imprinting the feel of another body against hers. "Thank you for spending the night with me."

"It was a pleasure."

"For me, too."

Rhianna drew back and studied Jules's face. Close up, each feature was highly individual. Combined, they assumed an androgynous beauty that would turn heads, no matter who was looking. Rhianna committed every detail to memory. The gray-black eyes flecked with indigo. The sensual mouth. The strong chin and nose. The small vertical cleft in each cheek. A strange sorrow claimed her. She wished the numbness would recede from her chest so that she could feel more. It seemed wrong somehow that her heart insisted on beating no matter what. There was a moment the night before when she'd wished it would just stop, when her mind was washed clean by the tide of her senses and all she knew was bliss. She could have died in that instant and been happy.

She leaned in and rested her cheek against Jules's. A hand slid over hers, clasping it gently. The eyes that sought her own were catlike in their unblinking calm.

"Take a chance and say yes to me," Jules said very softly. "You never know what might happen."

Rhianna could not find an answer that felt truthful or even honorable. She drew back, avoiding eye contact. "I can't."

Jules released her without further protest and Rhianna murmured a final good-bye. She could feel the gouge of Jules's stare as she walked away, but she did not look back.

CHAPTER THREE

Even if she hadn't smelled the burro droppings as she drew close to town, Rhianna would still have known where she was from the sounds of hollering and gunfire. She had arrived back in Oatman just in time for the daily traffic jam. Someone's Suburban was blocking the main street. The owners had probably fled at the sight of an armed gang approaching with guns drawn. Burros milled in anticipation, sticking their heads in car windows. A brawl between rival gangs meant traffic would remain at a standstill and passersby would linger to watch the drama unfold. For the wild burro population mayhem spelled one thing. Lunch.

Back in its gold-rush days, Oatman was a tent city jammed with miners who used the small, hairy beasts to haul their supplies. When the gold eventually ran out, they cut the overworked animals loose and left them to fend for themselves. Unlike their owners, the burros prospered, forming herds and successfully surviving in the wild. These days, their descendents roamed free in the hills around the town and wandered down each afternoon to beg for food.

Rhianna resigned herself to a long wait in the heat of the day while the male posturing went on. This afternoon one of the Bitter Creek boys had chosen to pick a fight with one of the Ghostriders. The rivals and their associates faced off in the middle of the traffic, cussing each other out.

Someone yelled, "You stole my woman!" and a volley of shots rang out. A man went down and all hell broke loose.

Uncomfortable in her stationary car, Rhianna opened the door and inhaled the familiar scent of desiccated poop and gun smoke. A gray burro immediately sidled up to claim the rest of the sandwich she'd purchased during the four-hour drive from Palm Springs. As the animal munched, various gunfighters blew each other away and, after the requisite death dance, collapsed onto the dusty street. The crowd cheered and clapped.

A woman in Victorian saloon-whore chic kicked one of the fallen men in the ribs and yelled, "Get up you lazy, no-good, cheap drunk. You owe me two dollars."

When he didn't respond, she strutted past a group of visitors standing beside a minibus draped with a banner that read BEN HUR SHRINERS FOR CRIPPLED CHILDREN BURN UNIT, GALVESTON. Today's charity, Rhianna surmised, fanning herself with the sandwich wrapper.

After a few minutes, the dust settled and the "dead" rose to pass the hat around and show off their six-guns to city slickers who had never seen a Colt Peacemaker. The tourists who kept Oatman solvent were lured with staged shootouts, panhandling, sidewalk egg fries, ladies strolling in 1890s costume, vintage cars, and a main street that looked like something from a Wild West movie, only it was the real McCoy.

The town had been named in honor of Olive Oatman, a young woman kidnapped by Apaches and sold to the Mohave, with whom she lived for five years before being ransomed for a horse and blankets. Despite public pressure to denounce her "savage" captors, Olive reported that she had been treated kindly and was never subjected to "unchaste abuse."

During the gold-mining boom, Oatman had a population of thousands, but when the mines closed in the 1920s a mass evacuation all but emptied the place, and the town's demise was cemented thirty years later when it was bypassed by the new Interstate 40. Truly a ghost town, it struggled along like many on the old Route 66, until nearby Laughlin, Nevada, became a gambling success story and tourists flocked to the area.

Before long these visitors began showing up in Oatman on a quest for the Old West. The few mavericks left running the town were happy to oblige the heritage seekers with a dose of authenticity, and they didn't even have to erect phony saloons, old-time general stores, or Western-façade dwellings. It was all here, and the ramshackle, forgotten-past glory of their town was virtually unmatched in the West. No one had spent a dime on maintenance for the past half century. Not on buildings and certainly not on roads.

There was only one way into town, and that was on a stretch of Route 66 infamous for its hazards. The blacktop road had seen a series of washouts that left RVs haplessly spinning their wheels in sand-filled potholes. These continued for about twelve miles and the intrepid motorists who made it past this obstacle course could then look forward to the Sitgreaves Pass, ten miles of shoulderless hairpin switchbacks, most of them blind, zigzagging through desert hillsides that routinely disgorged boulders onto the road. According to Rhianna's employers, "flatlanders" were so petrified of this pass that they sometimes paid locals to drive their cars across it. Accidents were a regular event, adding to the excitement of the drive and ensuring the local tow-truck driver could afford to dress his wife in Versace.

Despite its treacherous access, Oatman was a thriving backwater with a few hundred residents, most of whom kept abreast of one another's business. Rhianna had been made welcome when she arrived, but she was aware of a mixture of dubiousness and friendly resignation in her reception. New arrivals seldom stayed long, and no one made a big effort to befriend them until it looked like they might hang around.

When she'd first applied for the job she saw on Craigslist, her employers had warned her to expect the worst, describing Oatman as "a one-horse town, and that's not just a figure of speech." In case she harbored naïve illusions about the West, they had also pointed out that she was likely to be "bored to tears after a week" and the reason they paid well was because she would "need some compensation to live in the middle of nowhere and if you have a nervous breakdown, therapy doesn't come cheap." They'd already lost several nannies who could not cope with the isolation and lack of entertainment, and did not want to employ another one who would abandon them after a few weeks.

The Moss family had their spread just north of the town. Lloyd and Bonnie Moss were part owners of one of the smaller casinos in Laughlin and left their eighteen-month-old daughter at the ranch to be cared for by a nanny. When they took time out from managing the casino, they went traveling as a family. On those occasions the nanny served as a house sitter and had to make sure the ranch hands showed up for work. The job was about as easy as any job got, with employers who were so grateful that they gave regular paid vacations and even the use of a car so Rhianna didn't have to damage hers driving around the area.

The Mosses were genuine people, nothing like the glitzy casino-millionaire couple Rhianna had expected once she found out who they were. Sometimes she was even tempted to tell them her real name and her story, but it was too soon to take that risk, and she didn't want them to be needlessly concerned for their daughter's safety.

Rhianna had seen to it that no one knew where she was, not even her own family back in Denver. To communicate, she used disposable cell phones to call them and a mail-forwarding service. When she needed to e-mail someone, she drove to Vegas and used public Wi-Fi locations. Only her lawyer knew where she was and he said, with all the precautions she had taken, no one would ever find her. Not even Werner Brigham.

Rhianna stared out at the sign for Jackass Junction and allowed herself a satisfied smile. This was the very last place on earth anyone would look for her. And even if they did, who was going to link a nanny called Kate Lambert with Rhianna Lamb, the fashion buyer. Even her paychecks couldn't be traced. She had arranged for the Mosses to make automatic transfers into a bank account her attorney had set up for her. She used a Visa debit card to draw cash and make payments. It was issued to a registered business name: Kate Lambert Enterprises.

Rhianna Lamb had disappeared off the face of the earth, and anyone who tried to locate her would find nothing but dead ends. She was safe, and if loneliness was the price she had to pay, she was fine with that. All she cared about was peace of mind. She would never have guessed how much that mattered until she had to live without it.

❖

"You're home!" Bonnie Moss collected Rhianna in a hug.

She was the cuddly type who wore her emotions on her sleeve. Her dog was exactly the same. Hadrian, an English mastiff, was too old and stiff to leap up, but he greeted Rhianna with a flood of drool and shoved his meaty brindle head into her belly, almost knocking her off balance.

"Lloyd's at work, of course," Bonnie said. "But he'll be home tomorrow morning." She waved at a long, lean ranch hand smoking a cigarette in front of the stables and called, "Percy, can you bring Kate's bag into the house when you've had your break." Barely pausing for breath, she walked Rhianna toward the front entrance, one arm loosely around her waist. "How was Palm Springs? See any movie stars?"

Rhianna smiled. Her employer lived in hope that she would run into a Hollywood celebrity wandering through Laughlin one day and invite them back to the casino, where they would sit down for a meal with her and Lloyd and overshare about clandestine affairs and scandals on movie sets. Copies of *People* magazine were piled high next to her bed, and she had installed a custom-built home theater that had made the front page of the local newspaper. This featured an art-deco lobby, popcorn machine, tiered seating for ten, projection room, and curtains in front of the screen.

"I thought I saw Bruce Willis," Rhianna said, wanting to offer a near-thrill. "But it was just a bald guy trying to look like him."

Bonnie sighed. "Well, guess what I scored? You know the original *Goldfinger* poster I've been trying to find. I got it on eBay for nineteen hundred dollars. Unrolled and unfolded with the NSS stamp and everything. I was dying. The bidding went nuts."

"That's great," Rhianna said as they walked through the cool haven of the hallway, across the den, and into the kitchen. "I can't wait to see it."

"I'm getting a new showcase built for the James Bond memorabilia. I thought I'd put it between Hitchcock and the leading ladies' wall." Bonnie opened the fridge and pushed Hadrian's big head aside so he couldn't lick the front of the deli drawer. "Juice?"

"Thanks. I'm parched. I got caught in the gunfight coming through town."

Bonnie groaned. "Yeah, I figured. They're having them every day because those Shriners are in town."

"Is Alice sleeping?"

"Yes, I had the Calloway twins playing here this morning, so she's completely exhausted. And so am I. That woman just can't shut up."

"I guess she's missing the city." Rhianna picked up the tumblers of pink grapefruit juice and carried them out to the back patio.

The Moss residence was a sprawling single-level home built around three sides of an inner courtyard with a gazebo at the far end. Beyond this lay a gated swimming pool and a children's playground. A private deck adjoining Rhianna's apartment at the rear of the house looked out over the playground to the rugged purple peaks of the Black Mountains. She usually kept Alice and Hadrian back there when the Mosses were away; it felt safer and cozier than the big house. Bonnie and Lloyd seemed perfectly happy with this arrangement and had converted her second bedroom to a nursery so that Rhianna didn't have to drag toys and a cot bed back and forth.

"Her marriage is falling apart," Bonnie gossiped cheerfully. "I think he's been seeing someone on the side. I don't know why anyone thinks they can get away with adultery. The wife always knows."

Rhianna sipped her juice and tried to look like she was interested. "Is it someone local?"

"No, there's a woman in Vegas. What a mess. And two babies to think about." Bonnie tugged the pink band from her ponytail and shook out her shoulder-length mahogany waves.

"Did you get highlights?" Rhianna asked, noticing threads of bronze that hadn't been there four days earlier when she'd set out for Palm Springs.

Bonnie nodded. "Lloyd hasn't said a word, but I like them."

"They look great. They flatter your face."

Bonnie thanked her and said, "I thought about going red, but I could never pull that off. You're lucky. You have that eye color that works with everything." She studied Rhianna pensively. "Have you ever thought about going really blond. Like platinum? You'd look sensational. You've got exactly the right coloring."

Rhianna's pulse jerked. "I think it takes a certain kind of person to pull off platinum blond."

"Yeah, I don't see you as a simmering sexpot."

Rhianna caught a flash of herself in Palm Springs, standing in front of the bathroom mirror flushed from sex and alcohol. "No, not my style at all."

Weakly, she set her grapefruit juice back down on the table. Her hands felt damp and she could feel guilty color climbing from her neck to her cheeks. All she could see was Jules, sprawling naked on the bed, sated from their lovemaking but still inviting more. They hadn't stopped all night. Even completely exhausted, they'd found their way back into each other as dawn crept through the gaps around the window covers.

A pang of regret squeezed a small sound from Rhianna's throat and she pulled herself together before she started to cry. She didn't want to dwell on her sexual encounter in Palm Springs. It only made her feel confused. She still had no idea whether sleeping with Jules had been a blessing or a disaster. Despite her trepidation she had been able to touch and be touched, and it had felt amazingly good, better than she'd expected. Even intoxicated, and even anxious at times, she had hung in there. It was good to know she could still function sexually, even if she hadn't been able to stay in her body throughout. Some time in the future she might be ready for more.

To calm her breathing, Rhianna stared down at the bonsai garden in the middle of the kitchen table and pictured herself similarly shrunken, a tiny little self sitting beneath the twisted limbs of the red maple. Invisible.

"Kate?" Bonnie stared at her quizzically. "You didn't hear a word I said, did you?"

Rhianna shook her head. "Oops."

"Tell me everything!" Bonnie craned forward, lowered her voice to a conspiratorial half-whisper. "Did you?"

"Did I *what*?"

"Meet someone." Bonnie's coffee-brown eyes sparkled with mischief. "And was he hot?"

"I hate to disappoint you," Rhianna said, "but I wasn't looking for beefcake."

"Wrong place if you were." Bonnie opened a cookie jar she'd carried to the table earlier and extracted a Snickers bar. "I mean, all the cute guys in Palm Springs are gay, aren't they?"

"Put it this way, none of them were hitting on me."

Globs of saliva trembled off Hadrian's jowls as he watched his adored mistress eat the candy he wasn't allowed. Rhianna took pity and got up to fetch a dog biscuit.

"Tell if I'm being too nosy," Bonnie said, "but why the heck aren't you married? I've been wondering all these months but I didn't want to ask. You know, in case something had happened. I mean, why else would you want to move out here? Lloyd and I figured there had to be a story to explain *that* mystery."

Rhianna hated having to deceive people who had been so good to her. Carefully, she said, "There was a man. He made life difficult for me."

Her throat constricted and she knew something had changed in the timbre of her voice because tenderhearted Bonnie immediately stretched out a small, plump hand to take hers.

"Was he violent? You can tell me, sweetie. It won't go any further."

"Yes, he terrifies me."

"I knew it." Bonnie gave a self-satisfied smile. "I told Lloyd the very first time we ever saw you that there was a man responsible for that look in your eyes. I'd recognize it anywhere. I used to volunteer in a shelter back in Sin City. I saw it all the time."

A look. Yes. Every time she confronted her own face in a mirror, Rhianna saw that lingering shadow, too. "It's in the past now and I'm a long way from home. I'm sure he's chasing some other poor woman these days."

"Don't you worry about a thing," Bonnie said. "You're safe with us. Anyone shows up on this property looking for you, Lloyd'll take his head off."

Rhianna gave Bonnie's hand a brief, grateful squeeze. "I'm not worried. Even if he knew where I was, he's not going to come all the way out here."

"I know what I'm going to do." Bonnie reached down and absently fondled Hadrian's head. "I'm going to tell Percy to keep an extra watchful eye on you when we're not around. I know he's scrawny as a stray dog, but that old cowboy is a dead shot and real protective of his kin. That's how he sees us, you included. We're all he's got."

"Thanks, Bonnie." Rhianna felt surprisingly calm. Even telling half the story was better than holding it all in. "It's good being able to talk about it."

"And I have a great idea," Bonnie said. "I'm going to drive us all into Laughlin this afternoon and get you the best snub-nose .38 special money can buy."

"A gun?" Rhianna shook her head emphatically. "No, I think that's dangerous. What if Alice got a hold of it?"

"Children don't find guns unless adults are careless. This is not up for discussion. I am buying you a weapon. Period."

"Bonnie, I've never even held a gun. I have no idea how they work."

"That's what Percy's for. He could teach a gerbil to shoot straight." Bonnie got to her feet, a woman with a mission. Hanging her head inside the French doors, she yelled, "Percy, are you in the house?"

When there was no reply, she marched off and returned five minutes later with the weathered ranch hand. He had his hat tucked under one arm, and Rhianna had a feeling he had just plastered his stringy gray hair back with some spittle on the flat of his hand. Probably tidied his mustache the same way.

"I was just telling Kate that you'd be happy to teach her how to shoot," Bonnie said.

"Sure would." Percy was economical with words. The most he usually said to Rhianna was "Howdy."

"We're going to the gun dealer's this afternoon," Bonnie said.

"Fixing to purchase what?" he asked.

"I thought maybe a Smith & Wesson AirLite."

"Depends what she wants it for." Percy's blue-sky gaze inched toward Rhianna.

"I suppose a nine millimeter is an alternative," Bonnie mused. "A semi-automatic. Maybe a Ruger."

Like he thought carefully about every word, Percy drawled, "I heard you got yourself some man trouble."

Great. Bonnie was going to announce her problems to the entire of Oatman. "He couldn't take no for an answer," Rhianna said. "But, honestly, there's nothing to worry about."

She was wasting her breath.

Percy hooked a thumb in his belt, his hand dangling over the holster at his hip. "No harm taking precautions."

"Accuracy isn't that important," Bonnie noted. "Most times if you have to use a gun it's a close-quarters situation, so a snub-nose would work fine, and you can carry it in your purse."

"How come you know so much about this?" Rhianna teased. "You sound like the mafia."

"At the casino, most of the management is licensed to own a gun," Bonnie replied seriously. "We make sure they know how to use one."

"Do you keep a handgun in the house?"

"Of course. Handguns, rifles…but they're all in the gun safe."

They. Rhianna couldn't imagine owning one weapon, let alone an arsenal. Her father had tried to get her to carry a small Derringer when Werner Brigham had first started stalking her. Wonderful in theory, and dangerous in practice. She had refused, seeing herself threatening Brigham with a gun only to have it snatched and used against her. She'd also been one hundred percent certain that she could never shoot another human being.

Rhianna let her gaze fall to the gun at Percy's side. That had changed. Just like so many other things. She pictured Werner Brigham in front of her, stroking that strange dagger of his, softly talking to her as if she were an animal he was about to kill, but he wanted her cooperation so he could avoid sustaining bruises in the process. Yes, she could pull the trigger. She could watch him go down and feel nothing. She could even point the gun again while he was writhing in front of her, and blow him away. Disturbed by this dark truth, she said, "I think it's a good idea for Percy to teach me, but I could learn with one of your spare guns, couldn't I?"

"Oh, honey, I don't mind buying you one all of your own," Bonnie insisted. "It's only a few hundred dollars. Call it a bonus."

Rhianna didn't want to seem ungrateful, but if she had to get a gun license for a weapon of her own, she would have to show photo identification. The last thing she needed was for Bonnie to see her real name and start asking questions. Sounding as innocent and thankful as she could, she said, "That's really sweet of you. How about this? If Percy starts teaching me with one of your guns, then we can figure what kind might suit me best, and we'll go buy it."

"Get her started with the .22, maybe," Percy said.

"Good idea," Bonnie agreed. As though Rhianna might feel cheated by the smaller caliber offering, she added, "Don't worry, you'll trade up. You'll be shooting cans off the fence with a .38 in no time."

Rhianna liked the sound of that. "Thanks for thinking of me, both of you."

"It's my pleasure." Bonnie beamed. "I don't ever want you feeling vulnerable when you're out here by yourself."

Percy endorsed this sentiment wholeheartedly. "Want to take a man down with a single shot? Stick with me."

Rhianna smiled. A bullet with Werner Brigham's name on it. That was a reason to get out of bed in the morning.

CHAPTER FOUR

The client was ordinary. His hair clung to his skull in a thinning sandy thatch threaded with gray. His face was clean shaven with a nondescript nose, fleshy lips, and a soft chin. Women would probably find his bland looks comforting, and men would not feel threatened, despite his height and build. He was on the heavy side, but it wasn't muscle. He carried the flab of a man who had been active once but no longer put in the hours.

Carl Hagel, managing partner at Sagelblum, in-house shorthand for Salazar, Hagel & Goldblum, stepped to one side of the conference room door and said, "Mr. Brigham, let me introduce your new lead counsel, Julia Valiant." As the client stood to shake hands, Carl completed the formalities. "This is Werner Brigham. I think you know his mother, Mrs. Audrey Brigham."

"Naturally." Jules produced a watered-down version of the professional smile expected of a woman. The client's handshake was half courtesy, half grateful squeeze. "I admire your mother's charity efforts for children with cancer."

Audrey Brigham had personally requested that Julia head her son's no-expense-spared defense team five months earlier during the pre-trial phase. According to Carl, she'd showed up at Sagelblum's Denver office with several clippings about Jules, including one that named her a "Super Lawyer" and claimed she was "the sex offender's dream defense counsel," not exactly the accolade her parents had dreamed of when they mortgaged their house and sold half their possessions to pay for her education.

Jules had been a little over halfway into a year's leave of absence from the firm when Audrey Brigham slapped her money down on the table. She had seriously considered abandoning her overseas studies to take the case right away; it was unwise to say no to such a woman. Not only was Mrs. Brigham a major player on the charity circuit, she was also a formidable political fundraiser with influential friends. She had offered Sagelblum a performance bonus only an idiot would refuse, conditional upon Jules stepping in as lead trial attorney.

Declining was not an option, but the year in England reading philosophy at Cambridge University had been Jules's promise to herself when she graduated from law school at NYU, and she could not bear to sacrifice her studies. Instead she'd cut short the European tour she'd planned for the final months of her absence, agreeing to take over Brigham's defense when she returned. She had three weeks to get herself up to speed before the trial date.

Carl chatted for a few minutes to bolster the client's confidence. He made a big deal of Jules's acquittal record, one of the best in the business, then said, "If you'll both excuse me. Sid Lyle will join you as soon as he gets back from court."

Jules thanked him and opened the file she'd carried into the conference room. Watching the client closely, she said, "Rhianna Lamb."

She had his attention and repeated the name in a musing tone, letting it linger. There it was. The tip of his tongue crept along the parting of his lips, moistening them. His pupils dilated. The Adam's apple bobbed briefly above his blue shirt collar. He gave himself away so completely, the jury was going to see a pathetically fixated predator. That would have to change, along with the clothes. The necktie would be a problem, if today's choice was any indication. The knot was too large, the sheen too costly, and the pattern too bold. This was the tie of a man with an ego. Or one so impressionable he had seen the likes of Puff Daddy sporting this look and wanted to convey similar panache. Neither would play well with a Denver jury.

Jules was pretty familiar with their whims, having led a number of criminal defense teams this side of the Rockies. Sagelblum was a national firm that sent its senior trial attorneys all over the country to work with local counsel from its regional offices. Jules usually enjoyed her Denver assignments. The place had somehow managed to weld its historical Western sensibility and friendly informality with progressive urban development and efficient infrastructure.

Most of the district court judges were efficient and reasonable. They would be well disposed toward the client, she thought. The Brigham name carried some clout in Colorado, and while the man himself had a certain old-money aura that could raise some hackles among jurors, he also seemed earnest enough to secure their sympathies.

She tested his reactions again. "Is Rhianna beautiful?"

The question seemed to take him by surprise. Blinking, he said, "Very."

"Please," she prompted with an attentive smile, "describe her for me, Mr. Brigham."

"She is a classic beauty," he replied promptly, "not one of those cheesy *Deal or No Deal* models. You know what I'm talking about. They all look like they were made in the same factory. She's not trailer trash with a lot of makeup and a fancy hairdo."

Jules gave an encouraging nod. "Elegant?"

"Yes, although not in that studied sense." He warmed to his theme. "She's more demure than obvious. I would say 'classy'…the marrying kind."

"I still don't have a strong sense of her."

This was untrue. Jules had looked through photographs, video footage, and an extensive file on the woman Brigham was initially accused of kidnapping and sexually assaulting. Rhianna Lamb was a prosecutor's dream plaintiff, a natural blonde with long hair framing an innocent face with wide, soft cheekbones and enough puppy fat to make her look about sixteen. She had a clean record and a sexual history roughly comparable to that of a nun.

At the time of the alleged assault, she had held down a job in a traditionally female occupation, working as a fashion buyer at a department store in the upscale Cherry Creek shopping precinct. She volunteered at an animal-rescue shelter and took turns caring for the severely disabled child of a neighbor. She was a dutiful unmarried daughter, one of three respectable siblings who had never had a day's trouble in their registered-Democrat lives. She had placed her house on the market and left town after Werner Brigham was released on bail, and would only provide the DA with her parents' address, claiming she was "traveling" and not at any fixed abode.

Jules concluded from these maneuvers that the woman was not completely helpless. She'd had sufficient presence of mind to get out of Dodge and hide where Brigham could not find her. People did not abandon home, job, friends, and family without cause. Whatever the client said, one thing was perfectly plain. He had terrified the shit out of this Lamb woman.

From all accounts, the plaintiff had been a model student at her local high school and, later, at the second-tier college her parents had scrimped to afford. Naturally, she had waitressed at a family restaurant to help pay her own way. Months of dirt-digging, and thousands in private-investigator fees, had failed to turn up a single enemy or embittered ex-lover who could take the stand to reveal another side of Ms. Goody Two-shoes. There was no short-lived stint as an exotic dancer, no nude photos on the Internet, no sleazy MySpace revelations, no secret affair with a professor, no credit-card debt, no DUI, not even a parking ticket.

The only boyfriend they'd found was a computer geek who said he had respected her too much to hassle her for sex, so they dated, but their relationship was platonic. Lamb's best friend, Mimi Buckmaster, was a cello-playing vegan whose worst vice appeared to be baking eggless muffins no one liked. Other close female friends included a Sunday-school teacher, a social worker, a bank clerk, and a woman who designed Hallmark greeting cards. All in all, they had zip.

No one at Sagelblum could believe it. Rhianna Lamb did not wear tight jeans, chew gum, smoke, or drink beer. She attended church, listened to blues, and friends said her favorite movies were *Forrest Gump* and *Titanic*. She was, in fact, so boring and decent, at the age of twenty-eight, that she was universally described as "nice."

Jules could not imagine a more condemning epithet. Personally, she was thankful no one would ever say that about her, but professionally, she was bothered. In her experience no one was so "nice," so consistently, that they had nothing to hide. The investigators had to be missing a piece of the puzzle.

Irritated, she tuned in to the client once more. Werner Brigham was still waxing lyrical.

"She runs, so she has that athletic build but," he pronounced in an approving tone, "she's still feminine and graceful. She probably had ballet lessons as a girl. You can see that in the way she holds herself."

Ballet lessons. This was the first time she had ever heard a sex offender speculate on his alleged victim's background in dance. And Brigham was an offender; Jules felt dead certain about that. He had freely admitted to stalking Rhianna Lamb and to an incomplete sex act he insistently described as "a consummation." In his version of events, these actions were the culmination of a courtship and a preliminary to marriage. Brigham was a man who believed his own fiction.

"She has similar refined tastes in clothing to my mother," he shared in a reflective tone. "I think the two of them will be good friends. That's an important consideration."

And a sentiment best left unshared with members of the jury. Brigham was apparently a stranger to the norms of dating. Was he also a stranger to reason? Several of the senior trial attorneys on the team thought so. Their private notes, for her eyes only, were circumspect but ominous.

Mr. Brigham displays a marked inability to perceive his actions as they may be interpreted by others...

...if the client was not a well-connected man of wealth and education, he would be at risk of certification...

...the manner in which the client professes his devotion to the plaintiff must be adjusted and controlled by counsel if he is to take the stand.

Finally, there was Sid Lyle's assessment. Never one to mince words, he'd passed her a scrawled note during her first pre-trial conference. It read, *This guy is a fucking fruitcake.*

In a half-decent world, they would plead him out and he would serve time, or at least end up in a state mental hospital. But Salazar, Hagel & Goldblum had a reputation to keep up and high-end real estate to pay for. They took cases to trial.

Jules had no problem with such pragmatism. She hadn't worked her ass off for the shingle on her corner-suite door to start sweating about shades of guilt and innocence. If she didn't like defending well-heeled clients who had made errors in judgment, or were innocent and targeted for the wrong reasons, she could always trade in her Mercedes, sell her costly hideaway on Lake Tahoe, and cross the street to the DA's office. None of which were options she planned to explore anytime soon.

Werner Brigham had retained the best legal team money could buy, and she was the lead trial attorney who would walk down the courthouse steps with him when he was acquitted. Jules could sleep okay with that. She was paid handsomely to do a job, and she made a point of doing it better than most of her rivals.

"I understand you intended to propose marriage to Ms. Lamb the night of the incident," she said.

"I had the ring custom-made for her. She wouldn't even try it on." Brigham looked aggrieved.

"That must have been upsetting."

The client extracted a narrow gold case from inside his jacket; at first glance it could have passed for a lipstick. He flipped it open, extracted a slender silver toothpick, and set about working it between his front teeth. Between oral forays, he said, "That ring cost me fifty thousand dollars, not that money is an object. I knew from overhearing a conversation between Rhianna and her best friend, Mimi, that blue diamonds are her favorite. So I chose one with a blue diamond in the center and white princess diamonds on the sides. Princess...to express my vision of her."

Jules ran through the argument. *Does a man purchase a fifty-thousand-dollar diamond engagement ring for a woman who has not encouraged him? Does he risk embarrassment by informing family and friends that he is planning to marry in the near future if he has no hope of such a union?*

Werner Brigham is accused of a heinous crime. But his only "crime" was to mistake the mixed messages of a respectable, inexperienced single woman for natural shyness. You see, ladies and gentlemen, my client, in this day and age, is an old-fashioned man. A man from a prominent Denver family. A man brought up to respect women, but also to believe that men must take the lead in matters of romance and courtship...

Jury selection would be critical. They needed older women, preferably seven or eight of them, women who devoured Harlequin romances and still did their sons' laundry. And they needed young, poorly educated men who would find nothing remarkable in the idea that one of their sex could be confused by a woman and innocently do the wrong thing. With good management, they would be able to identify the closet Neanderthals who thought "no" meant a woman was playing hard to get and male sexual aggression was "normal." The world was full of them.

"Why do you think Ms. Lamb turned you down?" Jules was unable to take her eyes off the glinting toothpick. There could be nothing left to dislodge, but Brigham was probing almost viciously around his gums.

"She was overwhelmed," he replied. "It's been like that throughout our relationship. When you consider our different positions in life, that's hardly surprising. Women have always chased me for my money."

"Did Rhianna chase you?"

"No, quite the opposite," he said with disdain. "That's my point."

"You're saying Rhianna was not impressed by your wealth?"

"Exactly." He nodded.

"Do you have any idea why not?" Jules invited, wanting to see how Brigham would approach the topic without coaching.

"She's sensitive and unassuming. Obviously she is anxious about the social gulf between us and does not want me to see her as the grasping type. That's why my flowers embarrassed her." When Jules raised an eyebrow in query, he explained, "Each week, I sent her a large bouquet. She asked me to stop."

"And did you?"

"Of course not. I knew she was only worried about the

extravagance." He flicked a dismissive hand through the air as he laughed this off. "She genuinely didn't realize that a two-hundred-dollar bouquet is nothing to me, yet it could fill that second-rate abode of hers with beauty. That's all I ever wanted for her…to surround her with beauty. Isn't that what all truly feminine women want?"

He studied Jules with faint derision, leaving no doubt that she had failed the true-femininity test herself and was now being invited to speculate on the motives of her more acceptable sisters. Jules wondered what he saw in her that he disapproved of. At work, she kept her hair loose and shoulder length to send the right signal to clients and juries. She always wore a suit and a few carefully chosen items of jewelry—a simple gold initial pin her grandmother had given her when she graduated, a signet ring, small, thick gold cuff earrings. Today she was in Armani, a dark charcoal jacket and pants teamed with a patterned claret silk blouse.

She would have worn a skirt and classic Chanel or Ferragamo pumps if she had to appear before a judge. For a trial, she also changed her color scheme. A shell in ivory, pale pink, or soft olive green, and a less austere suit with a feminine cut. Juries appreciated eye candy, and she made sure to offer just enough, wearing her jackets a little shorter and her skirts slightly tight around the hips, so male jurors got to see a firm ass as she strolled back and forth. At the same time, for the benefit of the women she needed to win over, her skirts were long enough that she wasn't flaunting legs better than theirs, and she kept her jackets buttoned to disguise breast perkiness and nipples that made themselves obvious when her adrenaline surged.

"It sounds like you consider Ms. Lamb the ideal woman," Jules said. "Could you tell me why?"

The toothpick hung in the air an inch from his mouth, firmly clamped between thumb and forefinger. He wore a pinky ring on the hand in question, a smooth bloodstone cabochon set in pink gold. The ring drew attention to the affected angle of his pinky finger, which pointed straight up at the ceiling. That would have to change.

"Well, for a start, she's completely natural. Most women with her hair color get it from a bottle, but I happen to know she sees her hairdresser for only a cut. I personally checked that." He eyed Jules's jet black hair suspiciously, then continued his musings with the confidence of a man who knew his topic well. "I suppose people would call her a blonde, but I like to call her hair 'moonbeam' in color, a personal vanity." With a self-effacing chuckle, he explained, "Poetry was my major at Columbia. You could say Rhianna is my muse."

Jules winced. Oh, yes, the jury would have plenty to talk about over their hot lunches. "You have some works published, don't you?" She recalled an entry amidst her voluminous file notes.

"In the *Columbia Poetry Review* and, most recently, in *Pleiades*." He paused, as if to allow this information to sink in. When she did not react, he said with faint condescension, "Obviously, you are not acquainted with the *belles lettres* or you would recognize the prestige of those publications. I also won the Maxine DeKamp award for best undergraduate poet in my year."

Or, in jury-speak, Brigham is a Mommy's boy who writes poems instead of holding down a man's job. Jules had already reworked that angle in her mind.

Mr. Brigham is a published, award-winning poet. While this is strictly a personal passion rather than an occupation, his hobby provides evidence of his romantic side. Ask yourselves this question: What is a sensitive man with a fifty-thousand-dollar diamond ring in his pocket planning when he takes a limousine to the home of the woman he is in love with? That's right, ladies and gentlemen, he is planning a romantic dinner and a marriage proposal.

Mr. Brigham had reservations at the elite Palace Arms Restaurant for that evening and, as you have heard, the restaurant manager knew in advance that the dinner was an engagement celebration. My client placed a prepaid order for two bottles of high-priced champagne and a red-rose bouquet from the city's leading florist. Who does this without a reason?

The man you see before you made an error in judgment. He's only human. For his trouble, he has had his heart broken and his reputation destroyed by a malicious media. He has resigned from his job, lost friends, and seen his hopes of marriage and children go up in smoke. Hasn't he been punished enough?

"So you see, calling her a blonde gives the wrong impression." Brigham was still glued to his theme. "I don't know about you, but I always picture a tramp when people talk about a blonde. And that's not my Rhianna at all. She's morally impeccable, or I would not have decided to marry her."

"How can you be certain about her morality?" Jules inquired blandly.

"I used to watch her house in the evenings. No male visitors. And I took pains to be present at the social events she attended to make sure she was unmolested by men." He paused, seeming to bask in his own certainty. "Sometimes she has female friends visit, but never a man."

"You watched her house." As soon as Brigham stepped into the courtroom, the jury would smell Eau de Creep.

Fortunately, he seemed to grasp that he was entering hazardous terrain. With earnest indignation, he explained, "I wasn't watching her house to *spy* on her. I *care* for her. These days genuinely virtuous women are rare and their innocence makes them vulnerable. I was only trying to protect her from afar, before I have a husband's right to do so."

"I see."

He colored. Lowering his voice to a wet hiss, he said, "I have every reason to believe my future wife was a virgin when we met. How many do you suppose there are these days? Wouldn't you want to protect that asset?"

Jules made sure her face betrayed nothing. He sounded very sure about the virginity, too sure for a man who claimed he had not been "fully intimate" with the woman in question. How she was supposed to stop Brigham from convicting himself was a sobering prospect. They could keep him off the stand, but in a case like this, with a Pollyanna plaintiff like Rhianna Lamb, the defense strategist thought it would be a mistake and Jules agreed. Somehow she had to find a way to cast this client sympathetically. It would be essential to undermine the object of his one-sided fantasies. A virgin rape victim was every defense attorney's worst nightmare, and this client couldn't wait to proclaim Lamb's virtue.

"How often did you and Ms. Lamb actually date?" Jules asked.

Brigham resumed picking his teeth as he considered the question. Jules must have showed her faint distaste because he said, "Excuse me. Mommy is always telling me to confine my oral hygiene to a bathroom." He lowered the pick and rolled it between his fingers. "This was a gift from my late father, a small heirloom handed down in my family. I believe it belonged to Thomas Jefferson originally."

Jules nodded, disinterested. "Your dates with Ms. Lamb?"

"Well, I was seeing her almost every day until she...left town." Rage made his eyes gleam pale silver-gray, the pupils near pinpoints. "I blame the police for that, filling her head with ridiculous distortions of the truth. They have their own agenda."

"Why do you feel that way?"

"It's everywhere. Political correctness." He got busy with the toothpick again. "The feminists run things now, and they're out of touch with the way normal men think."

Jules studied the files on the tabletop as she counted to ten. "Tell me something, Mr. Brigham. Are you comfortable having a woman represent you at your trial?"

His eyes narrowed as if he suspected a trick question. "Why not? You come highly recommended."

"I'm also a feminist."

A bark of laughter expelled the toothpick from its parking spot between a couple of teeth on the lower jaw. Brigham pounced on the tiny silver spear before it could roll across the table. Snatching it up, he tenderly inspected it.

"I'm not threatened by women like yourself," he declared in a condescending tone. "In fact, I have the utmost respect for those of you with accomplishments that set you apart. The thing is, my mother considers herself to be a feminist, but you don't hear her blaming men for everything wrong in this world." As proof of his enlightenment, he said, "When I marry Rhianna I will give her the choice to be a stay-at-home wife or have a suitable job."

"You still wish to marry Ms. Lamb?"

"I'm willing to overlook her mistakes, and I take full responsibility for my own failings." He gave a pained sigh. "She wasn't ready, and instead of being patient and understanding, I became overwhelmed. But Mommy has spoken to me about this matter and it will not happen again. I guarantee it."

"Are you saying Ms. Lamb's allegations are true?"

"No! Absolutely not. I'm saying my behavior was not without blemish, but the police blew it up out of all proportion and persuaded her to press charges."

"You did not rape her?"

He flushed dark red.

"You will be asked that question when you take the stand," Jules said without emotion.

"I know." He mumbled something beneath his breath. "I realize the prosecution will try to trick me into incriminating myself. It's your job to make sure that doesn't happen."

Jules reminded herself that she was being paid a pile of money to keep this client out of prison, whether he made it easy for her or not. And just in case she needed a bigger incentive than usual, Audrey Brigham's performance bonus was two million dollars. The sum would be split between members of her son's defense team for a not-guilty verdict, with half earmarked for Jules.

Focusing once more on the information she needed to gather, she said, "Getting back to your dates with Ms. Lamb. Is there one that was especially memorable for you?"

He pondered for a moment, as though weighing many such occasions. "We had lunch together when she got her promotion to senior buyer."

"Can you tell me about that?"

"It was destiny. We ran into each other at a café. There were no tables and she asked if she could share mine. The connection was instant. I carried her parcels to her car. From that day forward, I knew we were meant to be together."

"How did you know that?"

"I took one look at her face and I realized she was the woman I had been waiting for, the angel of my hopes. It was love at first sight."

Holy crap.

Ladies and gentlemen, this case should never have come to trial. It should have been resolved in private like any other personal misunderstanding between adults. If Ms. Lamb were a different type of woman, more experienced in the ways of the world, more knowledgeable about men, she would have handled this situation very differently. I have no doubt of that. But Ms. Lamb did not know how to be assertive. She is a kindhearted person. She did not want to hurt Mr. Brigham's feelings by saying no, clearly and unambiguously. Because of her decency and sweet nature, she sent my client mixed signals that would give any man the wrong impression. And here we are.

Chapter Five

Jules was not a daydreamer. But that didn't prevent her from lapsing into vivid sexual fantasy when she was supposed to be all over Werner Brigham's defense prep. In the ten days since her brief sojourn in Palm Springs, these slips in concentration had made her crazy, and they were only getting worse. She was waking up in the middle of the night, lying sleepless with need until she got herself off. In meetings with the chief defense strategist, a woman who bore a fleeting resemblance to Kate, all she could think about was sex. Three days ago, she had stalled her Mercedes at a set of lights, causing a rear-ender. She didn't even bother to dispute responsibility. In a sea of rush-hour traffic, she had been miles away, deep in fantasy, thrusting her tongue inside a woman she knew nothing about. A woman who didn't want to see her again.

Her imagination had embroidered a vivid tapestry of sweaty, relentless sex that made her so moist, so constantly, she had to increase the changes of underwear in the overnight bag she kept at work. This week, certain that someone would detect the musky evidence of her arousal, she'd swapped her panties for fresh ones each lunch hour. Disastrous scenarios rotated in her mind: Herself exuding pheromones that caused chaos in meetings. A married partner hitting on her in an elevator. The hunky butch who made the FedEx deliveries losing control and locking her office door so they could fuck on her desk.

Despite the frigid air-conditioning, Jules's skin felt hot and damp most of the time, as if she'd just stepped out of a humidifier. This afternoon had deteriorated into another fight for control over her libido, and she had escaped from a meeting after her nipples got so tight she knew everyone was looking at them. Normally, she would have had her jacket on, but she kept breaking into a sweat, so she'd taken it off. What a nightmare. Even Carl Hagel, a man so in love with himself he sought his own reflection in wineglasses, had been talking to her breasts.

Jules was astonished that a casual fling could have reduced her to this state. It wasn't as if the sex had been spectacular. It was good, no question about that. But Jules never expected much of one-night stands. No one could possibly figure out another person, sexually, in the course of a few hours. In her experience, the buildup was usually more exciting than the event.

Admittedly, Kate had been unusual compared with the norm. Jules had been surprised that she was into light bondage, but she had a sense something else was going on. Kate didn't seem remotely familiar with BDSM conventions, and Jules had concluded that she was just experimenting. She'd probably chosen to play out a long-standing fantasy with a stranger because she felt ashamed or self-conscious. Some people didn't want a regular partner to know they had a yen for kink.

Normally, Jules wasn't at home playing bottom in a D/s scenario, but she'd been intrigued by the request and had decided to indulge Kate. She seemed such an unlikely dominant, Jules had wondered if a completely different person would emerge during the ritual of power exchange. In the end, she had no idea whether Kate had found what she was looking for by acting out her fantasy. Jules could imagine her playing the scene over and over in her head without knowing why she was compelled by it, and expecting some kind of revelation when she finally explored her desires in real time. Judging by the next morning, she must have been disappointed.

Her own reaction was quite the opposite, a fact that surprised Jules. She supposed it made sense that she could enjoy surrendering responsibility for a change, but she would never have gone there with a sexual partner who had something to prove. Kate was another story. She didn't seem driven by a need for ego gratification. In fact,

Jules suspected something about the bondage scenario had made her feel safe. The moment the restraints were tightened, her unease vanished and she lowered her guard. Her dominance was not harsh or calculated, only a confident assertion of her needs. She was open and tender, and in their most naked moments, Jules felt an affinity with her she'd seldom experienced with any lover.

Maybe that was why the encounter preyed on her mind so relentlessly. She wanted to have sex with Kate again, to find out if she'd simply imagined that fleeting connection. Yet that desire alone could not explain the depth of her erotic fixation. Staring at the spectacular city and mountain view from her office window, she tried to talk sense to herself. She'd had one-night stands before. The experiences were quickly folded away and forgotten, and there were plenty more where they came from. She certainly didn't dwell on any of the women involved, or ponder ways to engineer a repeat encounter. Why was the interlude with Kate any different? Sure, being tied up was a novelty, but it was no big deal compared with some of the play Jules got into.

Maybe she should hit a bar and find a woman to have sex with. Obviously the encounter with Kate had triggered a hunger she'd been smothering for too long. Jules often neglected her personal needs, prioritizing work ahead of all else. Gym workouts did not substitute for physical contact with another woman. That was why she'd decided to go to Palm Springs almost as soon as she'd returned from England.

While she was overseas she was living in a college town, but very few of the lesbians she met were available. Everyone seemed to be in relationships. Jules wanted to avoid complication, and she was busy in her spare time anyway, studying and traveling. Somehow she just didn't get around to having sex with a succession of women, as she'd anticipated.

A disconcerting thought crossed her mind. What if her preoccupation with Kate wasn't about sex, or even strong attraction? Another plausible explanation presented itself. Ego. A woman had said no to her and all hell was breaking loose. It would have been funny if her work wasn't affected.

Jules laughed. Was she so competitive by nature that she had to have a rematch? She wasn't used to rejection, and she didn't like it one bit. How often did she offer a woman something more, after they'd slept together? Never. Jules seldom had girlfriends and her recent attempts at "long-term" relationships hadn't made it past their first anniversary. She liked to believe that she didn't have the time or energy to keep a partner happy, but she knew there was more to it than that. If she was completely honest, her failures came down to making poor choices.

It was one thing to avoid settling down in her twenties, but Jules was thirty-three and she wanted to be a success in every aspect of her life. Having the perfect relationship was an essential ingredient. With that goal in mind, she had stumbled into several live-in relationships with women who seemed to have the makings of good corporate wives. She hadn't been in love with any of them, but that detail hadn't bothered her. She didn't suffer from illusions about love and romance. If magic happened that would be a bonus, but she didn't expect any lightning bolts, and so far none had materialized.

Jules was convinced that if two people shared similar goals and ideals they could build something worthwhile together. Her parents were a perfect example.

She had once asked her mother about their early married life, whether they were madly in love and couldn't keep their hands off each other. Clarice Valiant had looked at her like she'd lost her mind and said her marriage worked out fine because she and Jules's dad had an understanding. Love had grown between them over the years, they had mutual respect, and they were good companions. Neither of them had expected fireworks when they married, so they had not suffered the disappointment that could afflict couples drawn together by mere animal attraction. One could not build a solid future on such shifting sands.

This philosophy made sense to Jules. The Valiants were pragmatists and she was no exception. She owed her parents a great deal and had always been guided by their common sense. The opportunities she had in her own life were the result of their sacrifices. The very least she wanted to offer them now, having built the successful career they'd dreamed of, was the possibility of a grandchild. They had been devastated when she came out, not because they were homophobic, but because they believed their hopes of grandchildren were extinguished.

They had never spoken a word to her about their disappointment, but Jules saw it in their faces whenever they mentioned new additions to the family. Nieces and nephews with new babies. Cousins marrying. Jules had a picture in her mind, a Thanksgiving where she was at the table with an amazing partner and they announced that they were expecting a baby. Her parents would be ecstatic, and so would she. Jules liked kids and wouldn't mind having one if she could find the right woman to settle down with. So far, that wasn't panning out too well.

Her thoughts drifted back to Kate. Was the wife hunt a factor in her fixation, too? She didn't know the woman at all, and "potential wife" was not what she'd seen in the bar that evening. All the same, after spending a night with Kate, she'd been willing to keep an open mind and see her again. She hadn't expected to be turned down flat. If Kate had intended to inflame her desires by playing hard to get, it had worked. The trouble was, Jules didn't think she was playing.

She leaned back in her chair and weighed her options. She could impose self-discipline and wait for her libido to settle down. Or she could sleep with another woman and hope that would put the encounter with Kate into perspective. Or she could do what she really wanted to do—find the wretched woman and talk her into bed again.

The solution was a no-brainer. Jules took her cell phone from her pocket and silently thanked Gilbert Desjardines for teaching her everything she knew about slippery investigative techniques. Smiling to herself, she dialed Casitas Laquita and exchanged some pleasantries with Denise, one of the owners. Then she lied through her teeth.

"Listen, the reason I'm calling is to ask a favor. I'm supposed to be hooking up with a woman I met last time I stayed. She was in the next room. Kate…er…"

"Oh yes, I remember." Denise didn't supply the last name, as Jules had hoped.

"Small problem." Jules persevered. "I had her cell-phone number but it got washed with my jeans. I was wondering—"

"You know I can't give out guest information," Denise interrupted with a note of regret. "I'm sorry."

"Of course. I would never ask that." Jules thought fast. "Actually, I was wondering if you could send her something."

"Sure."

"I really like her," Jules confided. She had been staying at the inn regularly for three years and never with the same woman. She and the two owners had sometimes shared a laugh about her footloose habits, and Jules was sure they would help her out with a real romance if they could. "I thought if I gave you my credit-card details, you could send her some flowers with my name and number. Then she'll call me and we can make our plans."

"I don't see why not," Denise said after only a slight hesitation. "Red roses?"

"No." Jules wanted to send a more subtle message. "Make it peonies and irises." Peonies were sensuous and romantic, and irises lasted longer than most cut flowers. They would come into bloom and look beautiful for days. Kate would be thinking about her every time she saw them.

"I think she'll like that combination," Denise said. "She seems kind of sweet and old-fashioned."

Jules grinned. Now for her coup de grace. "There's a florist in Vegas I like. They deliver everywhere. I'll give you the number."

She felt sneaky as Denise read the phone number back to her and then took down the credit-card details. But she told herself all was fair in love and war, and even more so since this was a matter of lust and ego gratification.

"What would you like the card to say?" Denise asked.

"'I can't stop thinking about you.' And my name, of course."

Denise chuckled. "You sound smitten."

"Just a little." Jules hoped she sounded innocent. "Thanks for doing this. Oh, and don't forget to have them put my cell number on the card, too…while you're playing Cupid?"

"No problem. I'll call the order in right away."

"I owe you," Jules said.

Denise wished her luck, and Jules gave it thirty minutes, then phoned the florist. Sounding as vague as she could, she said, "I placed an order for flowers about a half hour ago. For Julia Valiant."

"Yes, ma'am. I have the order right here." The clerk sounded young.

"I just realized I might have given you the wrong information for the delivery. I'm sending gifts to a few people for my boss, and I think I was looking at the wrong name. Did I tell you a Mrs. Kelly Smith in Winchester?"

"No, ma'am. This delivery is for Ms. Kate Lambert in Oatman, Arizona."

Jules scratched the information down. "Peonies and irises?"

"Yes. Is the delivery information correct?"

"Phew. Yes, it is. I thought I'd better check. My boss gets mad if I screw up."

The girl laughed. "I know what you're talking about! They'll be delivered on Monday. That's the soonest FedEx can do it."

"Excellent. You've been very helpful." On an impulse, Jules said, "One thing more. Could you include some miniature red roses. Just buds."

"Oh, the tiny ones? They are so cute!"

"If there's an additional charge, please add it to the card." Jules ended the call and slid the phone back into her pocket, crowing, "Candy from a baby."

Bonnie stormed across the back patio, through the open French doors into the kitchen, where Rhianna was feeding Alice.

"That old fool!" She slumped down at the table. "Whatever I say, he's got an answer."

Rhianna passed her a Coke. "He's a lonely, stubborn old man. I think he's just doing this to get attention."

"Well, he sure as hell got mine." Bonnie cracked open the soda and gulped some down. Catching her small daughter's transfixed stare, she calmed her voice and leaned over to kiss Alice's head. "Mommy's upset but there's nothing to worry about. After you've had your lunch, we're going to play with your farm animals."

"So he hasn't done *anything* about it?" For Alice's benefit, Rhianna kept her tone light as well.

Their feud with Walter Entwhistle had started out as a boundary disagreement when the Mosses put up a new back fence just after Christmas. During the past two months, it had deteriorated into a standoff over his latest act of retaliation. Not only had he taken down ten feet of fence where he claimed it crossed into his land, but he'd replaced it with a huge pit. For several weeks the pit had grown wider and deeper by the day; then, all of a sudden, old man Entwhistle had hired some hands and started stripping out scrub and cactus from around his property. This had all ended up in the pit, an obvious hazard to people and animals.

Lloyd and Percy had fenced off the Mosses' side of the pit for safety, only to have Entwhistle knock the fence down, claiming it still encroached. Finally, yesterday, after a visit from the county sheriff, he'd erected a sign proclaiming PRIVATE PROPERTY—TRESPASSERS SHOT.

Bonnie was beyond incensed. She'd tried reason, home-baked goods, and emotional blackmail about his late wife, whom she'd helped during the illness that finally claimed her life. She'd begged Entwhistle to consider Alice and Hadrian, who was hard of hearing and almost blind. All he could say was that if they stayed away from his property, she wouldn't have anything to worry about.

"I don't understand why he's doing this." Bonnie was in tears. "We've been good neighbors to him."

"It's four months since Mrs. Entwhistle passed," Rhianna said. "I think he's really feeling the loss and this is a big distraction for him. Some people create that for themselves when they're not ready to deal with something deeper."

Bonnie sighed. "I know. I'm trying to be understanding, but just go down there and take a look. Those barrel cactus with prickly pear piled on top, some of them have spikes three inches long. And he's started dumping all the waste from his henhouse there, too.

We won't be using the hot tub anytime soon. Very romantic, sitting under the stars breathing in the smell of chicken poop."

Rhianna groaned. "Did he say when he was planning to fill it in?"

"Oh, he rambled on about mulching after summer when it's had a chance to rot down some. I get the impression he's not in any hurry."

"I could try talking with him," Rhianna offered. "He always waves if he sees me and Alice."

"No, he already thinks we're ganging up on him. Anyway, it's not your problem. Lloyd and I need to deal with him." Bonnie peeled a banana, her round face crinkled in puzzlement. "He could have dug that pit anywhere. He's got all that land east of this place, and the hill out west."

"Yes, but then we wouldn't have to pay him any mind." Rhianna wiped Alice's face and hands with a washcloth, picked some noodles from her dark honey curls, and released her from the chair harness.

As soon as she was steady on her feet, the little girl toddled into the den and opened her toy box. Dragging out plastic cows and horses, she called, "Mommy, look."

"I'm coming, sweetie. Get all the pieces out for the big barn and we'll do some building." Bonnie got to her feet and asked Rhianna, "Are you still going to Denver next week?"

"Yes, on Wednesday." Rhianna's stomach bunched. "I'm really sorry."

"It's fine. We knew you had this commitment when we hired you."

"I hope it's only for a week or two. I'll call as soon as I know."

"Don't worry. You'll probably be back home before we are."

Bonnie and Lloyd had decided to go to Europe on vacation before they heard she needed to be away again, this time for weeks. Rhianna had offered to resign when the trial date was finally confirmed rather than cause a problem for her good-hearted employers. She had warned them ahead of time that she had personal matters to attend to in Denver and would be traveling back and forth to resolve these.

She had been intentionally vague, and they had never probed. The Mosses had always made it clear that they respected her privacy.

"Kate." A troubled look appeared in Bonnie's eyes. "I'm not sure how to say this. But Lloyd and I care about you. You're much more than an employee to us and I wish…I mean, if you ever need to talk, or if you need help…" She hesitated. "If you have financial worries…anything. Please don't be embarrassed to tell us. We're here for you."

Rhianna sighed. Obviously her employers knew she was hiding something. How could they not? Smart, attractive young women did not suddenly decide to become nannies and take jobs miles from anywhere.

As Bonnie stared at her, Rhianna decided to acknowledge what was unspoken. "Things aren't as simple as I've said," she began awkwardly. "I know you can see that. But I promise you, I'm not a bad person. I haven't done anything that I need to run from."

"You don't have to tell me that." A flush crept over Bonnie's cheeks. "I know you're a good person. No one can hide their true self all of the time." She closed her fingers gently over Rhianna's arm. "You remind me a lot of a woman I used to work with. She disappeared seven years ago and I never saw her again. For weeks, I had a feeling something was wrong but I didn't ask. You know how that is—you don't want to be nosy. But I always wished I had. I think she needed help, but she didn't know who she could trust."

Wanting to offer some comfort, Rhianna said, "I'm sure it wasn't that she didn't trust you. Maybe she was just trying to protect you by not telling you something."

"Is that what you're doing?"

"In a way, but mostly I'm trying to protect myself."

"It's about that man, isn't it—the one you mentioned?"

"Yes."

Bonnie seemed lost in thought for a few seconds, then she said, "Kate, Lloyd knows people. They're not welcome in my home, but he stays in touch with them." Strained embarrassment tightened her face. "If you need for someone like that to go to Denver with you and…take care of the problem, just ask."

Rhianna laughed softly. "Are you offering me a guy called Joey with a big neck and some anger-management issues?"

Bonnie shrugged innocently. "Knuckle-draggers have their uses."

"You're a friend. But no. I can handle this by myself."

A small petulant voice called, "Mommy? Soon, please."

"I'm being summoned." As Bonnie headed for the den, she glanced back. "The offer's on the table. Remember that when you're there. All you have to do is pick up the phone."

Chapter Six

I can't plead guilty." Brigham was so outraged he dropped his silver toothpick. "I refuse to confess to a crime I did not commit."

"Given the circumstances, the deal is a reasonable one," Jules said with evenhanded calm. "You're facing a rape charge. The DA is willing to reduce that to second-degree assault. That's a class-four felony instead of a class-two. You'd serve eighteen months."

"Prison? That's out of the question."

"Mr. Brigham, if you are found guilty as charged, you are looking at eight to twenty-four years. At a minimum you'll serve a mandatory five."

"But they're not going to find me guilty," the client declared with the confidence of a man who thought he could buy an acquittal.

To some extent he was correct. Jules had handled worse cases and gotten the charges dismissed. And if by some unhappy stroke of fate the jury did not see things her way, there was always the appeal process. Sagelblum had a 90 percent success rate in that arena.

"It's your decision," she said. "I am obligated to discuss the DA's offer with you, that's all."

"Can't you people get the trial delayed again?" Brigham seemed to be having a cranky Monday. He had arrived late for the morning meeting and had complained about the cookies served with his coffee.

"You were arraigned over five months ago," Jules said. "Jury selection begins this week."

Colorado had a speedy trial law that required felony cases to be in front of a jury within six months of arraignment. Sagelblum had already obtained a three-week delay. The firm did not fall back on such tactics in criminal cases unless they were not trial-ready, which would be unusual. They had built their reputation by getting involved early and preparing an aggressive defense that was all about getting ahead of the prosecution. Everyone at the district attorney's office knew that with Sagelblum on board, the case would go all the way and they would have an expensive fight on their hands. In Brigham's case, the continuance had been sought so Jules had time to get back from England and prepare for her role.

"It's up to you," she said. "Take a plea or take your chances."

"You don't think I should accept, do you?" Brigham sounded incredulous.

Jules hesitated. It was tempting to steer this client toward a plea. In Colorado most criminal cases never went to trial, and most men charged with rape were eager to plead guilty to a less-stigmatizing felony. Prosecutors were seldom hard-line unless the media turned a case into a fiasco as they had with the Kobe Bryant prosecution. Normally, a plea bargain was a win/win for all parties. The victim would not have to testify and face humiliation and trauma in a courtroom full of strangers. Judges with clogged calendars could process out offenders. The DA could keep bodies moving and guarantee a conviction.

There was only one problem. Fees.

Sagelblum made the big bucks by going to trial, not pleading their clients out.

"We've already succeeded in getting the charges reduced," Jules said. They'd won a motion to dismiss the kidnapping charge. "If you can pay close attention during preparation and adhere very carefully to the testimony plan, I think we can be optimistic at trial."

"When will she arrive?"

"Who?"

"Rhianna."

"I have no idea."

"Is there somewhere they usually stay—witnesses and so on?"

"I hope you are not contemplating making contact with Ms. Lamb. A restraining order was issued against you, Mr. Brigham. Violating it would be unwise."

"You're right. It would look bad." His resignation sounded phony. "All I want is to apologize and let her know my feelings have not changed. I still want her to be my wife."

Jules had a feeling the plaintiff would be unmoved by this sentiment. She said, "Let me give you some advice. If you walk out of court a free man, put Ms. Lamb out of your mind and don't look back."

"Mommy said exactly the same thing."

"Let's be honest." Jules attempted an argument that would make sense to any self-respecting narcissist. "Some women simply don't know what is in their own best interests. Don't let this one ruin your life."

"I'm not expecting anyone." Bonnie looked up from her accounts reconciliation when the doorbell rang.

Rhianna rose from the sofa, where she'd been reading *The Very Hungry Caterpillar* to Alice. "Maybe it's old man Entwhistle coming over to apologize for being a jerk."

Bonnie snorted. "Don't hold your breath."

Rhianna swung Alice onto her hip and padded through the house to the front door, Hadrian trailing her. He couldn't hear the doorbell anymore, but he still performed guard-dog duty when he realized someone was there. He barked a couple of times, a low, deep sound that would scare the hell out of anyone.

When she looked up at the security monitor, Rhianna broke out in a smile and called, "Looks like your husband finally figured out that he screwed up over your hair. He's sent you flowers."

She heard the sound of Bonnie's eager footsteps as she unlocked the door.

"Kate Lambert?" The FedEx driver on the porch held out an impressive bouquet.

Rhianna supposed such a delivery would normally command an ecstatic response, so her horrified gasp shocked the guy. He took a step back and glanced down at his delivery board.

Bonnie rescued him with a loud squeal. "Oh, my Lord." She stepped past Rhianna to sign for the delivery. "They're stunning."

Rhianna lowered Alice to the floor. Her legs felt like they were about to crumple beneath her. Bile rose in her throat. She thought she was going to vomit on the highly polished floor.

Bonnie tipped the FedEx guy and closed the door after him, cradling the flowers like a newborn. "I don't even know what these are," she gushed, poking at a huge peony. "They're like roses, only so much bigger, and those petals! To die for. Whoever sent these sure has the hots for you!"

Rhianna stared at the heavy wooden door. There was still time to stop the delivery van from driving away. She could tell the driver to take the flowers back where they came from, along with a message that there was no Kate Lambert at this address.

Bonnie finally noticed her silence. "Are you okay? You're really pale."

"Let me see the card," Rhianna said, praying, *Please, God, don't let them be from him.*

Her shooting lessons had been going well, she thought distractedly. Maybe this was Percy's idea of an incentive. She swept another quick look over the flowers. No. Definitely not. Fear tightened its grip on her gut, squeezing until she felt sweat ooze from her pores. Had he found her? Was it possible?

Werner Brigham came from money. That meant he could pay for someone to track her down. That was why she'd been so careful. Her lawyer had told her exactly what it would take to get Brigham out of her life. One of them had to die, or Rhianna Lamb had to vanish without a trace.

She stared down at the envelope and decided she was being ridiculous. It was addressed to Kate Lambert. Wasn't that what she'd set out to do—to rebuild her life under a new identity? The flowers only proved one thing; she'd been successful. Someone thought "Kate" was a real person and had sent flowers to her.

Taking a deep breath to calm her nerves, she extracted the card from the envelope and gingerly turned it over.

I can't stop thinking about you.

Jules

A cell-phone number was typed below.

"Who the heck is Jules and why haven't I heard about him?" Bonnie was reading over her shoulder. "'I can't stop thinking about you!' Oh, be still, my heart."

Rhianna tucked the card hastily into the pocket of her shorts. How could this be happening to her?

Bonnie looked mortified all of a sudden. "They're not from *him*, are they? The problem?"

"No. Jules is a friend."

"A friend who blows serious money on a flower delivery and writes *that* in a card. Uh-huh." Happy again, Bonnie set off toward the kitchen, holding the bouquet aloft so that Hadrian couldn't chew on it. "We need to get these in water."

Alice gripped the hem of Rhianna's shorts and they both followed.

Bonnie lowered the flowers onto the counter and tenderly removed the cellophane. "Two vases, I think. There are so many."

The flowers were truly gorgeous, and so romantic Rhianna felt a delicious thrill just looking at them. It almost didn't matter that she had not given her last name to Jules, and that Jules had somehow found a way to track her down. Rhianna forced herself to think about that unpleasant fact. The woman had ignored her desire for anonymity and had deliberately invaded her privacy. What kind of person did that stuff? Rhianna knew only too well; she'd just escaped from one of them, and Werner Brigham used to send extravagant bouquets, too.

She stared down at the peonies, marveling over the baby-skin delicacy of their clumped ivory petals. A translucent blush of pink barely intruded on the budding inner core of each flower. Green straight iris stems peeped between the blooms, their dark purple tips just beginning to unfurl. The arrangement was set off with miniature rosebuds, all dark velvety red, none in bloom. It was hard to miss the symbolism. Jules had sent her a poem, written in flowers.

That was something Werner Brigham had never done. His opulent flower deliveries sent a message, and it wasn't a subtle one. Huge sprays of Thai orchids, dozens of red roses reclining in a bath of baby's breath, elaborate ikebana. They announced themselves as gestures from a man with money to throw away. There was no consistency, no thought of what might appeal to her. His choices were all about him.

Bonnie climbed the kitchen stepladder and passed a couple of large vases down from a high storage cupboard. "Arrange them out here if you want, then I'll help you carry them to your apartment."

"They're kind of big for the apartment. Let's keep them in the house."

Bonnie gave her a long look. "Why don't you invite Jules to come visit some time." She had obviously attempted a casual air, but Rhianna could tell she was dying of curiosity. "Lloyd could take him fishing up the Colorado or whatever, so he wouldn't be stuck here with us girls the whole time."

Rhianna lifted Alice into her chair harness and secured the straps. She sliced an apple and set the pieces on a plate, arranged like a happy face, with a couple of raisins for eyes. Alice had a picky appetite and Rhianna had found the best way to tempt her was to make her meals fun. She could already imagine the adult Alice, fussy around the house, washing her hands often, spending too long reading the menu at restaurants.

The little girl was very particular about everything. Her food, her clothes, even the bows in her hair. She amazed both Bonnie and Rhianna by putting away her toys without being asked and requesting a washcloth whenever she spilled a drop of paint or food on herself. Bonnie worried that such behavior was unnatural, but Rhianna thought it was a whole lot better than having to care for one of those toddlers who behaved like a wild animal. That might have been a deal breaker.

"Bonnie," she ruffled Alice's golden curls on her way to the counter, "Jules is a woman."

So far, Rhianna had not identified herself as a lesbian. She had asked the Mosses at their interview if they objected to gay or lesbian people working for them. The couple had been so outspoken in their disgust with homophobia and hypocrisy that she knew she didn't need to disclose any more personal information than necessary. Her lawyer had told her that the less other people knew about her, the fewer pieces they could put together.

During the six months she'd worked for the Mosses, she had met many of their more senior employees, folks invited to the house for outdoor parties and barbecues. Several were gay men and Rhianna was pretty certain one of the women was a lesbian. The Mosses were clearly gay-friendly.

Bonnie repeated, "A woman?" It seemed to hit her then and she sounded a little miffed as she said, "You should have filled me in sooner! There I was inviting single males to our barbecues and bugging Lloyd to find someone decent...now you tell me I've been barking up the wrong tree the whole time?"

"In a word, yes."

Bonnie got busy rinsing the vases and filling them with water. "You know, I wondered, because you never seemed interested in any of the guys. But I had no idea."

"I'm sorry. I should have said something."

"Why? I mean, I don't go around saying 'by the way, everyone, I'm a heterosexual.' It's no one's business."

"I would have told you from the start if I felt it might be a problem," Rhianna said. "I mean...with Alice. A gay person looking after your child. Not everyone would be comfortable with that."

"Well, they're ignorant. Name me ten lesbians who've been convicted of child molestation, and I'll name you a thousand heterosexuals."

Smiling, Rhianna located a pair of shears and began to trim the stems and place the flowers in water.

"I mean it about your friend," Bonnie said. "Invite her out here when you get back from Denver."

Rhianna caught a flash of herself and Jules stepping out onto the patio as the sun rose behind the Black Mountains and spilled its bright gold beams across the jagged horizon. Nice idea, but she was pretty certain cozy, domesticated togetherness was not what Jules had in mind when she suggested they hook up occasionally. She was amazed all over again that Jules had bothered to send a romantic bouquet when she only wanted another casual encounter. A woman like her couldn't possibly be short of dates.

"I'm not looking to get involved with anyone right now," she told Bonnie. "But thanks. It's really kind of you to offer."

"Well, for entirely selfish reasons, I'm happy that you're single, but I hope you change your mind about that before too much longer. No one is an island."

Rhianna laughed. "Do you know how funny that sounds, living out here in the desert?"

Bonnie joined her laugher and trimmed a couple of iris stems. "I should get back to those accounts. I'll put Alice down for her nap."

After Bonnie carried her sleepy daughter away, Rhianna finished arranging the flowers and carried the vases one at a time to their respective destinations, the larger to the hall table near the front door, the smaller to her apartment. She set the modern crystal container down on her dressing table, then took the florist's card from her pocket. Good manners dictated that she should call Jules to thank her. She also wanted an explanation. How had Jules managed to obtain the name and address Rhianna had not divulged to her? What else did she know?

She stared down at the phone number for a long time before she dialed. Although she'd mentally rehearsed a message to leave on the voice mail, the sound of Jules's voice shocked her so much that she couldn't speak at first. All she could remember was that same warm, low drawl in her ear as they had sex for hours.

"Kate?"

A real person. She hadn't expected that. "Oh, I thought I'd be talking to a machine."

"I saw the area code on caller ID and figured it was you. It's good to hear from you."

"Well, I'm sure you must have expected me to call," Kate said dryly. "To say thanks for the flowers." Before she could get as far as a comment on the invasion of her privacy, Jules preempted her.

"I want to apologize for hunting you down when you didn't share your personal details with me. You have every reason to be angry, and I'll understand if you toss the flowers in the trash and hang up right now." She paused and in a velvety tone said, "I promise, if you want to end this call, I'll respect your choice and never contact you again."

Rhianna stared at the flowers. Their faint sweet scent already pervaded her room. What did she really want? Her uncertainty surprised her. She had been so determined to keep to her plan, it had only occurred to her on the drive back from Palm Springs that she had no reason to refuse to see Jules again. Just because having sex had not freed her of her demons, she shouldn't necessarily give up on the woman she had slept with.

She'd been stunned to awaken after their night together still feeling displaced in her own skin. Worse still, her body bore such plain testimony to the pleasure she'd experienced, it only made her numbness more acute. But perhaps repeat encounters might change that. Or perhaps she just needed to give herself more time.

No one made an overnight recovery from rape. Why should she be any different? She'd had intensive therapy for two months after the attack, and then she became fed up. All she wanted was to stop thinking about that night and move on. She wanted to build a new life in a place where no one knew anything about what had happened and the people she worked with treated her just like anyone else. She was fed up with the pity and embarrassment, with people falling silent when she walked into a room.

Living a sane life had become impossible for her in Denver, and when Werner Brigham was released on bail after the preliminary hearing, she had known the protection order would make no difference. He would come after her again, and this time she would not get away.

"Kate, are you there?"

Rhianna wondered how her real name would sound from those lips. The thought set off a small warning explosion in the back of her mind. This was why she had to be careful about getting close to people. The first thing she wanted to do was tell them the truth. She hated living a lie, having to pretend to be someone other than herself. But she could not afford to relax. It was too soon. She hadn't come this far, lost so much that mattered, just to give herself away because she wanted to hear a sexy woman speak her name.

"I'm here," she said. "How did you find me?"

"Actually, I didn't find you. I cheated. I asked the owners at Casitas to send the bouquet on my behalf."

A flood of relief engulfed Rhianna. Jules hadn't traced her after all. She'd agonized over the registration form when she'd checked into Casitas, wondering how she could avoid providing an address when it was probably required for billing to a credit card. For a few moments, she'd even considered paying for her room in cash, then she realized she was being silly. It didn't matter if she wrote down an address for Kate on a form at a hotel or a doctor's office. No one in the world knew that Kate Lambert was Rhianna Lamb.

"So they didn't give you my details?" she confirmed.

"No. Although, since you just called me from your address, I have the landline number now."

Rhianna rolled her eyes. She had assumed Jules knew where she was, so it wouldn't matter if she used the Mosses' phone to call. Not that it made any difference. She reminded herself yet again that it was okay for people to know where "Kate Lambert" lived. In fact, it would only arouse suspicion if she behaved secretively. She had assumed a new identity, and if she wanted to avoid drawing attention to herself, she needed to act like a normal person.

Curious, she said, "Why did you want to get in touch with me?"

"Because I haven't been able to get you out of my mind." The answer was almost a cliché, but Jules did not sound flippant.

Rhianna wasn't sure what to say. "I'm flattered, but—"

"Just hear me out. I know you're not looking for a girlfriend, but does that mean you've taken a vow of celibacy?"

"I guess I'm trying to avoid complications. I don't want to mislead anyone about what I can offer."

"Then we have that in common," Jules said. "Come on, Kate.

Don't you think if I wanted a regular partner I'd have one? I'm quite a catch."

"And modest to a fault." Rhianna laughed.

"Just stating the facts. I have a well-paying job, a big house, a nice life. Finding someone to share all that would probably take me a week. If I wasn't fussy and if I bothered to look."

"Why don't you?"

"Because I know my limitations. I can't make long-term relationships work. I've tried."

"Me, too."

"Is that what happened to you?"

"What do you mean?"

A short silence followed, then Jules said as if she were measuring each word, "I can recognize damage. It's not rocket science."

Rhianna eased her white-knuckle grip on the phone and flexed her fingers. What was Jules trying to say? Did she think getting tied up was weird? She seemed to be into it at the time. Embarrassed, Rhianna said, "I don't *have* to tie someone up to have sex, you know. It was just a spur-of-the-moment thing."

"I'm not talking about *that*. I like games."

"Then what?"

"It was just a feeling." Jules's tone was very casual. "I could be completely off base. So…I have a suggestion. Let's meet again and prove I'm wrong." When Rhianna didn't answer, she teased, "I guess you saw that coming, huh?"

Rhianna's heart thudded loudly in her ears. "Okay, let's meet."

"When?"

Right now. Rhianna let herself imagine Jules naked in her bed, staring up at her with those shadowed eyes, the pupils huge and black. Saying the things she said. *Come on. Do me. You know I want it.* Tasting the way she tasted—wet honey, bitter almond, and salt. Rhianna could feel the slick aftermath of her, clinging to her mouth and chin. She'd held nothing back. Rhianna had wanted total control and Jules had given it to her. A gift. Rhianna had known it, and yet she'd thrown it back at Jules the next morning, walking away like it meant nothing. Suddenly, she wanted to make up for that rebuff, but she wasn't sure how. She certainly couldn't reciprocate in kind. It wouldn't matter how well she knew someone; she would never be able to surrender herself completely.

"I wish you were here." The words were out before she could get a grip on herself.

"Me, too." Something changed in the timbre of Jules's voice. "I want you."

"Mmm." Rhianna's nipples tightened.

"God, I could come so easily right now." Jules sighed. "I've been like this all week."

Rhianna hesitated. "I can still feel you."

A soft groan teased her ear. "Do you know how wet you just made me?"

"I wish I could touch you," Rhianna whispered.

"Tell me what you want."

"To have you in my mouth. Sucking until you're hard and swollen and you just have to come." Rhianna heard a soft groan and a metallic click. Jules had just locked her door. The knowledge swept through her, making her nerves tingle. She got off her bed and did the same. "I've been thinking about you, too. Ever since Palm Springs."

"Thinking what?"

"Mostly about you fucking me."

A sharp intake of breath made static on the phone. "Jesus." Jules's voice fractured slightly. "We can't have this conversation. I'm at work."

"And I'm in my bedroom. Lonely. Dripping wet—"

"Tease," Jules said hoarsely. "I can't wait to have you again."

"You could have me right now." Rhianna wasn't sure what wicked instinct had possessed her, but she felt incredibly aroused and aware of her own power. Jules was far away, stuck in an office somewhere, trying to look like she was in control. Only she wasn't.

"Stop," Jules gasped out. "I have to be in a meeting in ten minutes. I'm serious."

"And I have to come. Really, really soon," Rhianna said sweetly.

"Are you touching yourself?"

"Do you want me to?"

"Yes. Talk to me. Tell me what you feel."

Rhianna shuffled farther up the bed and unzipped her shorts. Her panties were soaked. She worked her fingers over the narrow ridge of her clit and along the channels on either side. "My clit is really hard, and I'm slippery and open. All ready for you."

"I'm right there, between your legs, waiting. You know what it's going to feel like when I fuck you, don't you?"

"Yes." Rhianna let her fingers glide back and forth, keeping her pressure light, teasing herself. "You're so good, I want you inside. Deep and hard."

"Oh, God." Short ragged breaths. "You're making me sweat."

For a split second, Rhianna wondered what on earth she was thinking. How could she be doing this? What if Bonnie picked up the phone and overheard? What if she came to the apartment for some reason and found the door locked? *That's your common sense talking*, she thought, and proceeded to ignore the voice of reason, pushing her shorts and panties down and kicking them off. She wanted this. She'd been wanting it ever since she got back from Palm Springs. Pretending otherwise was pointless.

"I wish you could feel how open I am," she murmured. "Come here. I want my legs around you."

"You want me to fuck you?"

Rhianna gasped. "Yes. Please."

"Like this? Spreading you wide and making you take me? Is that what you need, baby?"

Rhianna closed her eyes and shut out everything but Jules's voice and the steadily building tension between her legs. Her sense memories of their one night together were still intact, and she plugged into them, recalling every sensation. She tilted her hips, rising against the pressure of her hand.

Jules kept talking to her, urging her on. She centered the pressure of her fingers where it was unbearable. Transfixed, she groaned, "I'm so close."

"Me, too," Jules moaned.

"I can't believe it. I never come so fast." Rhianna clamped her thighs together on her hand, rocking and bucking.

She could hear sounds at the other end of the phone. Raw, yearning groans and murmured words she could not make out. The taste and smell of Jules seeped through the thin walls of memory, flooding her with desire. If she'd ever felt this way about one of her few other lovers, she couldn't remember.

"Don't stop. Now!" she cried. "Do it. Come on. Come inside me." She felt herself spill and pulse, soaking her hand and shivering with pleasure.

A stifled cry of release held her riveted, clutching the phone like it was a part of Jules she could cling to. They were silent, only breathing. Rhianna felt as close to Jules as if they were locked in a lovers' embrace, and there was much more between them than words through a telephone.

"When can I see you?" Rhianna asked.

"I could be in Palm Springs on Saturday." Jules's voice had a rasping edge to it.

Rhianna caught her breath with some difficulty. "I can't. I have to go away for a while." She didn't want to think about what was ahead. Not now. But she needed to let Jules know she was serious about getting together. Nervously, she offered a partial truth. "I'll be in Denver visiting family."

Jules laughed softly. "There is a God, after all. I'm working in Denver at the moment. We could meet."

Rhianna recoiled at the thought. The timing couldn't be worse. She had no idea how she was going to cope with the stress of being back in Denver, about to give evidence at her attacker's trial. She couldn't add another whole dimension to the trip. "I'm not sure if I can," she said evasively. "I mean, my mom has made plans."

Her excuse sounded weak. Like she had cold feet already.

Jules didn't seem to notice. "Call me on this number as soon as you get in. My firm has an apartment downtown. You can come stay for a night or two."

"I'll have to see how it goes," Rhianna said.

"I don't think so," Jules responded slowly and firmly. "Your mom will just have to cope without you."

Rhianna rolled onto her side and drew her knees up. She felt flushed and heavy with post-orgasmic lassitude, and the truth was, the thought of seeing Jules made the dreaded prospect of the next week or two almost bearable. "Okay," she said, "it's a date."

"Don't plan anything for the next day," Jules warned her. "I'm going to keep you up all night."

CHAPTER SEVEN

"Mr. Brigham?"

Werner hastened to his feet and offered his hand. He felt proud of himself for having sufficient cosmopolitan flair not to hesitate in this courtesy when tall, muscular Gilbert Desjardines loomed before him.

The man was not what he'd expected for a private investigator, not the modern-day Humphrey Bogart of his imaginings. Desjardines was black, not that Werner had any problem with colored people being in responsible jobs. The Brigham family had always employed black women as housekeepers and nannies, and his mother often said there was no decent fried chicken without a black cook in charge of the kitchen.

Werner could also call to mind black police officers he'd encountered, and private security personnel. It made complete sense that there would be black private eyes. However, this one was not the clean-cut, suit-and-tie black man he'd seen on television commercials. It appeared that Gilbert Desjardines was drawn, like many of his race, to a more flamboyant look. His suit was pale green and he wore a skintight pink shirt unbuttoned at the neck to reveal not one, but at least four heavy gold chains. His taste for flashy jewelry was equally apparent in the diamond rings on several of his fingers.

This was, Werner decided, not a look a white man would ever get away with. However, he wanted to assure the investigator that his appearance would not be held against him, so he said, "I've heard reports that you are the best there is, Mr. Desjardines. That's why I'm here."

This remark was greeted with a tooth-studded smile, and Desjardines waved him into an office that was the last word in idiosyncratic décor. If someone had asked Werner what the domicile of a pimp might look like, this is what he would have described. The walls were a very dark purple, most of the furnishings bright yellow, and there was even a faux leopard rug on the floor. In the far corner of this startling work environment, a mulatto woman who perfectly fit the setting was doing something to a coffee machine.

She batted her heavy eyelashes in their direction and said, "Kawfee?"

Werner might have imagined he was hallucinating if he couldn't smell the rich aroma of a good brew. He thanked her and tried not to stare as he sat down on the yellow leather sofa near Desjardines's desk. She was a fake blonde, of course, with a pile of frizzy curls held high on her head with a dramatic pink comb. This accessory matched the shade of an indecent top that clung to improbably large breasts. She completed this shameless outfit with a velvet miniskirt, black lace hosiery, and high heels of the type no respectable female would wear.

When she bent to serve the coffee, Werner had to lean away for fear of suffocation. Her cleavage was virtually in his face and her perfume was sickeningly sweet. He felt like telling Desjardines that only a certain class of customer would be impressed by a secretary who looked like an exotic dancer. Instead, he said, "Thank you, ma'am."

"Mr. Brigham, meet Damonique Nova, my business partner." Desjardines handed Werner a card with the woman's absurd name on it. "Spousal fidelity testing, she's da bomb."

Whereupon the blonde inquired in her grating accent, "Are you a married man, Mr. Brigham?"

"Not yet," Werner said. "But I hope to become engaged shortly."

"Congratulations. I sure hope things work out for you." She

wiggled her hips as she crossed to the door. To Desjardines, she said, "I got a skip trace to take care of. You good, baby?"

He made some kind of hand signal and the door closed, leaving Werner to wonder if he had made a wise choice in coming here. These people did not strike him as seasoned professionals.

He got to the point quickly. "I'm a client of Salazar, Hagel & Goldblum. I could not help but notice your card among papers on my attorney's desk recently, and there is a matter I believe you may be able to assist me with. I pay well."

Desjardines sat down behind his big desk, the only decent piece of furniture in the room. "I'm listening."

Werner lifted his briefcase and laid it on the desk. Feeling pleased with himself for thinking ahead, he unlocked the case and flipped it open. As he had anticipated, the investigator leaned forward with a look of astonishment on his face.

"Man, what you thinking carrying that much cash around with you?" he asked.

"This is for you. Fifty thousand dollars."

"Put it away," Desjardines said. "I don't deal drugs and I don't launder cash."

"I'm not interested in any of that," Werner said impatiently. "This is for your services. I want to hire you to…er…tail someone for me."

"Who?"

Werner poked around under the neatly stacked bills, pulled out Rhianna's photograph, and slid it across the desk. "This is my fiancée-to-be. She's going to be in town very soon because she's a witness in a court case."

"Ah, you want protection? Now we don't exactly do that, but I got a cousin, Marcel—"

"No, not protection. I want you to watch her. Find out where she's staying and who she sees. Then, when she leaves town again, follow her wherever she goes. I have reason to believe she may be living under a false identity."

The investigator stared at him. "Now, why would she do that?"

"She has fragile mental health."

Desjardines studied the photograph, then returned it to the case and closed the lid. He pushed the case back across the desk and shook his head. "You talking to the wrong man."

"Fifty thousand dollars is nothing to me," Werner assured him. "I can pay more. Name your fee."

"You're not hearing me." Desjardines stood up. "You want to make a bad situation worse for yourself?"

Infuriated, Werner said, "All I want is her new name and address."

"I can't help you." The investigator crossed his office and flung open the door.

Werner rose and crossed the room to stand in the doorway. He refused to be intimidated. "Do you have any idea who I am?"

"I know who you are." Desjardines seemed bigger suddenly. "Go talk to your lawyer. Ask *her* why this is a crazy-ass idea if you don't believe me."

Rattled, Werner slammed out of the office and caught the elevator down to street level. He stood on the pavement with his heart pounding and sweat damping his top lip. Where had he parked his car? As he looked up and down the street, it occurred to him that this was indeed the wrong neighborhood to loiter in with fifty thousand dollars in his briefcase. He could see Mommy's disappointed face when the police brought him home, mugged and minus the cash.

At times like this, it was important to look calm and confident and behave like he knew exactly where he was going. *You* own *this street,* Werner told himself. Adopting a casual stride, he set off north, aware that he was already attracting a few second looks. The neighborhood was only getting worse. After a block or so, Werner concluded that he must have parked in the other direction. He chose a post to lean against, then took his cell phone from his pocket like he was answering a call. As he pretended to talk, he watched the traffic slowing for the nearest set of lights. A car caught his eye, a late-model SUV lavishly fitted with chrome and a custom paint job. Rap music boomed from its open windows, and an individual had a hand draped over the door tapping away to the tuneless beat. Costly jewelry glittered from his fingers.

In that moment a brilliant plan dawned on Werner. He had tried going about this the right way, but thanks to Desjardines, he was now forced to explore alternatives. Slipping his hand inside his briefcase as covertly as he could, he withdrew a wad of bills, crammed them in his pocket, then locked the case. The lights would change at any moment. He needed to act fast or lose his opportunity.

A youth stood nearby wearing shorts that did not cover his underpants. Werner imagined he was the type who spoke in a vernacular incomprehensible to anyone whose first language was English. He approached the boy and said, "Excuse me, young man. Do you want to make five hundred dollars?"

The kid looked him up and down dubiously. His response sounded like, "Whatchu talkin' bout?"

"Go tell the driver of that car that I would like a conversation with him. Tell him this is about money."

"Yo." The kid stuck his hand out. "Hit me."

Werner thought assaulting this character was probably not in the interests of his health. As he tried to interpret the invitation, the kid rolled his eyes.

With exaggerated patience, he said, "Put your down payment here, man."

Werner found a hundred in one of his pockets and poked it into the hand. He said, "You may consider that a gratuity."

The kid sidled off, and a few minutes later, the lights changed and the SUV crawled past Werner, then slid to a halt. A stringy black man in a ball cap and a satin jacket got out of the passenger side and mooched over.

"I hear you is asking for a meeting with my man, Mr. Notorious Hard?"

Werner refrained from scoffing at the name. He took the wad of twenties from his pocket and handed it to this go-between. "Please pay that young man over there five hundred dollars. You may keep the rest for yourself as payment for your services."

The man in the ball cap gave a courteous nod. This was how it worked, Werner thought. He had seen television shows about gangs. Everything came down to respect. They were unhappy when they did not receive their due. He could understand that. He felt exactly the same way.

After the kid had been paid, Werner spoke to the go-between in his most deferential manner. "Please inform Mr. Hard that I am looking for a superior individual to perform a surveillance job. No violence. Clean work. I will pay twenty thousand in cash to the businessman who can carry out this assignment for me."

No need to go crazy. Twenty thousand was surely sufficient to secure the attention of a man whose vehicle was probably his office.

The go-between adjusted his ball cap and signaled toward the car in some kind of sign language. With the cordiality Werner should rightfully have received from Desjardines, his new friend said, "Mr. Notorious Hard is the superior individual who can do this business for you. Walk with me, Mr. Moneyman."

Jules stepped out of a meeting to take Gilbert Desjardines's call.

"That fool was in here this morning. Put fifty on the table."

"You told him to take a walk?"

"Yeah. He wasn't happy."

Jules sighed. She would be thrilled when this case was over. At the best of times, defending an alleged sex offender was challenging. But most of them understood the gravity of the situation and conducted themselves accordingly. Brigham was a loose cannon.

"Any progress on Lamb?"

"I have people on the parents' house and the best friend."

"Do something for me, Gil. As soon as she shows, put a security tail on her as well." The last thing they needed was for Brigham to violate the restraining order on the eve of his trial.

"I'll call Marcel."

"If anyone sees Brigham hanging around, I want to know."

"You want me to put someone on him, too?"

Jules vacillated. She'd thought about it, but Sagelblum was squeamish about placing a client under surveillance. Understandably, no one wanted to pay the bill to be spied on by their own legal team.

"No, it's an overreach," she said. "If we can keep him away from her until the trial's over, that works."

She ended the call and returned to the conference room. These were the final few days for the defense team to fine-tune their strategy. Jury selection would begin tomorrow, and the makeup of the final twelve would dictate certain aspects of their approach during trial. But right now, they were rehearsing their key witnesses once more, and Jules was testing her opening statement in front of the team. Everyone was tired. At this stage, all-nighters were routine and the team's energy was fueled by strong coffee, adrenaline, and the goal of another reputation-enhancing victory.

"Take a break, people," she said from the doorway. It was after one and their day had started at seven. "Go eat lunch." She stopped Sid Lyle on his way out. "Want to walk and talk?"

Sid was her secondary and the local counsel on the team. Sagelblum never contracted out a case. Instead the firm pulled in a local attorney, if none of their branch offices was licensed for the jurisdiction, then obtained admission to practice. Or they used a lead counsel from a branch office, as was the case in Denver. The partners had discovered long ago that you couldn't send a high-octane Los Angeles trial lawyer into a hick-town courtroom and expect him or her to win over the jury and a judge who had never made the big time himself.

At the same time, bringing in a national trial attorney provided a buffer. Local counsel sometimes had vested interests, and politics could prevent them from adopting the most aggressive tactics. They still had to do business in their jurisdiction once the trial was over. If anyone got pissed off, it was useful to have someone to blame— the fancy defense attorney brought in from elsewhere by the client made an ideal scapegoat.

Jules had worked with Sid before and found him to be a

straight shooter. He was not a Yale wunderkind in an Italian suit; he was a down-home guy any mother would love. Polite. Genuine. Ordinary looking, with a wedding ring and some middle-aged spread. Pictures of his four kids crowded his desk. His oldest was fighting in Iraq, his second was a local high-school football hero. His young daughters were twins and had appeared on television with their mother, spearheading a local campaign to buy state-of-the-art artificial limbs and equipment for young amputees from disadvantaged backgrounds.

Everyone saw Sid Lyle as a man of the highest ethical standards. If he told a jury a client was innocent, they wanted to take him at his word. In a case like this one, Jules would have him question the weakest witnesses to lend their testimonies greater weight, and she would refrain from using him on cross. If anyone was going to look like a villain, it had to be her.

She said, "Brigham tried to put a tail on Lamb this morning."

"We should have taken the DA's offer," Sid said.

"I agree."

"You want me to talk to him again?"

"Yeah, and this time frighten the shit out of him," Jules said. "He thinks a Brigham won't be sent to prison in this town. His grandfather was a governor. His mother knows Nancy Reagan. He doesn't get it that the law applies to people like him, too."

"Can't we take a run at getting him certified? His mother could make it happen."

"Carl won't buy it."

"Carl would sell Christ a ticket to his own crucifixion," Sid said in disgust. "Brigham needs help, and that's giving him the benefit of the doubt."

"I hear you. But he's not our responsibility. Our job is to keep him out of trouble until we have a verdict. After that, he's on his own."

"I'll see what I can do." Sid sounded weary. "Some cases…you just know it's going to end in tears."

❖

Love is always in the air at baggage claims, Rhianna thought as she waited by the carousel at Denver International. Around her, people clung to one another, made pickup arrangements, chatted blithely like no one could hear them except the person at the other end of their Bluetooth. Fragments of conversation cluttered the air. Every second sentence was "I love you."

Or that was how it seemed.

Rhianna resisted the urge to break out her new prepaid cell phone to prove she, too, had someone special who wanted to know the moment she'd landed safely. She watched smiles break across eager faces, hands swing together, lovers kiss. Her parents didn't know when she was coming in. That was intentional. Rhianna planned to take a taxi to her best friend Mimi's place in LoDo, then call them and arrange to meet at a cousin's home.

Her mom thought she was being overly dramatic, but her dad supported her. They all agreed that this would be over soon and she would no longer need to live her life in fear, wondering if she would turn a street corner and be dragged into a car.

Rhianna caught sight of her two bags and hauled them off the carousel onto a trolley. The Denver weather was supposed to be cool, typical for March, so she wheeled past the crowd to a line of seats near one of the exit doors and opened the case that held her woolen coat. She was back here, she thought suddenly, and her heart began to race. She slid her arms into the coat, tugged the zipper closed on her bag, and flopped into one of the seats to calm her breathing.

She had almost been tempted to cancel the trip, to call her victim advocate and tell her she could not go through with the trial. For the first time since Werner Brigham had invaded her world, she was starting to feel safe and could actually laugh. Missing friends and family was the big drawback with her new life, but she could imagine a time when she could return to visit. Werner Brigham could not possibly stay interested in her forever, especially if he couldn't find her. Sooner or later, he would give up and turn his attention to someone else. All she had to do was wait.

Recently, during one of her occasional phone calls, her father had suggested they plan a family vacation. He thought they could go on a cruise. He and her mom had been saving for a couple of years toward a dream holiday, and they had enough to include her. One of her brothers and his wife would join them. It would be like old times when they all went camping together, only the food would be edible.

Rhianna loved the idea and they'd agreed that after the trial, when the crazy man was locked up, that's how they would celebrate. A wayward thought crossed her mind as she stared at the people milling in the arrivals area. What if something came of her affair with Jules, if that's what it could be called? What would her parents think if she wanted to bring a girlfriend along on a family holiday? So far, she'd never asked them to accept someone as her partner. She'd never brought anyone home for Thanksgiving or Christmas, other than Mimi one year when Mimi's parents were out of town. None of her relationships had been that serious.

Rhianna wondered why that was. She had a group of good friends, and somehow they'd fallen into the habit of going out together. They were all single, all in their twenties, and she'd known most of them her whole life. Gradually, over the past several years, some had started pairing off and getting engaged, and the circle had grown smaller. Mimi was the only one who knew Rhianna was a lesbian, although she was sure a couple of the others had guessed.

Rhianna had been meaning to come out to them ever since she came out to herself after she graduated from college, but she'd been a coward. Although none of her circle was anti-gay, as far as she knew, Rhianna had always worried that something would change if she told them who she was. It wasn't as if she wanted to live a "gay lifestyle" 24/7, going to GLBT community events, getting involved in politics, or mixing only with gays and lesbians. She had never wanted to be pigeonholed that way; she didn't see why she needed to make a public statement out of her personal feelings.

The few people closest to her knew, and if anyone else had ever asked she would not have lied. But no one had. Rhianna knew she was guilty of deceit by omission, and she knew that allowing people to make assumptions was taking the easy way out. But so what? Everyone had things about themselves that they didn't discuss, and she was not one of those exhibitionists who thought the whole world needed to know what color panties she wore. There would be no MySpace if everyone was like her.

That was one of the reasons the thought of this trial made her feel ill. Bad enough that she would have to see that loathsome man sitting in the courtroom next to his lawyers, acting like he was innocent. But the idea of having to take the stand and explain what had happened, to answer disgusting intrusive questions, to hear it implied that she had somehow invited her attack—Rhianna had no idea how she was going to cope.

For the next two days she was supposed to be spending time with Norman Clay, the prosecuting attorney, reviewing her testimony again. She'd already been back and forth from Denver several times since she'd moved to Oatman. Thanks to the preparation she'd received, she knew what to expect when she took the stand. Mr. Clay had warned her that a big-city trial attorney would be coming in to represent Brigham. The last time they'd spoken, he still didn't know who that would be, but Rhianna imagined a slick, handsome lawyer with a ski tan and a perfect smile.

The defense would try to make it look like she was to blame for what had happened, but Norman Clay said that strategy would be an uphill struggle because she was a credible plaintiff. All she had to do was be herself and tell the truth. He had made one request, that she get her hair color changed back to blond by the time she appeared in court. He thought her new look was too sophisticated.

Rhianna had made an appointment with a hairdresser for Friday afternoon and was even getting extensions so she would appear in court with the blond ponytail she used to have. She supposed it was a good idea. At least Brigham would not get to see how much she had changed her appearance. The less he knew about her, the better.

She checked her wristwatch. It was almost 7:00 p.m. Idly she wondered what Jules was doing and whether she was home. Her stomach fluttered. She still couldn't believe she had actually had phone sex, something she'd snickered over in the past when one of her friends had bragged about doing it. She would never have imagined the experience could be so erotic. Even now, just thinking about it made her wet, yet she was mystified by the appeal. How could she get so aroused just talking on the phone? Was it healthy?

She pictured Jules at work, impeccably dressed, about to go to a meeting but getting all flustered and wanting to have sex instead. The thought made her blood run lusciously hot, flooding every sensitive spot. Her clit tingled. Her nipples perked. She felt gloriously female, powerful and desirable. This was how sexy women felt, she thought. They knew they could make someone want them. Rhianna had never experienced that heady self-awareness until now. Until Jules.

Impulsively she took her new cell phone from her purse, along with the card Jules had sent with the flowers. She dialed the number and held her breath.

"Jules Valiant." Her voice seemed flat and distracted.

Rhianna almost hung up, sensing she had probably called at a bad time. But she wanted at least to say hello and confirm their date for Saturday night. Nervously, she said, "Jules, it's me…Kate. I'm at the airport."

In a heartbeat the tone changed. "It's so good to hear your voice. Don't move. Don't get a taxi. Don't even think about going to your parents' place. I'm coming to get you."

Rhianna laughed. "You can't do that. Our date's not till Saturday."

"Are you seriously going to pretend you called me just to say hello?"

The smoky drawl somehow insinuated its way from Rhianna's ear to her throat, stifling the breath she needed to draw. "No," she admitted, taking in a sharp gulp of air.

"Good. Because I've finally finished work and I can't think of anything I'd like more than to see you."

"I'd like that, too." Why pretend otherwise? Rhianna smiled helplessly. With all the shit that had happened to her over the past eighteen months, she was owed one good thing, and Jules was certainly that.

"Are you at the baggage claim?"

"Yes." Rhianna wished she'd worn something more interesting than jeans and a simple sweater. Maybe she would go change in the ladies' restroom.

"Take the elevator down to level four," Jules instructed. "I'll be at the curbside pickup in twenty minutes. Dark gray Mercedes CLS550."

"I was planning to see a friend later," Rhianna said feebly. Fortunately she hadn't told Mimi for certain which day she would arrive. She had a house key and a standing invitation to show up whenever she was in town.

"She'll understand," Jules said. "I'm on my way to the parking garage at work."

"Okay. Good. I mean…fantastic." Rhianna hesitated, then spilled exactly what she was thinking. "Jules…I can't wait to see you."

"Don't sound so amazed. My ego can't handle it."

"Then I guess I'll have to make it up to you," Rhianna teased recklessly.

"You know I'm going to hold you to that, don't you?"

Rhianna knew there was a hot, dark gleam in Jules's eyes. "I was hoping you might."

CHAPTER EIGHT

Jules shoved Kate's luggage into the designer apartment used by Sagelblum trial attorneys when they were in town. The ride from the airport had been exquisitely tense, the conversation, erratic. She felt knotted inside, not quite able to believe her own turbulent emotions. She couldn't think. She was awash with craving, a prisoner of Kate's every unconscious movement: The quivering copper of her hair as the Denver breeze plucked at it on the way to the car. The curve of her neck as she lowered her head to get in the passenger seat. The slope of a wrist, the hitch of a shoulder, the way one of her knees angled in against the other as she sat.

When they spoke, Jules was lost. Her blood stirred at the shape of Kate's mouth. She wanted to stroke a finger around it and tease the shadow beneath her lower lip. Kiss her. Fuck her. Not let her sleep. The force of these desires troubled her. She supposed she was used to calling the shots with women. Kate's ambivalence about their budding liaison had made her uneasy. Perhaps that could explain her intense desire. Was she desperate to somehow stake a claim? How juvenile.

Normally, she didn't get possessive, even in the few relationships that lasted longer than a month. Neither did she harbor strange anxieties or agonize about the future. Self-torment was not her style. And she never chased women; it was the other way around. What had gone wrong this time?

The moment she saw Kate standing at the baggage claim, it crossed her mind to wonder if she'd finally stumbled on The One.

The thought shook her. Worse still, it stayed with her, lurking in the back of her mind as a tempting explanation for all that was strange about their fling so far.

Jules was not prey to flights of fancy or delusions of presentiment, but she could not escape the sense that Kate was significant. At the same time she felt that at any moment she could vanish, and that she'd only allowed Jules into her life because of some mysterious agenda. Jules feared she would still be groping in the dark, trying to fathom the role she'd been assigned, when she was discarded. This possibility had both decimated her peace of mind and heightened her anticipation during the twenty-minute drive to downtown Denver.

Hoping Kate hadn't noticed her distraction level, she nudged the apartment door closed with a knee and wheeled the luggage out of the way. Kate removed her coat and hung it on the decorative stand just inside the entrance; then she strolled lightly into the living area, her head tilted back so she could take in the full splendor of the room's central feature. A vast modern chandelier fell from the thirty-foot atrium-style ceiling like a flock of torn crystal ticket stubs, each swaying and pivoting in the faint rush of the air-conditioning.

She executed a slow twirl, her smile radiant. "This is amazing."

"Yes." Jules plucked a smile from the chaos of her responses. "I never get used to it."

All at once, she was frantic with the urge to throw Kate down on the floor, or across a table, or over the back of furniture. The only other time she'd felt like this was back in the days when she snorted coke at parties, before she stamped out every habit that could undermine her career. What was her excuse tonight? She supposed lust could undo common sense, self-control, even self-respect. She had already been keyed up, expecting to see Kate on Saturday. Having her arrive early had somehow unglued her. She felt thrilled but awkward, self-conscious at the thought of their phone call, even worried about their next lovemaking. What would Kate expect of her? Jules didn't want to disappoint.

She tried to get a read on the woman exploring the room. Would they have to go through the motions of dinner and conversation? No doubt Kate would need to freshen up after her flight. Jules ran through the possibilities. While Kate was showering, she could make a light meal. They could listen to seductive music as they dined, then sit a few feet apart on the sofa occupying that weird fugue state people slid into when it was unseemly just to grab each other.

Did Kate even want to grab her? Jules followed her progress as she moved through the room, brushing her fingers over furnishings and surfaces until she came to the windows. There she paused, seemingly entranced by the city nightscape. Surely, if she felt the same aching need Jules did, she would not be ten feet away, distracting herself by twinkling lights. She would not be fondling inanimate objects when her hands could be occupied with a warm body.

For a few excruciating seconds, Jules was filled with resentment. How could a stranger evoke such messy and inexplicable emotions in her? She felt vulnerable and desperate. Kate's remoteness was maddening. This whole scenario seemed mirage-like. She was daunted by the sense that she could plunge in with wild abandon, only to find everything evaporating.

Determined to seize control, of at least the situation if not herself, she said, "I'll show you where things are."

Kate turned toward her. "Can I ask you a question?"

"Of course."

"Did you specify the flowers for that bouquet or did the florist just put something together?"

"I chose them myself." Jules wondered if this was a test.

"I thought so."

Kate left the window and dawdled toward her, stopping within arm's reach. Her eyes were bright and more green than brown. A tiny melting smile found its way to her mouth, making it so kissable Jules had to choke back a small animal sound of longing. Heat flooded her face. She could not believe she was giving herself away like this. Where was her sophistication?

"Mostly, I don't like getting flowers," Kate said. "But I make exceptions for peonies and irises." Her smile broadened. "I wonder how you knew that."

The words were so softly spoken, Jules had to move closer. She could smell mint on Kate's breath. Scent invaded the air, emanating from both of them. Commercial perfume masked the rougher notes of perspiration, body, and clothing. Jules recognized the salty traces of her own wet arousal in the mix. Her hands trembled and she slid them into her pockets.

She regarded Kate cautiously, seeking some idea of where they stood with each other. None of the usual cues were apparent. Kate offered no long, hot looks. No coy smiles. No "accidental" touch. Where was the woman who had seduced her over the phone just two days ago? Jules wanted her here, now, in the flesh. Was physical proximity a problem? Would Kate only articulate her desires with a thousand miles of desert and mountain between them?

Jules followed her instincts. "I've been thinking…"

"Yes?" Kate's expression was politely attentive, like she was about to hear the recipe for a meal she would never cook.

"I have some urgent work to do. How about if I get that out of the way while you shower and make yourself comfortable?" She indicated the curved stairwell. "My bedroom and office are on the top level along from the balcony. Just come on up when you're ready."

No pressure. No demands. Jules intercepted a glimmer of relief in Kate's eyes and realized she had hit upon the right move at the right time. Although Kate hid her emotions well, she was probably nervous and needed a chance to relax. Jules already knew from Palm Springs and their phone sex that Kate liked to dictate the nature of her encounters. If that's what it took, Jules could be accommodating.

"The guest room is over there." She pointed to a door. "I'll bring your luggage."

"Thank you." Kate walked with her through the living room back toward the front entrance. "Jules?"

"Yes?"

"I'm happy to be here."

"I wasn't completely sure," Jules admitted. "I mean, I know it wasn't your plan to visit with me tonight."

"It's probably better this way," Kate said. "I have a lot to do while I'm in town. Maybe I can stay tonight and tomorrow, instead of Friday or Saturday."

"Tonight *and* tomorrow?" Jules repeated. She couldn't be *that* ambivalent if she was already thinking they would spend two nights together.

"If it's not a hassle for you." A glimpse of teasing danced in Kate's eyes.

"Are you crazy?" Jules grinned. "I have to work during the day tomorrow, but otherwise I'm all yours."

Voir dire could drag on into next week until they had twelve acceptable jurors for the Brigham trial, but other than that she was in good shape, workwise. She would have plenty of time on the weekend for the usual last-minute push, especially if Kate wasn't going to be here. The change in dates sounded good for both of them.

Jules met Kate's gaze and immediately felt jarred. Something in the shape and set of her eyes triggered a match with another face. She combed through memory, and Rhianna Lamb's image popped into her mind. Sharpening her recall as best she could, she made an automatic comparison.

There was a superficial similarity, she supposed, but the two faces were actually quite different, even taking hair color out of the equation. Kate's delicately boned features made for real beauty, whereas Lamb was just a conventionally pretty girl-next-door. Their bodies were very different, too. Kate was almost too slender and moved with the grace of a nymph. Lamb played soccer, and a video of her in a game revealed a shapely, solidly built woman whose body language spoke of an outgoing personality. Kate was the complete opposite. Her innate reserve was obvious.

Jules laughed inwardly at herself. Lately she'd seen flashes of Kate in everyone from Sagelblum's chief defense strategist to television news anchors, to the woman behind the United ticket counter at LAX. She reminded herself that she didn't need to prowl the faces around her for Kate substitutes. The real thing was standing right in front of her.

"You look beautiful," she said spontaneously. "I meant to tell you that before."

Kate reacted with innocent surprise, as though she seldom received compliments. She lifted a hand to Jules's lapel and let it rest there. Her quiet smile was beguiling.

She said, "I'll get clean. Then you can get me dirty."

"Let's fuck, then make love," Jules said, circling like a hawk.

Rhianna moved out of reach. The backs of her thighs connected with the bed. She said, "Be gentle."

Jules unbuttoned the pale shirt she was wearing and pulled it free of her low-slung jeans. She had on a tank-style sports bra. Her nipples stood out beneath the thin white knit. Her hand dropped to her belt buckle. She asked, "How gentle?" as she tugged her fly open. "Am I only allowed to use my tongue, or can I get inside you?"

Rhianna sat on the edge of the bed, riveted by the slow, deliberate movements of Jules's hands. "That depends."

The jeans fell. Jules stepped out of them. The shirt followed. Her eyes glittered with intent. "What do you have in mind?"

Rhianna hitched herself fully onto the bed and leaned back, propped on her hands. Her thin silk robe fell away from her thighs. She opened her legs slightly more. "I want to take it slowly."

The double entendre was not lost on Jules. With a small, hungry grin, she said, "I can give it to you any way you need."

"Make me wait," Rhianna said. "I want to come in your mouth first."

Jules's hands slipped between Rhianna's knees, easing them apart, making her aware of the pulse that beat at her core. Wetness collected beneath her, gluing her robe to her butt. She felt her knees jerked up and sideways, exposing her fully.

Jules leaned over her. "Slowly, huh? You're sure about that?"

Her voice grew hoarse. "It's just, you're so wet. And I'm…not the patient type."

"Well, that's not my problem," Rhianna said. "If you can't exercise control, I'll take care of myself and you can do the same."

"Jesus." Jules stroked a few dark strands back into the short, stark ponytail at her nape. Her hands were not quite steady, neither was her breathing. Her eyes skated restlessly from Rhianna's face to the parting of her thighs, revealing her struggle to contain herself.

Rhianna smiled, reveling in the havoc she had caused. At the same time, she was bemused by her own wayward daring. She had never spoken this way to a lover. She had always been happy to kiss and touch and reach mutual satisfaction without the need to tease and control and to feel her own power. She wondered how far she could push before Jules pushed back.

Sagging back onto the bed, she said, "You're still not naked."

"Neither are you." Jules peeled off the sports bra.

Rhianna watched but did not remove her robe. "You work out," she observed as the briefs went south.

"Uh-huh."

Jules was tanned, trimmed, and so tense Rhianna could almost feel the pounding of her pulse. "You almost have a six-pack. I like it."

Jules took a pillow and dropped it on the floor. "Show me where you want my mouth."

Goose bumps needled Rhianna's skin. Shivering, she slid both hands down and held herself open. "You know what to do."

The words were barely out before she was jerked down the bed until her tailbone reached the edge. Jules cupped her ass and stared up at her with flushed cheeks and a dangerous gleam in her eyes.

"After this," she said, "I'm going to fist you and you're going to let me."

"Perhaps," Rhianna said as she felt the hot, slow glide of a satin tongue.

Jules worked with infinite patience, caressing and stroking her into swollen readiness. She inched so delicately around Rhianna's clit, the sensation was unbearable. Every tiny slithering nudge, every hint of pressure, the almost imperceptible nibbles made her nerves scream for more. Rhianna arched her back and tilted her hips, whimpering as Jules replied with more of the same feather-light torment.

When her clit was finally enfolded and Jules began to suck, Rhianna groaned, "Yes! Oh, yes. Don't stop."

But just as her responses gathered momentum, the intensity ebbed. Jules drifted away, completely breaking contact, leaving Rhianna's climax out of reach. Then her mouth flowed warmly and her tongue lapped far too daintily. Rhianna felt so tight and hard and empty, she whined in frustration.

"Jules, please. Make me come."

Another suck carried her closer, but again the pressure subsided before she could climb the steep incline to release. Jules was merely toying with her, and Rhianna needed to come so badly, she couldn't wait. She reached down, but the tip of her forefinger barely soothed her aching clit before her hand was knocked away.

Jules raised her head and stared lazily over Rhianna's torso. "Slow and gentle. Isn't that what you wanted?"

"I need more."

"Now?"

Frantic with unsatisfied desire, Rhianna mumbled, "Yes."

Jules planted kisses on Rhianna's belly, then changed position and dragged her gently up the bed. Kneeling at her side, stroking and kissing her, she worked her way to a nipple. Her mouth slid wetly and tenderly over the tight knot of flesh and she bit softly, just enough to send a small jolt straight to Rhianna's clit.

In desperation, Rhianna tried to touch herself again. This time Jules covered her hand and bumped it hard against her throbbing crotch, squeezing until she begged, "Please. Just fuck me."

Jules moved over her. Her voice was low and rough in Rhianna's ear. "Are you mine?"

"Yes, I'm yours," Rhianna gasped.

And Jules gave her exactly what she wanted, sliding between her legs, filling her, kissing her, pounding into her. "You feel so good," she said, "wrapped around me this way."

She thrust faster, meeting the rise of Rhianna's hips with deep, hard strokes. Her thumb worked Rhianna's clit, making her brim with pleasure. Rhianna's senses spun out of control. Everything seemed to zero in at her core. Sweet tension rose in steadily building waves until she had to let go.

"Now," she cried, stiffening and squeezing down.

Then she was flooding and opening, pulsing helplessly with each spasm. She gave herself over completely, aware only of the fierce unraveling within. She no longer knew whose pulse she felt, or whose flesh ended where; their bodies were seamlessly fused.

When time slowed, she opened her eyes to find Jules staring down at her with rapt tenderness. Her expression was so unguarded, her longing so naked, something burst into life deep inside, where her spirit had wintered too long. Rhianna's eyes flooded and she cupped Jules's cheek and drew her into a long, profound kiss. They rocked together, sweating and shuddering until she felt Jules start to withdraw.

"No," she said weakly. "You're not done."

Jules's breath rushed out and she shifted position to straddle Rhianna's thigh. "Are you sure?" she asked, easing her free arm beneath Rhianna's waist.

"You said I would let you. Remember?"

"Bold words." Jules laughed softly.

Rhianna moved her muscles, playing along the fingers still buried deep inside. "I'm waiting," she said.

In the thin light of dawn, Jules rolled onto her back and stared across at Kate. Everything hurt. Her jaw. Her nipples. Her back. Her sex. She flopped a hand onto Kate's chest.

"We should sleep," Kate murmured foggily.

Jules doubted she could. She wanted to spend what was left of the night watching the woman in her bed. Dragging herself closer, she said, "I have to go to work in a few hours. Shall I leave you a key?"

"Yes," Kate said, heavy-eyed.

"You'll be here when I get home?"

Another yes.

"Kate, I'm not ready to say good-bye."

"I don't think we should." Kate's voice was dreamy. She was drifting.

"I feel something for you." Jules needed to say the words before she could question the emotion.

Kate mumbled, "Let's talk later."

"Promise me something." Jules felt foolish, asking. "Promise me you won't leave without talking to me."

Kate forced a few blinks, obviously trying to keep herself awake. "I promise."

"I want to see where this could take us," Jules said in a rush.

"Are you proposing we get serious?" Kate's voice was light, but her eyes were watchful.

"Yes, I think I am." Jules hesitated, unfamiliar with the emotional terrain she was in. "Kate, have you ever thought about settling down? You know, home and garden. Kids. A couple of dogs. Family vacations. The whole nine yards?"

Kate's focus sharpened. "Is that what you're looking for?"

Why pretend? "Ultimately. With the right woman. Yeah, I want it all."

For a few seconds, Kate seemed lost in thought. "I always expected that's what I would have in my life by now," she said softly. "I've had girlfriends, but we never got that far."

"I've lived with several women." Jules stared up at the ceiling, surprised that they were having this conversation and that she was the one who had started it. "I don't know what I was thinking, really. We were never on the same page."

"You didn't notice that before you moved in with them?" A hint of mischief seeped into Kate's tone. "I hadn't picked you for the impulsive type."

"I'm not," Jules said. *Except where you're concerned.*

"What type are you?"

"No one's ever asked me that."

"Well, that certainly sheds some light on the whole 'not-on-the-same-page' issue," Kate murmured. "You still haven't answered my question."

"My type," Jules mused. "Responsible. Logical. I'm driven and goal-oriented. I want what I want. I'm very determined."

"No? Really?"

Jules laughed. "Since we're doing personality tests, how about you?"

After a long pause, Kate said, "I'm the caring type. I don't like pretension or phoniness. It's funny how some things change. I used to be more of an extrovert, but now I value my privacy."

"You forgot to mention how you drive women mad with lust," Jules said. "Me in particular."

"And you forgot to mention how gifted you are in bed."

"You find me pleasing?" Jules let her hand drift down Kate's torso.

"I do."

"Does that mean you'll date me?"

"Let's see what happens," Kate replied in a noncommittal tone.

"You could try to sound more enthusiastic." Jules attempted a teasing note, but something went wrong and she could hear her own anxiety.

"Jules." Kate rolled toward her and nuzzled into her neck. "Relax. I'm here, aren't I?"

"Yes." Jules cradled her, breathing in the scent of sex and warm body.

She wasn't sure why she was in turmoil when she should be falling into a sated sleep. She kissed Kate's hair and forced herself to think rationally. They had another night. Kate seemed receptive to the idea that they would keep seeing each other. They didn't have to settle their entire future now. She held Kate more tightly.

"I don't think it was an accident that we met in Palm Springs," she whispered. "I think it was meant."

"So, you're a fatalist, too?"

Jules met Kate's dreamy amber-green stare. "I never thought I was until you."

CHAPTER NINE

Rhianna looked straight ahead as she made her way to the witness box. The courtroom seemed smaller than she remembered from her walk-through with Norman Clay the previous Friday. It had been empty and she had been able to fully appreciate the innate dignity of the high plaster ceilings, cherrywood panels, and orderly straight-backed pews. A sense of awe had driven her worst fears away. She was to have her day in court, to tell her story and accuse her attacker in the hallowed halls of justice.

Even now, with people milling around and a drone of noise gathering as she approached the front of the room, Rhianna still felt safe in this physical symbol of civilization. The rule of law was the glue that enabled communities to function. The right of an individual to be heard was nowhere more fundamental than in a courtroom. *Everything will be all right,* she thought as she climbed the steps to the stand and the bailiff closed the gate after her.

She stared up at the American flag and the man sitting at the bench below it. According to the prosecutor, Judge Oscar P. Tuttle III was a levelheaded magistrate who had no time for fools. He was a big man with a domed head and chins that overlapped. Rhianna met his eyes briefly just before the clerk told her to raise her right hand and swear to tell the truth. After the oath, she had to state her name and spell it. She could feel so many eyes on her that she could not quite stop her voice from shaking. She wanted to look directly at Werner Brigham, to show she was not intimidated, but she wasn't ready. Instead she allowed herself the comfort of a quick glance at her parents, who were to her left, sitting a couple of rows behind the prosecutor's table. Her mom gave her a discreet wave and her dad looked teary eyed, but they both had an air of stoic determination about them.

Just as she'd been told during the trial preparation, the prosecutor got up and walked to a spot near the jury and started asking her questions about herself. These were intended to introduce her to the jury. Norman Clay's calm, supportive expression helped settle her nerves, and Rhianna remembered to look at the jury as she spoke. She knew they'd been instructed not to show emotion. All the same, she caught some tiny encouraging nods, enough to suggest she'd made a good first impression. Relieved, she took the victim advocate's advice and found the friendliest face among the twelve so she could keep coming back to that juror.

Eventually she would have to look over to the other side of the room, at her attacker, but for the moment she enjoyed the petty satisfaction of ignoring him. He was hating it, she imagined. Already she had caught a hum of noise from the table where he and his high-priced defense team were sitting. Resisting the urge to snatch a look in their direction, she focused on each of the prosecutor's questions, carefully listening, then waiting for a couple of seconds before she answered.

Finally, Mr. Clay worked his way around to the one that signaled her testimony was beginning. "Ms. Lamb, you have alleged that on the evening of Saturday, July 30, 2006, you were the victim of a sexual assault. In a statement given to Denver police about the attack, you identified the man who attacked you as Werner Elbert Brigham. Do you see Mr. Brigham in this courtroom?"

Bracing herself, Rhianna looked to her right. He was there; her brain registered his disturbing presence. But her eyes refused to budge from the woman sitting next to him. Her heart plunged and her lungs froze on the sharp breath she drew. *No!* She started to tremble and she could feel the blood leaving her face. Panic clamped her jaws. Her temples started to pound. She blinked in disbelief.

Jules Valiant was sitting next to the man who had destroyed her life. Impossible. She stared harder.

Jules stared back, her eyes flinty.

"Ms. Lamb?" Norman Clay sounded alarmed.

Rhianna knew what was expected. They had rehearsed this moment. Shaking uncontrollably, she forced her arm up and pointed. The accusation was a croak. "That's him."

"Ms. Lamb?" This time the voice came from behind her and Rhianna realized the judge was leaning in her direction. Covering his microphone, he asked, "Do you need a moment to compose yourself?"

To Rhianna's horror the only sound she could expel was a sob, and she realized tears were streaming down her face.

The judge promptly ordered the jurors to leave the court, then said something to Mr. Clay. Rhianna stood, along with everyone else, but the entire room lurched and the wood-paneled walls seemed to melt. A sea of noise swept over her, and she was vaguely aware of an arm around her waist as her legs buckled under her.

"Get a medic in here!" Norman Clay yelled.

Rhianna closed her eyes as her head spun out of control. She was aware of being lowered to the floor. She could hear her mother arguing with someone. Fuzzily, she turned her head and tried to speak above the clamor of voices. Before she could form a sentence a male voice ordered, "Step back," and someone gently slapped her cheek. "Ma'am, look at me."

Rhianna blinked up at a man in a paramedic outfit. He asked if he could examine her.

She agreed and said, "I'm okay. I nearly fainted, that's all."

As he listened to her heart and took her blood pressure, she stared past him. A bailiff was leading Werner Brigham out of the room. A group of people stood in a huddle at the defense table, Jules among them. Her face was drained of color. She must have felt Rhianna's gaze, because she looked directly at her. For several bleak, painful seconds their eyes locked, then Jules turned away.

❖

"I heard about the swoon," Carl said. "Didn't think Clay had it in him to stage something like that. Jury ate it up, huh."

"Carl, I'm not calling about that." Jules spoke rapidly into her cell phone. "I can't try this case. I need to excuse myself."

"On what basis?"

"Conflict of interest."

"What, you're covertly working for the DA?"

"Carl," Jules paused to steady herself, "the plaintiff spent a couple of nights at the apartment last week."

"Are you fucking kidding me?"

"I had no idea who she was. She's been going by another name."

"You slept with her? In the firm's apartment!"

"Like I'm the only one doing that," Jules retorted. "At least I'm not married and cheating on my wife."

She didn't need to name names. Sagelblum attorneys had been using the penthouse as an extramarital love nest ever since the firm bought the place. Carl gave the culprits a halfhearted rap on the knuckles if he heard rumors.

"So, what are you saying?" he asked. "You've got something serious with this woman?"

Highly unlikely now, Jules thought. "I'm saying we don't need Brigham coming after us claiming misconduct."

"So get him acquitted. There's no basis for a complaint unless he's convicted."

"Sid is up to speed," Jules said. "He can try the case. I'll work with him every step of the way."

"Forget it. Audrey Brigham bought *you*."

"Tell her Judge Tuttle has a problem with me and it's in her son's interests to remove me."

Carl snorted. "Get serious. She's not that stupid."

"You think it's a better idea for everyone to find out that I slept with the plaintiff in a rape trial? Norman Clay is going to be all over this."

Carl was silent for a few seconds and Jules knew exactly what he was doing—devouring a Junior Mint. Slowly, thoughtfully, he said, "I don't think so."

"Oh, please. I'm a Salazar, Hagel & Goldblum superlawyer. Ask any prosecutor in the country if he'd take me down. You know the answer."

"Hear me out." Her boss sounded remarkably calm for a man whose firm was about to become a laughingstock. "This is a he-said-she-said rape trial. It's all about the plaintiff's credibility. Clay thinks he's batting a thousand because he's got the fucking Virgin Mary on the stand. Not anymore."

Jules caught her breath, filled with unease. "You actually want us to use this?"

"Sure I do. Go talk to our learned friend. Tell him we're going to come clean, and they can't hide behind the rape-shield law because we won't be approaching this as evidence of sexual history. By the time you're through, his poor little victim is going to look like a sex-crazed dyke who led a rich, gullible man down the garden path."

Jules said what she thought. "Huh?"

"Rhianna Lamb is not the girl next door. She's a cunning con artist with a plan to extort money via an out-of-court settlement. She wanted Brigham to attack her."

"There's something I'm not seeing. How does her being a lesbian furnish us with this compelling new argument?"

"We're already saying he misunderstood her rejection because he's a fifties throwback. What if there's more to it than that? What if she was intentionally sending mixed messages? Is a virgin bride going to come up with a plan like that—no. But a woman leading a double life? Pay dirt!"

Jules followed this magical thinking. "Her lesbianism tanks her credibility, and the fact that she concealed it from him proves she had an agenda?"

"It's a slam dunk." Carl chortled. He liked to toss around infamous phrases from the War on Terror playbook.

"You'd hang my reputation, and this firm's, out there to win this thing? Rhetorical question."

Carl Hagel was the bionic attorney. He had the killer instincts of a barracuda coupled with naked avarice and a nerveless demeanor that suggested either supreme arrogance or supreme confidence. No one liked him, but at Sagelblum it was universally agreed that he was the best of the best, and the next time any of them committed a heinous felony he was their man.

"It's not going to come to that," Carl decreed with the bland certainty he brought to every high-risk strategy. "I'll tell you what's going to happen. You're going to let Clay know his case is dog food. Tell him you can pull the trigger on his client any time you want and you'll sleep okay. He's going to ask her what she wants to do, and she's going to tell him it never happened."

Jules's stomach churned. "You can't be certain of that."

"Yes, I can. Because that's what she does. That's how she got herself in this mess in the first place. She can't say no like she means it. She skipped town when the shit hit the fan last year. Backing down and avoiding confrontation is her MO. And you know what's really fucking inspirational about this?"

He was going to tell her, regardless, and in a chilling, disgusting way, everything he said made sense. Jules pushed her hair back from her face. Perspiration kept a few annoying strands clinging to her forehead.

"Knowing what could go wrong," Carl continued happily. "And knowing you've got the power. That's going to mess with her head like you won't believe. Just step back and watch her lose the jury."

"Christ." Jules sagged against the nearest pillar. "You really are a devious bastard."

Her boss chuckled like she'd just paid him the ultimate compliment. "I'm thinking, if she slept with you, she slept with other women, too. I'll get Desjardines onto it."

"I'm not happy about this, Carl." Jules knew exactly how lame that sounded.

"You're the one who fucked up," her boss said. "Now make the problem go away."

"But won't it help our case if they know I'm a lesbian?" Rhianna asked. "I mean, wouldn't it prove there's no way I encouraged him?"

Norman Clay rolled a pen between his thumb and forefinger.

"No, it will prove that you're not the nice woman the jury thought you were."

"A lesbian can't be nice?"

The look he gave her wasn't stern so much as disappointed. "You should have told me."

"Why? What's it got to do with anything? This wasn't a crime about a lesbian, it was a crime against me—an innocent person."

"Rhianna, we don't live in an ideal world. It shouldn't make any difference if the person on the stand is white, black, Catholic, Muslim, pretty, ugly, straight, or gay. But it does, because juries are made up of flawed human beings. All it will take is one homophobe out of twelve. What are the odds?"

"This is a nightmare." Rhianna rested her head on her hands, unable to block out the memory of Jules sitting in the courtroom next to that man. "I can't believe this is happening."

"The defense attorneys want to go to trial without a hassle. If we agree to continue as planned, they'll agree not to raise the matter of your sexuality."

Rhianna felt obtuse. "I still don't get why it's such a huge deal. I know what you're saying about prejudice, but can't the judge issue instructions about that?"

He shook his head. "We can't open the door, trust me on this. If we do, Julia Valiant is going to claim you engineered the events that night to set up her client for a sting. To force the Brighams into a big out-of-court settlement. Your lesbianism, and the fact that you've chosen to conceal it from most people, makes you seem... less than honest. Even opportunistic. That how she's going to argue her theory."

Jules would do that? "I *wanted* a man to rape me? That's insane." Rhianna looked around for something she could throw at a wall.

"They intend to portray you as a manipulative deviant."

"Did she actually say that? Julia Valiant, I mean. Did she tell you that?" An even more hideous possibility crossed her mind. "Do you think she knew who I was all along?"

"It's hard to say, but we're not talking about a small-town law firm. Salazar, Hagel & Goldblum play hardball. They hire detectives and jury consultants. They have a research team that prepares files on every witness. And if a few dirty ticks will help them win…Julia Valiant is one of the most ruthless trial attorneys in the country. That's why Audrey Brigham hired her."

Rhianna forced herself upright instead of sagging down on the table like she had no spine. Her heart flatly refused to accept that Jules had intentionally set her up. Was everything that had seemed real and meaningful between them mere illusion? Had Jules staged a farce to gather ammunition for the trial? The chance meeting in Palm Springs, the rash, romantic gesture of the flowers, the passion and the tenderness. Rhianna could not believe that the woman she'd shared herself with had been planning to betray her all along. Would Jules sink so low?

"Mrs. Brigham is offering a two-million-dollar bonus for an acquittal," Clay said. "I heard half of that will go to Ms. Valiant."

A million dollars. People sold out their mothers for less. Was that the kind of person Jules was? Rhianna felt like the wind had been knocked out of her. Everything was going horribly, unspeakably wrong.

"What do you think I should do?" She wiped her tears. "Should I just withdraw the charges and save everyone a lot of trouble?"

"It's too late for that, and if you refuse to testify, I'll subpoena you."

"I don't understand. Why can't I just change my mind and not go through with this?"

"Because the people of the state of Colorado have charged Brigham with a crime. The trial will proceed whether you want it to or not."

"Will the jury know anything…about me and Jules?"

"No. They'll only hear the evidence set before them. And when Ms. Valiant cross-examines you, be on your guard," he cautioned. "Listen carefully and answer her questions as simply as you can. Remember, she's not your friend."

CHAPTER TEN

Jules was soft-spoken and charming. None of her initial questions seemed confrontational. The jury could not take their eyes off her. Rhianna felt the same way, but she forced herself to look somewhere else every time she caught herself staring. This morning, for the first day of the cross-examination, Jules was playing the feminine card. Her suit was silver-gray silk, shot with violet. The skirt was snug fitting, and beneath the jacket, a fine pale lavender sweater clung to her curves. Her hair swung loose, a sleek curtain that spilled forward when she glanced down, giving her a reason to tuck it fetchingly back now and then when it strayed too far onto her face.

She did this just before she strolled back toward the witness box to continue her pedantic review of Rhianna's testimony. "Would you state once again what you believed about Mr. Brigham's invitations?"

"I thought he was asking me to date him." Rhianna reminded herself once more that the jury saw her as a straight woman.

"And you declined because you did not wish to date him. Correct?"

"Yes."

"And the reasons you stated were that you did not find Mr. Brigham attractive and you were not looking for a boyfriend. Did you have a boyfriend at that time?"

Somehow the woman who had lain with her head on Rhianna's

belly, and her hand fisted within, managed to make that question sound breezy. Rhianna wanted to shake her. "No."

"Was there another man you were interested in at any time during your acquaintanceship with Mr. Brigham?"

What was this? Had Jules decided to sneakily tease out the information about her sexuality, after all? Rhianna counted to three and said mildly, "No."

"So you were not willing to go on a social outing with Mr. Brigham even to discover if the two of you might become friends?"

"I could see that he wasn't interested in being my friend."

"What made you believe that?"

"I think most women can tell when someone is interested."

"So, you consider yourself a good judge of men because most women are? It's what—genetic?"

Norman Clay stood. "Objection."

"Rephrase your question, Ms. Valiant," Judge Tuttle instructed. "And Ms. Lamb. The court is not interested in your views on most people, only those pertaining to yourself."

Jules resumed. "Please describe how you know when someone is showing a romantic interest in you."

Rhianna almost laughed. Unable to help herself, she said pointedly, "Flowers. The people who send me flowers usually want something, and in my experience it's not friendship."

Impassively, Jules said, "Mr. Brigham frequently sent you bouquets, so you felt this was a sign of romantic interest?"

"Yes, which is why I phoned him and asked him to stop."

"He continued to send them, didn't he?"

"Yes."

"Did that seem odd to you?"

"Yes."

"Was it your conclusion that he did not take your rejection seriously?"

"Yes."

"What did you do about that?"

"I started throwing the flowers in the trash or giving them away."

"Did you tell him you were doing this?"

"No."

"Why not?"

"I thought if I ignored him, he would give up and leave me alone."

Jules apparently wanted the jury to notice this point. As if a couple of them might be hard of hearing, she strolled along the box and repeated crisply, "Ms. Lamb avoided confronting Mr. Brigham. She thought if she ignored him, he would leave her alone." Stopping dead, her hands on her hips, she faced Rhianna and asked pleasantly, "In your experience, have you found such a fainthearted, indirect approach to be successful in discouraging men?"

"Objection."

"Sustained."

Jules smiled. "Let me see if I understand this correctly. Having found that no did not work with Mr. Brigham, you thought saying nothing at all might be more effective?"

"Yes."

"Over what period did you ignore Mr. Brigham?"

"Nine months."

"Did it work?"

"No."

"So for nine months he continued to behave like he was still courting you. He sent flowers, he made calls inviting you on dates, he hung around your workplace hoping for the chance to see you. Do you think this was the behavior of a man who knew his advances weren't welcome?"

"I don't know."

"It never occurred to you that he just wasn't *getting* it?"

"Objection," Clay said. "Your Honor, Ms. Lamb cannot be expected to have read the defendant's mind."

"Ms. Valiant, is this line of questioning leading somewhere?" the judge asked.

"It is, Your Honor," Jules said. "This witness testified on direct examination that she believed the defendant knew his advances were not welcome. Yet she now appears to be contradicting herself. The jury needs to understand exactly what Ms. Lamb believed."

"Proceed."

"Ms. Lamb," Jules said earnestly. "Based on Werner Brigham's conduct, did you believe he understood that he was wasting his time and that you had rejected him?"

Rhianna repeated the question in her mind, trying to figure out why Jules was spending so much time on this one minor point. "I'm not sure what he thought."

"Let me rephrase. How do you normally deter men who are romantically interested in you?"

"Saying no usually works." Rhianna tried to keep the acid from her tone. Norman Clay said juries don't respond well to witnesses who showed anger, even if provoked. "If a man doesn't listen, I say it more loudly. Which was what I had to do with Mr. Brigham. In fact, I had to scream."

This statement created a small ripple among the jurors, and Jules narrowed her eyes very slightly. "So, you claim Mr. Brigham knew his overtures were not welcome. Yet you also claim you weren't sure if he understood he had been rejected. Which is it?"

"Objection. Your Honor, Ms. Valiant is confusing the witness."

"Are you confused," the judge asked.

Rhianna glanced at Norman Clay. The prosecutor's face gave no clue as to his thoughts. Jules had backed her into a corner with this circular argument and was making her sound like a ditz.

"No, Your Honor." Ignoring the frown of consternation on Mr. Clay's face, she said, "I think Ms. Valiant wants me to explain why her client was chasing a woman who didn't want him. I've asked myself the same question many times." She looked past Jules to Brigham. "All I can say is that it's hard to form an opinion about behavior that makes no sense."

She glanced toward the jury in time to catch a couple of unconscious nods. Something flickered in Jules's eyes as they slid over her. Rhianna's nipples reacted and she checked to make sure her pastel pink jacket wasn't flapping open. The color made her wince. Norman Clay had seen to it that she could have passed for a coed from the most conservative Bible college below the Mason-Dixon Line. Beneath the jacket she wore a white blouse with a Peter

Pan collar, and a pleated skirt in tones of pink and dove gray. Cuban-heel Mary Janes completed her yesteryear preppiness, the black-patent kind Catholic girls wore to mass, and a large black velvet bow secured her fake ponytail high on her head.

Rhianna had expected jury members to see straight through this contrived look, but by the time Norman Clay had questioned her for a couple of hours, she realized that she was not a real person to them. She was the well-behaved daughter or sister everyone wished they had back home instead of the one who gave attitude and dressed like Britney Spears. She could see why her sexuality was off-limits. If she was asked directly, she would have to tell the truth, of course. The defense had agreed to stay away from the topic, but Rhianna wondered if Jules was planning to reveal her anyway, by inference.

Filled with trepidation, she surveyed the courtroom. Jules was not the only one checking her out. Werner Brigham had been feasting his eyes on her ever since she took the stand, and he kept shifting in his seat like he needed to use the restroom. He had combed his limp, sandy hair back for the trial and oiled it firmly in place. The style drew attention to his flaccid face and weak chin. Rhianna tried not to look at him. The feverish intensity of his stare made her flesh crawl.

"Ms. Lamb, with the benefit of hindsight do you think you could have done more to make your rejection emphatic?"

"I got a restraining order," Rhianna pointed out.

"After six months, yes. Can you see why that delay might imply some ambivalence on your part?"

Anger flared deep inside Rhianna. "It wouldn't have mattered what I said or did. Mr. Brigham was not interested in *my* wishes."

Jules smiled. "In that case, I'm surprised you accepted an invitation for a dinner date with him on the Saturday of the alleged assault. Do you see why that decision might seem illogical?"

Rhianna was silent. Something had changed in the way Jules was questioning her. She was still being pleasant, but the cross-examination suddenly seemed more serious.

"Please answer the question. Doesn't it seem illogical that you would go on a dinner date with Mr. Brigham?"

"Yes. But—"

Before Rhianna could explain herself, Jules asked, "Did Mr. Brigham seem happy about the date?"

"It wasn't a date, it was a meeting."

Jules conceded this point with an apologetic nod before repeating, "So, Mr. Brigham seemed happy?"

"Yes."

"What did you wear to this encounter?"

"A dress and pumps."

"Please describe these."

"The dress was a dark blue sheath style, a cocktail dress. And the shoes were Prada sling backs with high heels."

"That's quite a contrast from the outfit you're wearing now." Jules gave the jury time to reach the same conclusion. "Why did you wear provocative clothing to a meeting with a man you were trying to discourage?" Without taking a breath, she said, "Strike that— You felt this meeting would send a clear, unambiguous signal to Mr. Brigham that you were not interested. Correct?"

"Yes."

"Did you think if you looked pretty he would be more receptive?"

Rhianna hesitated. "Yes."

"The court has heard you characterize your romantic experience with men as limited. Do I understand you correctly?"

"Yes."

"So, you have not faced a situation like this before. Let me qualify that. Would you say you have never been so ardently pursued by a man?"

"Yes. Never."

"When women find themselves genuinely upset about a man's pursuit, it's been my experience that they will say virtually anything to make him leave them alone. Was that how you felt before going to dinner with Mr. Brigham?"

"Yes."

"During the nine months in which Mr. Brigham courted you, did you ever consider telling him that you were interested in another man?"

"I thought about it."

"But you decided not to?"

Rhianna was aware that Jules had somehow framed her questions so that all she could do was agree with everything. Irritated, she said, "Yes."

"Was that because you were not interested in any other man?"

"Yes, and because I didn't want to cause trouble for another person by misrepresenting a friendship."

"By 'friendship,' do you mean a platonic friendship of the type you have described having with men?"

"Yes."

"Would you say that most of your understanding of men derives from platonic friendships?"

"Yes, and from growing up with a father and two brothers."

"Did your father approve of your having dinner with Mr. Brigham?"

"I didn't discuss it with him."

"Because you thought he would prevent you from going?"

"Objection," Clay barked. "If Ms. Valiant is done testifying perhaps we can return to the facts."

"Withdrawn." Absently, Jules stroked her hair back, a movement that tightened her jacket across her breasts and called attention to her striking face.

Watching her, Rhianna crashed into a wall of feeling. Her memories were so fresh, their physicality was tangible. Her body still bore marks. She still felt raw in her most secret places, and she was achingly aware of all that had passed between them. There was no retreat to be found within. Her mind was an occupied country, with Jules the invader. All she could see was the two of them hot and naked, clinging to each other. She could not stop reliving those moments, craving more. Her inability to evict Jules from her mind was torture. What did it take, she wondered. How much worse did the betrayal need to get before she could just hate the woman as she deserved?

Whatever happened, however this played out, Rhianna almost didn't care. She had already lost. One day soon she would leave

Denver, with all of this behind her, and she would never see Jules again. She knew it made no sense to feel shattered by that realization, but she did.

Jules pitched her question another way. "Why did you withhold the details of your dinner engagement from your father?"

"I knew he would worry."

"Did you expect he would try to talk you out of it?"

"Yes."

"So you didn't tell him. Obviously it was important to you to have this dinner. Why?"

"I thought if we could just have an adult conversation, I could reason with him."

Jules frowned. "Having a meal with you placed Mr. Brigham in violation of the restraining order against him. Was that your intention?"

"I didn't think about it."

"Witnesses will confirm that you drank expensive champagne and were seen smiling and laughing with Mr. Brigham. Complete strangers will testify before this court that you appeared to be flirting. Yet you have stated that you were extremely shocked when Mr. Brigham proposed marriage to you during the course of the meal. Is that correct?"

"Yes." Rhianna wanted to ask, *How can you do this?* She felt frazzled. The effort of controlling every reaction and second-guessing before she opened her mouth was wearing on her. She just wanted the cross-examination to be over so that she could go home and forget any of this had ever happened.

"Help me understand," Jules said. "You chose to wear flattering clothes. You were drinking champagne and flirting with this man… a man who had been courting you for nine months. Yet you were amazed when he offered you a fifty-thousand-dollar diamond ring. Ms. Lamb, you are either very naïve or you are lying. Which is it?"

"Objection!"

Jules made a helpless gesture with her hands and looked up at the judge. Her air was one of patient forbearance, as if she knew hers was a lone voice of common sense, and she did not expect anyone to acknowledge it. But she still dared to hope His Honor would come down on the side of reason.

"Overruled," Judge Tuttle said tonelessly. "The witness may answer."

Rhianna said. "I am neither."

"I suppose there is a third alternative," Jules said coldly. "You didn't give Mr. Brigham a clear answer to his proposal, did you? In previous testimony you stated this was because you were afraid."

"Yes."

"So…Not lying. Not naïve. But afraid."

"Yes."

"And in this state of fear, you agreed that Mr. Brigham could escort you home?"

"Yes, but there was a driver, and I thought—"

"Ms. Lamb. You entered the car of your own free will. You did not state an unequivocal no to the offer of marriage. You have testified that in the car Mr. Brigham spoke of the home he wanted to share with you as his wife. He talked about having children. Yes or no?"

"Yes."

"Did Mr. Brigham treat you courteously during dinner and in the car?"

"Yes."

"You were friendly toward him, also?"

"I was polite."

Jules sighed. "Ms. Lamb, do you have an aversion to sexual intimacy with men?"

Rhianna's heart threatened to choke her. "I don't have enough experience to answer that."

"Of course, because you only have platonic friendships with men. You are an attractive twenty-eight-year-old woman. You must have had plenty of offers, through high school, college, in your working life. But you had never had sex with a man until Mr. Brigham. Correct?"

"Yes."

"Were you saving yourself for marriage?"

Rhianna clamped her hands firmly together in her lap to stop them from shaking. "I had not met a man I wanted to be intimate with."

"I see. There's nothing to be ashamed of," Jules said sympathetically. "Fear of sexual intimacy is a clinical condition for which sufferers seek help all the time."

"I'm not—" Rhianna cut herself off before she could fall into the trap Jules had set. If she claimed to have no problem, Jules would end up drawing from her an admission of her sexuality. Carefully, she said, "I didn't think it was mandatory for a woman to sleep around to prove herself normal."

She glanced toward the friendliest face in the jury and saw a chilling mix of puzzlement, sympathy, and dawning comprehension. Trying not to panic, she stole quick looks around the other faces. Dismay, cynicism, suspicion. She was losing their support.

"Ms. Lamb, do you want to fall in love and settle down one day?"

Rhianna thought, *Bitch.* "Yes."

"Yes, I thought so." Jules offered the jury a mild, apologetic smile, as if she knew she had tried their patience with her dreary cross-examination. "Let's cut to the chase. The reason Mr. Brigham could not figure out where he stood with you, Ms. Lamb, and the reason he could be forgiven for thinking you were just playing hard to get, is that you gave him mixed messages. It probably wasn't your intention."

Jules continued in a resolute but compassionate tone. "I put it to you that you could not reject Mr. Brigham emphatically because in your heart you wanted what he was offering. A home, a family, social position. You went to dinner with him, and you willingly accompanied him to his home because you were hoping you could overcome your fears. You knew you could cement an engagement by having sex with the man who wanted to marry you. But when you tried to go through with it, things went wrong, didn't they?"

"Objection. Must we endure this catalogue of assumptions while we wait for Ms. Valiant to get to the point?"

The jury was mesmerized. Several people cast pitying looks at

Rhianna. Even her parents were staring with stupefied expressions as if they thought there could be some truth in Jules's twisted version of events.

Judge Tuttle ran a thumb over his chins. "Ms. Lamb may answer."

"That's not what happened," Rhianna responded to the question.

"Really?" Jules gave her a stony look. "An innocent man was caught up in *your* confusion, and you don't want to take responsibility so you cry rape. Isn't that what's really going on here?"

"No!"

"You thought you could change this pattern for yourself, but in the end your pathological disgust for sex with men got the better of you. Once again it destroyed your chances of a real relationship. Mr. Brigham is just one of a long line of men you've confused and disappointed. Isn't that the truth you don't want to face?"

"No. I was raped!" Rhianna tried to calm herself, but she was crying. "I told him to stop and he didn't. He had a knife. He threatened me."

"I know you want to believe that, but your mixed messages and your history of platonic friendships tell the real story, Ms. Lamb. I venture to suggest that you have been too embarrassed to seek professional help about your condition. And to complicate your dilemma, we live in a society that endorses virtue in unmarried women like yourself. Mr. Brigham himself was well aware of your innocence and valued it highly, as he will testify in due course."

Like she truly regretted what she had to say, Jules shook her head. "You unwittingly toyed with a man who only wanted to cherish and protect you. Who wanted to *marry* you. In the heat of the moment, Mr. Brigham may have misjudged your reactions. That remains to be seen. However, you placed this respectable man in that position."

"Objection."

Rhianna wanted to shout, *Now? You wait until* now *to object?*

"Ms. Valiant," the judge said in a warning tone.

Jules raked the jurors with a compelling gaze as though

personally challenging each of them. To Rhianna, she said, "Get help, Ms. Lamb. Don't destroy a man's life because you have a hang-up."

"Objection! Now Ms. Valiant is using the cross-examination to make her closing arguments!"

"Sustained."

Jules did not even offer one of her mea culpa smiles. Staring at Rhianna, she said gravely, "It's time to tell the truth. You hoped you could get over your problem enough to snag an eligible bachelor. But you find sex with men repugnant, and it would not have mattered who Mr. Brigham was or what he did. You would have felt the same way. Isn't that true?"

Rhianna was silent.

"Yes or no, Ms. Lamb. May I remind you that you are under oath." Sternly, Jules said, "I'll repeat the question. Sex with men repels you, doesn't it?"

"Yes," Rhianna whispered.

"Ladies and gentlemen." Jules's tone was not triumphant. She did not strut or gloat. Her eyes were eloquent, her face genuinely sad. She looked breathtaking. "That was a yes."

CHAPTER ELEVEN

To destroying the witness without losing the jury." Carl raised his glass.

Jules acknowledged the toast and drank with her team. "We're not out of the woods yet, people."

"You saw the jury." Carl's smile was smug. "They feel sorry for her. Sure, they think she had sex and didn't like it much. But they also think that's her problem, and we're going to hammer that point home."

Sid Lyle leafed through some notes on his legal pad. "I've located an expert witness on female sexual-aversion disorder. Dr. Virginia Zempel. She's available."

"Oh, yeah. We're making sweet music." Carl tilted his chair back and contemplated the view from their sixteenth-floor hospitality suite. "How are we doing on those other guys she never slept with?"

"We talked to the computer-geek boyfriend again," Sid said. "Apparently she complained to him about guys pressuring her for sex. That's one reason he never tried for second base himself. The joke is, we don't even have to call these witnesses. Clay is doing it for us."

"I'm loving it!" Carl beamed. "He drags these jerks onto the stand to prove she's as pure as the driven snow and we're going to nail them. They'll be sharing how she's a frigid tease who makes normal guys feel rejected. It's not sexual history, because hey! She doesn't have any."

Jules stared into her wine and reminded herself that she had gone easy on Rhianna. She could have been a lot tougher and still owned the jury. But after all this she wanted to see Rhianna again, so she needed to leave a door open. She tried to tell herself that the outcome of this thing was by no means certain. Their defense was flimsy at best. But juries hesitated over a guilty verdict in rape cases if reasonable doubt could be established. Werner Brigham would not be sent down for a mandatory five-year term if they believed he was a bewildered but well-intentioned schmuck who had misunderstood what was going on. The fact that he'd proposed would weigh with the six middle-aged women on the jury, and every one of the men would empathize with a guy who had paid for an engagement ring and a fancy dinner and thought he would get more than a good-night kiss.

"The prosecution can't pull anything out of the hat," she said. "They've painted themselves into a corner with the virgin-victim strategy."

Carl loosened his tie happily. "The only way we're losing this is if our client fucks himself in the ass."

"I'll straitjacket him," Jules said. "We can let him run off at the mouth a bit on the virtuous-woman issue. That won't do us any harm. But if Clay goes for a narrative cross, we'll be right in the danger zone."

Sid nodded. "No kidding. We need for *this* client to keep it zipped up."

"I'll talk to his mother again," Carl said. "If there's one woman he pays attention to, it's her."

A couple of hospitality staff entered from the kitchen with more fruit and cheese and refilled everyone's wineglasses. The team went on to dissect the plaintiff's testimony some more, marveling that she had been so dumb as to get in the client's car of her own volition, and poring over her police statement. Rhianna had claimed that Brigham threatened her with a knife. The cops had conducted a search for the weapon and come up empty-handed.

Rhianna had waited three long days before reporting the "rape," and she had done all the wrong things: showered, burned her underclothing, and told no one what had happened. The subsequent forensic examination had turned up no DNA evidence or collateral physical injury; however, internal trauma consistent with rape was present.

Sagelblum had initially hoped that another male could be implicated in her physical condition so that they could claim their client had been falsely accused, probably for financial reasons. After all, she could have slept with anybody during those three days. However, Rhianna had spent that period holed up in her childhood bedroom at the home of her parents. Even if there had been another male in the picture, there was no opportunity for him to have seen her in private. The prosecution was sitting on a stack of statements concerning her movements for the days after the alleged attack. The stories were all consistent.

Jules had her own theory about Rhianna's reactions. She hadn't told anyone she was planning dinner with Brigham because she knew they would talk her out of going. In the end, admitting she had been raped was as good as admitting she had been foolhardy and paid the price. Instead, she must have spent those three days deeply traumatized and planning her next move. In desperation, after being stalked by a man for months, and then raped, she had decided to leave Denver and assume a new identity. When she confided in her parents, they had dug deeper and found out about the attack. They were the ones who initially phoned the police.

Perhaps Mr. and Mrs. Lamb had believed they could stop their daughter from leaving town by convincing her to press charges. Jules could imagine them naïvely expecting Brigham to be taken off the streets and remanded in custody until his trial. Audrey Brigham had offered a settlement of five hundred thousand as soon as he was arrested. But despite her family's unglamorous financial position, Rhianna had rejected the offer without attempting to negotiate for more.

Jules wished she had just taken the money and used it to buy herself a life. If Brigham had been a nobody without the means to hire a good defense team, Rhianna could probably have expected to see a conviction. A public defender would have ensured his client copped a plea. But Sagelblum was going to fight this thing all the way to the appeals court if necessary. Even if the jury brought in a guilty verdict, the case wasn't going away anytime soon.

Jules picked up a small bunch of grapes and absently consumed a couple. One way or another, Rhianna was not going to escape Werner Brigham. The thought shook her, and she stared out at the city lights. Could she blow the trial without anyone noticing? Could she claim bad luck and a client who alienated the jury?

Jules choked back loud laughter. Carl wasn't stupid. He had shown up to watch her cross-examination, and Jules knew he planned to make himself a fixture at her table until the verdict came in. He didn't have to spell out his reasons. She would do exactly the same thing if their positions were reversed. As far as Carl was concerned, her cut-throat instincts were on trial. She had to prove her loyalty to Sagelblum by displaying a personal disinterest in Rhianna. If she seemed ambivalent, Carl would take over and go for Rhianna's jugular. If she lost, there would always be questions, and if Audrey Brigham discovered what had occurred, Sagelblum would face a serious financial hit instead of the big payday Carl anticipated.

She had no choice, Jules thought. Whatever it took, she had to win.

The trial lasted for less than a week, and when the jury still hadn't reached a verdict after two days, Rhianna had prepared herself for the worst. But when she finally heard the clerk announce, "Not guilty," shock crushed her lungs all the same. She registered Norman Clay's disappointment, her family's anger and dismay, the embarrassed glances of several jurors, the jubilation at the defense table. But a strange numbness set in almost immediately, and the events of the morning took on a surreal quality. She felt incredibly calm and focused. Her one desire was to get away as fast as she could without having to speak to anyone.

"Let's go," she told her father before he could wind himself up. He was normally a patient man, but he had been pushed to his outer limits. Rhianna knew his doctor had increased his blood-pressure medication just before the trial commenced.

Shaking hands with the prosecutor, she said, "Thank you for everything, Mr. Clay. I hope we never find ourselves in these circumstances again."

His relief was palpable. Rhianna supposed in her situation some victims would have harangued him.

"I'll show you a way out of here to avoid the circus," he said.

They left via a back entrance and as they drove past the district court a few minutes later, she saw Werner Brigham and his mother holding a press conference in front of the imposing white building. At their side, Jules Valiant stood with the rest of the defense team and various public-relations hirelings Rhianna recognized. These "family spokespeople" had been stage-managing media relations ever since the arrest, making sure to give the impression that their client was the "real" victim.

"They call this justice?" her father ground out from the driver's seat. "It was a farce."

"Don't get started, Desmond," Rhianna's mother murmured. She always used his full name when she meant business; otherwise it was just "Des."

They drove in silence for a few minutes, then Rhianna said, "I won't be staying tonight. I need to get back to my job."

Her mother turned awkwardly in the front seat. "Darling, it won't hurt to wait until tomorrow. I don't think you should go anywhere today. Not after this."

"I'm fine," Rhianna said. "The sooner I get on with my life the better."

"Your mother thinks it's time you gave us your address," Des Lamb said. "And I agree with her."

Rhianna didn't put up a fight. She had already decided it was wrong to keep them in the dark anymore. As the car slowed for a set of traffic lights, she took a notepad from her purse, jotted down the details, and passed the slip forward.

Her mother took it eagerly. "Is Kate Lambert your employer?"

"No, that's my new identity. I'm employed by Bonnie and Lloyd Moss, looking after their baby."

This comment earned an irritated grunt from her father. "We put you through college so you could work as a nanny."

"Des, let it go." Her mother stroked a soothing hand over the skin at the back of his neck.

"No! This is what that asshole has done to my daughter. I'm going to kill him."

"Dad, I won't be doing this forever, and the Mosses are good people. You'd like them."

"So long as you feel safe, Des and I are fine with it." Her mother cast a wobbly smile in her direction.

Rhianna studied her father's profile. He was flushed with anger, and the rigid set of his mouth betrayed the emotions he was trying to hide. She hoped he wouldn't do anything stupid.

Carefully, she said, "Don't worry about me. Oatman's a safe place and I've even been learning how to shoot. You were right, Dad. It makes me feel stronger knowing how to handle a gun."

Her father heaved a sigh. "Wonderful. My daughter now has to be armed because our wonderful legal system couldn't put a nut behind bars."

"You might not be able to get a flight out today," her mother said, changing the subject in a thin voice. "They're all overbooked these days."

"That's not a problem." Rhianna had decided not to use her return flight. Brigham would expect her to head for the airport, so she had other plans. "I decided to cancel the return. I'm going to call Hertz now and arrange for a car instead. We can swing by their downtown office. It's not far from Mimi's place."

"Get a medium-size," her father said. "You don't want to make that trip in one of those crappy compacts."

"You're going to drive all the way to Arizona?" her mother murmured weakly.

Tabitha Lamb viewed road trips as an invitation to disaster. If the unfortunate driver didn't get a flat tire in the middle of the night on a lonely stretch of highway inhabited by a family of cannibals who lay in wait for breakdowns, she would make a wrong turn and end up in Wyoming.

Rhianna's father snorted. "It's not Mars. What are we talking about? Nine hundred miles?"

"Pretty close," Rhianna said. "It's a two-day drive. I'll break the trip when I get to Grand Junction."

"Oh, my Lord." A maternal sigh.

Rhianna made the call to Hertz as her parents quibbled over the best route to take and where she should stop for food. "You guys can just drop me at the rental agency," she said once she'd made the reservation. "I'll pick up the car and go straight to Mimi's to get my stuff."

Her mother craned around. "You're not even going to have lunch with us before you set off?"

"No, I better get going. I don't want to be driving in the mountains *after dark*."

"The mountains," her mother echoed in horror.

"You know," Rhianna mused aloud, "I think they shot some footage for the movie *Deliverance* up there."

She exchanged a glance with her father via the rearview mirror, and they both burst into semi-hysterical laughter.

"I don't know what you two think is so funny." Tabitha Lamb's tone was chagrined. "And on today of all days."

The family fell silent.

Rhianna stared out the window at the familiar Denver skyline and felt her world falling in around her. If things had turned out differently, she could have come back here to stay. Maybe she could have returned to the person she used to be and the life she'd once had. And maybe she could have had a partner.

Not anymore. It was over. The best she could hope for now was a future she'd never planned on, in a place that held no past for her. She would make it work. She had no choice.

"Do you have to leave right *now*?" Mimi asked, plainly aghast.

Rhianna zipped her suitcase and lowered it from the bed to

the floor. She glanced at her wristwatch. "It's been three hours since they let him go. I need to get on the road before he shows up here."

"Rhianna, the guy was just on trial. You can't seriously imagine he'll start stalking you again. Don't you think he's learned his lesson?"

"You're assuming he acts like a normal person," Rhianna said. "He doesn't. You should have seen the way he looked at me after they read the verdict."

"Okay, even if he is a nut, you've still got some time. I mean, won't he be out celebrating. Isn't that what assholes like him do when their rich families buy them a free pass?"

"I can't take that chance." Rhianna felt clammy just thinking about Werner Brigham sitting at a table, twirling that silver toothpick in his mouth. "When I was testifying…when I said what I really thought of him, you should have seen his face. It wasn't just anger. There was something else. I can't explain it. But he's not going to give up, believe me."

"Okay, so he's obsessed and a weirdo. But your mom said all he could talk about when they put him on the stand was how much he loves you. I don't think he'd actually try to hurt you." Mimi flushed in embarrassment. "I'm sorry. I know he *did* hurt you, but it sounds like he was confused, not that I'm making excuses for him. I mean—"

"Mimi!" Rhianna was astounded. If her closest friend in the world could be sucked in by Jules Valiant's portrayal of Brigham, no wonder the jury found him not guilty.

"I just meant that maybe he's had a wake-up call."

"No," Rhianna said patiently. "He wants to own me. Men like him don't just give up and go back to watching Broncos games. They think they're entitled to have whatever they want. And if they can't have it, they make sure no one else can."

Mimi's deep blue eyes flooded with tears, and she tucked her light brown hair self-consciously behind her ears. "Your parents gave me one of your books about stalkers. I couldn't read all of it, I got so frightened."

Rhianna sat down on the bed and slipped an arm around her.

"Don't worry. I can take care of myself nowadays, and he's not going to find me."

Mimi grabbed her in a hug. "It's so unfair. You're a good person and none of this should have happened to you. I don't understand why they didn't charge him with something else. Even regular assault, if that would have gotten him convicted."

"We offered him a deal," Rhianna said.

At the time she had been outraged that the prosecutor would even suggest a lesser charge, but she could see the point in plea bargains now. Receiving some semblance of justice was better than nothing. In her case, the jury had deliberated for so long that Norman Clay said there must have been several holdouts who didn't want Brigham set free. But in the end, they had believed his version of events and not hers. They had swallowed everything Jules fed them. *They believed her, not me.* Rhianna was stunned by that simple, ugly fact.

"What kind of deal?" Mimi asked.

"Assault instead of rape, with eighteen months in prison instead of a mandatory five years. The defense turned us down."

Because Jules Valiant had gambled on an outright win. All or nothing. Having seen her in action, Rhianna could understand why. She probably helped real monsters get away with murder. Maybe she defended child molesters, too. Rhianna ought to be thankful that she'd found out exactly who Jules was before they started seeing each other. What if she'd been in love with her? At least she could walk away now without a broken heart.

"Where are you going?" Mimi asked, staring at the luggage.

Rhianna hesitated. She hated not telling Mimi the whole truth. They'd shared secrets since elementary school. "I'm taking I-70 through Vail to Grand Junction."

"Is that where you've been living? Grand Junction?"

"No, but that's where I'm breaking my trip."

"I wish you'd give me your new address." Mimi's small, bowed mouth formed a disheartened pout. "You know I won't tell anyone."

"It's for your safety," Rhianna said. "When things settle down, you can come visit me. Maybe I'll even move back here."

Mimi slanted a doubtful look at her. "If he comes calling I'll tell him you're on your way to Canada."

Another country. Should she consider that option? Rhianna could not imagine having to start again somewhere else for the second time in six months, but over the next few weeks she needed to come up with a long-term plan. She had always expected Oatman to be a stopgap, a safe hideaway until Werner Brigham was locked up. Now she would have to decide whether to make her identity change permanent and become Kate Lambert officially. Was she safe, or should she put even more distance between herself and the man who would soon be hunting her again?

"Yes, tell him Canada," she said, forcing a smile. "Better yet, Australia."

"Want me to pack some snacks for the trip?"

Picturing bean salad and a couple of oatmeal muffins that could double as baseballs, Rhianna shook her head. "I'm not hungry. I can pick up something along the way."

Mimi grimaced. "All they have on I-70 is fast-food chains. It's a nightmare. Do you still have that Rescue Remedy I gave you for the trial? I have a spare if you've used it all up."

"I have enough for the trip." Somehow Rhianna doubted a Bach flower remedy was going to get her through the next few days.

She froze at the shrill alert of Mimi's doorbell.

"I'm not expecting anyone." Mimi's features were tight with apprehension. She got off the bed and padded across the room. Her eyes flicked to Rhianna. "Do you think you should hide?"

"No. Let's see who it is before you open the door."

Nerves erupting, Rhianna followed her out into the main living area. Mimi's loft apartment was a typical LoDo conversion. High ceilings. Wood floors. Industrial décor. Her front door was wrapped in decorative beaten copper. A wide-angle door viewer was built into the center of a beaded spiral pattern.

Mimi looked through the peephole then whispered to Rhianna, "It's okay. Just some guy." Leaving the guard in place, she cracked the door open a few inches and they both peeped out.

A tall, stick-thin African-American man stood in the hallway.

He took off his ball cap. "I got something for Shameeka Washington. This her apartment?"

"I'm sorry," Mimi said. "I don't know anyone called Shameeka in this building."

"I got the wrong address, maybe. Sorry for the interruption." He hesitated. "You ladies chasing?"

"Do you mean drugs? You sell drugs?" Mimi glanced over her shoulder with an excited little smile, like their visitor was Santa Claus.

"Thanks anyway," Rhianna stepped in before her best friend could explore this idea, "but we're not interested. Have a nice day." She closed the door.

Mimi sighed. "My friend with the indoor garden got busted a month ago."

"Then you need to find another old Deadhead just like him. Don't get mixed up with people who probably have their own meth lab." She returned to the guest bedroom with Mimi trailing after her, wringing her hands.

"I think you're making a mistake," Mimi said as Rhianna pulled the handle up so she could wheel her case to the door. "You're letting this creep ruin your life. He's taken everything away from you. Your job. Your home. Your friends and family. It's not right. You could move in here and live with me. Then you wouldn't be alone."

"Mimi. If I stay here in Denver he's going to kill me. It's that simple. I'm not placing you at risk as well. But thanks for the offer." She collected her overnight bag from a chair nearby and perched it on top of the larger case. "I need to go."

"I'll ride down with you." Mimi's mouth trembled. Rhianna could tell she was only just managing not to weep noisily.

She sniffed a few times as they locked the apartment, and they both jumped when the elevator doors swung open before they could press the button. Rhianna couldn't believe her eyes.

"You!" Mimi glared.

Jules stepped into the hallway. Her gaze fell to the luggage. "Leaving?"

"What do you think?" Rhianna tried to look straight through her, but her eyes insisted on a lengthy top-to-toe feast.

Jules must have noticed the overt appraisal. Her pupils dilated and for a split second something hot hovered between them. "Can we talk?" she asked.

"She's got nothing to say to you. Bitch!" Mimi was only five foot two, but she was a kick-boxer. Rhianna could see her rolling her feet in anticipation.

She touched her friend's arm. "Go back inside. I can handle this."

Mimi protested, but in the end, with Rhianna standing over her, she stepped back into the apartment. "What's *she* doing here?" she whispered irately.

"I have no idea," Rhianna said very softly. "But she can ride down to the garage with me and say whatever she needs to say, then I'm out of here."

"Whatever. You know where to find me." Mimi stepped back with visible reluctance. "I love you. Be careful."

"I love you too. I'll phone when I get to Grand Junction." Rhianna headed into the hall again.

"You're on your way back to Oatman?" Jules asked as soon as the apartment door closed and they were alone in front of the elevator.

Ignoring the question, Rhianna jabbed the Down button. She had no plans to explain her movements to her attacker's hired gun.

"Could we go get a coffee or something?" Jules persisted.

"No. What are you doing here?"

"I want us to discuss this."

"What is there to discuss?" Rhianna retorted. "What's done is done."

"Rhianna, I had no idea. How could I?"

"What would you have done differently if you knew?"

"Quite a few things. If I hadn't found out at the last minute, I would have had some options."

"I don't believe you." Rhianna stared fixedly at the steel doors delaying her escape. "In exchange for money you ruin innocent people's lives. Men who should be in prison get to walk away. I think that says it all, don't you?"

"Maybe it does. Maybe things are that simple and I'm just a bad person." Jules looked like she hadn't slept in days. Her white shirt was rumpled and her hair was drifting from the band at her nape. Shadows bruised her eyes. "For what it's worth, I'm sorry. I know this hurt you, and I wish to hell none of it had ever happened."

The doors whooshed apart and Rhianna released the breath she'd been holding. Hauling her bags into the carpeted confines of the elevator, she said, "It's way too late for *sorry*."

Jules wasn't going to make things easy. "Oh, no. This is not how it ends." She came after Rhianna. "I want you to listen to me. I can help you."

"I think you've helped me enough." The doors slid together and Rhianna pressed the button for the parking level, then sagged against the rear wall, completely drained. "For God's sake, Jules, just go. We have nothing to talk about."

"I can't." Jules took a step closer, her eyes pleading. "I care about you. What we said to each other…in bed that night. I meant every word and I still do. Can we find a way to get beyond this?"

"You must be joking." Rhianna stared up at the floor display, frustrated at the slowness of the descent. "Are you obtuse, or just insensitive?"

"I know you're angry. You have good cause, but it won't solve anything. Neither of us gets to rewrite the past."

Rhianna willed herself to stay calm. In just five minutes, she would be driving out of here and her nightmare would be over. "If that's all you came here to say, could we ride down in peace now and go our separate ways?"

"Is that really what you want?" Jules tugged roughly at her collar. A couple of buttons flew off. "You want to run away from everything? From him. From everyone who cares about you. From me. You think that's your best option?"

"What are you saying? I'm a coward?"

Rhianna stepped out into the oil-stained chill of the parking basement. The concrete structure was virtually empty, and the rental car, a silver Ford Taurus, was parked about twenty yards away. Inhaling the lingering taint of stale exhaust fumes, she walked briskly toward it, dragging her luggage after her. The urgent tap of her shoes echoed in alternation with a more muffled step, as Jules kept pace with her. A short distance from the car, she caught Rhianna's arm.

"Stop! Please. I know you're afraid and you're trying to stay safe. That's why I'm here. Just let me help."

Rhianna stopped and released the suitcase. Wheeling around to face Jules, she blazed, "If you wanted to help me, you would have made sure Werner Brigham went to prison!"

"Actually, that was Norman Clay's job. I'm a defense counsel and I did what I get paid to do. Maybe if you'd trusted me enough to tell me one fucking thing about what was going on for you, we could have—"

"Oh, this is *my fault*. You're ethically stunted, but I'm to blame for my situation?"

"We were sleeping together!" Jules shouted. "We agreed that it was more than a fling and we were going to give it a chance. But even then you didn't tell me who you were or what was going on with you."

"We barely knew each other," Rhianna yelled. "Do you think I'd risk telling you?"

"How could we get to know each other if you didn't?" Jules was pale with anger. Her chest heaving, she grated, "What if I was some other woman and not involved in any of this? Were you planning to just drive out of my life, too?"

"No!"

"Really? When were you going to be honest with me?"

"As soon as it was all over," Rhianna said quietly.

Jules circled her, hands on hips. "I knew something was wrong. We were making love but you were on another planet. I should have listened to my instincts. Jesus, what was I thinking?"

"You weren't thinking and neither was I," Rhianna said. "We were too busy fucking."

She would not have believed she could feel worse than she did in the days immediately after the attack. But for the first time in this ordeal, utter despair overwhelmed her. She had come *this* close to seeing him locked up. If the woman in front of her had wanted to, she could have made that happen. And to think, Rhianna had been serious about starting a relationship with her. She swung a quick automatic look around the parking garage, watching for any movement, then opened the Taurus's trunk.

Reaching down for the lighter of her bags, she muttered, "I wish we'd never met."

"Don't say that." Jules caught her by the wrist.

Rhianna tried to jerk her hand free, but she met Jules's eyes and could not look away. The stare seemed to suck the oxygen from around them, and a strange undercurrent stirred beneath the emotional surface of the moment. Something primal welled up, smothering anger, grief, and reason. Shocked, Rhianna forced her gaze down to the hand clamped around her own. She could feel the weight of Jules's eyes on her. The bag fell from her fingers. Common sense and self-respect washed out in a low tide that left her unbearably exposed. She saw then what had been invisible amidst the swirling debris of her life, a sweet hope Jules had brought to life, the bright, shining glimmer of possibility.

Jules mattered; the realization shocked her profoundly. They didn't know each other at all, but no one had come close to touching her as Jules did, to slipping beneath her guard and wooing her inner self. Her pulse raced and a frantic sense of resistance hammered in the back of her skull.

"Let go of me." She forced the words from her dry throat.

"Rhianna." It was not so much a plea as a softly spoken invocation. Jules's face was etched with anguish. Its naked vulnerability seemed impossible. Tears brimmed around her eyes. Her mouth looked chewed. With none of her usual finesse, she blurted, "Please come back to L.A. with me. I'll take good care of you."

Rhianna crushed the giddy yes that fluttered from the cocoon of her heart. "I don't think this is a U-Haul moment."

Ignoring Jules's outstretched hands, she loaded her bags mechanically into the trunk and slammed it closed.

Jules's stare was unwavering. She lifted a shaking hand to her jacket and took an envelope from the breast pocket. "I want you to have this."

"What is it?"

"A hundred thousand dollars."

Rhianna could not process the information at first. She gazed at the innocent white envelope like it was a speck in the distance, looming before her, ready to burst open at any moment and reveal its shocking contents. Rage found a way to her then, marshalling its forces in the deepest recesses of her mind and sweeping all aside in her defense.

She took the envelope, ripped it in half, then slapped Jules hard across the face. "Fuck you," she said with icy disdain. "And you can tell your precious client from me, if I ever see his face at my window again, I'll kill him."

Chapter Twelve

Jules cupped her palm to her cheek and mumbled, "Damn," as Rhianna screeched out of the parking garage. So much for her powers of persuasion.

She picked up the two pieces of envelope and stalked back to the elevator. As she waited for the doors to open, she heard the sound of an engine and turned sharply, but the car that purred into view wasn't the silver Taurus. A Lincoln Town Car with dark tinted windows slid toward her and halted a few feet away, angled so its passenger could exit near the elevator. A rear door opened and, to Jules's astonishment, Werner Brigham emerged, brandishing a bouquet of at least five dozen red roses.

He did a double take at the sight of her, then seemed to collect himself. "Ms. Valiant, the architect of my good fortune. What an unexpected pleasure." Strolling toward her, he inquired archly, "Not out spending your reward money yet? Mommy sent the check up to your office by messenger this afternoon."

Jules didn't bite. "What are you doing here?"

"I believe this is Mimi Buckmaster's apartment building. I'm dropping these off for Rhianna. She's staying here."

His casual certainty implied rights he didn't have. Jules was puzzled. How could he know Rhianna was here? *She* only knew because Gilbert Desjardines and his crew had been tailing Rhianna since the trial began.

"You're too late," she said coldly. "Ms. Lamb left some time ago."

"Left?" Savage life flickered in his dead stare. "Are you saying she has departed?"

Jules shrugged. "I saw her loading luggage into her car."

He ran a large, limp hand slowly over his light brownish-blonde hair. "Do you know her destination?"

"Mr. Brigham, we spoke about this," she said. "For your own sake, stay away from her. If the police pick you up again, you'll have a lot of explaining to do."

He nodded like he was crestfallen, then asked hopefully, "Did you have occasion to speak with her?"

"Not really."

He eyed her stinging cheek and smothered a titter. "I can't help but notice the impression of a dainty hand on your face. A parting gift from my Rhianna?"

Jules wanted to smack him in the mouth over "my Rhianna." Keeping her cool, she said, "Ms. Lamb is not happy with either of us."

With a rueful laugh, he confided, "She slapped me, too," as though this shared experience placed him and Jules on common ground.

"No doubt you asked for it."

A narrow look sharpened his droopy face. The gloves were off, Jules thought. He was a free man. She was paid in full. Neither of them had any reason to cozy up to the other.

"You think I should have gone to prison, don't you?" he said.

"What I think is irrelevant. You are a client." Jules lowered her gaze to the roses and said pointedly, "Chasing her would be unwise. And besides, she's living out of state as far as I know. Maybe even in another country."

Brigham bounced the roses in his arms. His eyes were flat and rainy gray. "I'm going to have her," he said blandly. "And this time I won't be made a fool of."

Rhianna's words came back to her. *The people who send me flowers usually want something.* Jules had known the barb was also directed at her, and it had hurt. She hadn't sent the peonies to awe or coerce; she had wanted to touch Rhianna and she knew she'd succeeded.

Her hand tightened around the torn envelope and she felt angry with herself for her clumsy attempt to hand over the money. She should have waited. Nothing had gone according to plan and, when it became obvious that she couldn't engineer the sensible discussion she had hoped for, she had panicked and added insult to injury. What a pitiable move. Something had gone badly wrong with her suave and her instincts. Ever since the first time she saw Rhianna, her circuits had been jammed.

Jules was transported back in time to junior high, where she had first discovered she could get really wet just staring at a girl. The object of her inarticulate yearnings was Serena Anderson, five feet nothing of overdeveloped pubescence. Serena, whose long looks and breathy requests for spare ballpoints were invitations to daydream. The sight of her slowly sucking a lollipop had forced Jules to get better acquainted with her clit for relief. Serena's vague hints about sleepovers had tortured her night and day. For months, she could think of nothing but Serena naked in her bed, offering her body for limitless exploration.

Her desires had driven her to her parents' bedroom to unearth the cache of instructional materials other kids claimed they found under mattresses and in bottom drawers. All she'd discovered was her mother's contraceptive pills and several *Playboy* magazines with the centerfolds torn out.

Jules had spent six months in crush-hell until one day Serena offered her lips for a kiss good-bye because her father had been transferred and she was moving to another city. Her brave disappointment had communicated itself to Jules as an indictment. Many years later, she realized that Serena had expected more of her. But Jules had been so preoccupied with her own passion, and so convinced of its hopelessness, she had not noticed that it was shared. Serena had been waiting for her to prove herself. She needed to know that Jules valued her enough to take a risk.

Have I learned nothing? Jules understood exactly why she had failed to pass her first romantic test. She had invented a goddess where there was just a girl, and had then deemed herself unworthy. She thought she was less than Serena deserved. Twenty years has passed since that fraught good-bye kiss. But she still took very few risks with women. Puzzled by that realization, Jules forced her attention back to Brigham. While she had been engaging in self-recrimination, he had pulled out his cell phone and was staring quizzically at the tiny screen.

"Excuse me," he said when he realized Jules was watching him. "I need to make a call."

He waved toward his car, and the driver managed to draw closer without running them over. The man got out and, without expression, held the door open for his employer. Brigham tossed the costly roses onto the seat ahead of him and paused, leaning against the car with a self-impressed air. His pants seemed a whisker too short, Jules noticed for the first time. He wore them too high on his belly flab, and slouched like a tall girl who would never get a prom date. Now that his hands were free, he reached for his toothpick case and set about probing his teeth. Between delicate swiveling motions, he said, "I assume you'll be returning to Los Angeles very soon."

"Yes."

"I have a hypothetical question for you."

"I'm listening." If she knew what Brigham was planning, she could take the appropriate countermeasures.

"Let us say a woman disappears and a man is suspected of kidnapping her because of previous mistakes. Would he be arrested immediately, or would the police have to build a case first?"

Jules was not going to be drawn into his game. Warning herself to remain calm, she changed the subject without responding to him. "Does your mother know you're here?"

Brigham's color rose and his pupils dilated. "My mother has absolute confidence in me."

"That wasn't what I asked. You dragged the Brigham name through the mud. Do you think your mother wants you to pick up where you left off with Rhianna Lamb?"

He stuffed the toothpick back in its receptacle and climbed into the car. After the driver closed the door, the window slid down and Brigham said, "You are an excellent attorney, Ms. Valiant. But you've done your job. Don't cause me any trouble, and I won't cause you any."

"Are you threatening me?"

"Don't be melodramatic, Counselor."

"I'll only say this once," Jules warned coldly. "I promise you, if you go near Rhianna Lamb—if you touch a hair on her head—you'll wish you had never been born."

❖

The dining options were limited at two a.m. in Grand Junction. After checking in to a dreary Holiday Inn, Rhianna found the nearest Denny's and ordered a meal certain to give her indigestion.

A few booths away from her, a noisy domestic dispute was in progress. The couple insulting each other sounded drunk. At another table a man was complaining about his prime-rib dinner in a slurred monologue. A child sat opposite him, transfixed by a Game Boy. Not far from them sat the only other sober diner in the place. A trucker, Rhianna surmised from the rig at the far end of the parking lot. While she was waiting for her salad and chicken wings, he got irritated with the arguing couple and complained to the waitress. She offered him a complimentary stuffed waffle, which he accepted.

About ten minutes later, Rhianna's chicken wings showed up without the salad. She ate several in quick succession and washed them down with weak coffee. Someone turned up the music, probably to drown out the customers. The arguing couple decided to sing along to "My Heart Will Go On"—Celine Dion fans, obviously.

Rhianna wondered if it was worth enduring the impromptu karaoke in order to eat limp lettuce, or whether she should ask for the check before someone remembered her meal. Naturally, the waitress had vanished. Rhianna poured some more lukewarm coffee and stared out the window, thinking, *My life is over.*

Which was exactly the right moment for a robbery to take place, and the likely target had just stepped in the door. He looked around like he'd stumbled into a horror movie. The waitress wandered through the diner, slapped Rhianna's salad down in front of the kid with the Game Boy, and stared at the new arrival like she'd never seen a six-foot-five African-American man in a primrose yellow suit, an orange fedora with a zebra-striped band, cornrows, and bling.

She asked the obvious question, "Are you lost, sir?"

He said, "I can't have no Celine Dion. Not while I eat."

"I'll take care of it," she said and showed him toward a booth.

He didn't get that far across the room. Stopping at Rhianna's table, he flashed a diamond-studded smile. "Damn, you slammin'. What's up, baby?"

Despite herself, Rhianna found the smile infectious. Returning it, she said, "What can I tell you? Denny's at two a.m. on a slow night. It's not pretty."

He seemed to read this as an invitation. Extending his hand, he announced, "You looking at the real deal, baby. They jocking my style cos I just can't help myself. I'm Mr. Notorious Hard."

Her day couldn't get any worse. Why not complete it with a man who was probably a rap star being chased by a carload of gangbangers with a grudge? Tomorrow, this Denny's would no doubt be on the news as the scene of a bloody shootout. She would be one of the shaken survivors, explaining how she hid under a table and pretended to be dead.

Rhianna shook his huge paw. Remembering her rule to use her new identity at all times once she was out of Denver, she said, "I'm Kate Lambert. Feel free to join me."

Mr. Notorious Hard sat down and examined the menu as if he expected to find something delicious on it. When his coffee arrived, he handed the waitress a hundred-dollar note and said, "Let me break it down. I know you got some fine breakfast back there." To Rhianna, he said, "You hungry, baby?"

She said, "Well, my salad never came. I could eat some waffles, maybe."

"You take that down?" he asked the waitress, adding, "Don't make me look like a fool with no soggy, nasty breakfast."

She tucked the hundred away and managed a big smile. "Coming right up."

Someone changed the music, tactfully rolling with Puff Daddy's version of "I'll Be Missing You." Mr. Notorious Hard appeared to find this song poignant. Soberly, he shook his head and lamented, "Biggie, he the man. He just trying to do his thing. That was cold."

Rhianna had no idea what he was talking about, but said for good measure, "It's hard when bad things happen to good people."

Her sympathy appeared to strike a chord. "You sensitive," he said. "I like that. I wanna get with you, baby."

Rhianna poured more coffee in both their mugs. "Are you hitting on me, Notorious?"

He laughed. "You so fine, you got me hooked."

The waffles arrived, crispy and golden, and the waitress returned a moment later with a huge plate of steak and eggs. "That's the chef's personal tenderloin," she said.

They thanked her and Rhianna returned her attention to Notorious, saying, "You're very charming and you smell good, but I have a confession."

Notorious anticipated the issue. "Damn. Who's your daddy?"

It did not seem wise to answer honestly, so Rhianna cut into her waffle and replied, "Let's just say, I don't want to create a problem."

He took time out from carving up his steak. "Here's my scandal. I don't cuss. I don't hit my ladies. But I gotta be straight. Itty-bitty white girls, I just wanna get you home."

"That's very candid." Rhianna bathed a piece of waffle in syrup. "I'm sure you must be popular."

Her dinner companion chewed efficiently. Between forkfuls of egg, he said, "You ever been with a brother?"

"No." Rhianna didn't care that this was not the kind of conversation she would normally have. Her life was a disaster and all bets were off.

"Any time you looking for a man to give you that special feeling." Notorious took a card from his top pocket and slid it across the table.

Rhianna thanked him and put the card in her purse. They ate in silence for a few minutes, the focus of every other diner. Even the kid with the Game Boy had stopped playing to turn around and stare.

"You going to California?" Notorious asked.

"Arizona," Rhianna said, pushing her plate to the side.

"I got business there," he said. "You wanna roll in my Mercedes?"

Rhianna laughed. "You don't give up easily." She picked up her purse and fished around for her wallet.

"It's on my tab," he insisted, waving her money away.

"That's very kind of you." Rhianna stood. "If you'll excuse me, I'm tired and it's time I got some sleep."

Notorious reached for her hand and lifted it to his lips. After planting a courtly kiss, he said, "It's not my intention to hurt you, baby."

Rhianna was not sure how to respond to such a strange farewell, but she supposed he was worried he might have offended her. To reassure him that she had taken his flirtation in good humor, she said, "I had a terrible day before I came here, Notorious. Eating dinner with you was the only good part of it."

He grinned. "Keep my number."

CHAPTER THIRTEEN

Y ou had dinner with her?" Werner almost swallowed his toothpick. He could not believe the story he'd just heard.

"You asked me for her name," Mr. Hard pointed out, sounding affronted. "How you suppose I discover that if I can't get close to her?"

Werner didn't want to think about an enormous black man "getting close" to Rhianna. "The name, do you have it?"

After a long pause, Hard said, "Kate Lambert."

Werner had to stand up. He couldn't sit still. Lately he had contemplated speaking to his doctor about restless legs syndrome. It appeared he might be afflicted.

"Kate Lambert," he gloated softly. Twenty thousand dollars wisely invested.

"What you want with her?" The gangster actually had the effrontery to sound mistrustful.

Resenting the tone of his question, Werner replied, "As I said, I'm going to marry her."

"Damn. I thought you was a dreamer. *You* her daddy?"

Werner was familiar with this euphemism from eating in the kitchen with the cook and her grown-up sons occasionally. Mr. Notorious Hard was not referring to a parent. "Rhianna is my wife-to-be," he confirmed impatiently.

"How long you been with her?"

Werner remembered not to sound disrespectful, but this was a business conversation. "Mr. Hard, I'm not sure why this information is relevant to your assignment?"

"I've been thinking." The tone was reflective. "I told my momma I would be something. So I made my life all about the Benjamins. But what she think about this shit? That's got me stressing."

Belated scruples from a man who was probably a pimp. Werner rolled his eyes. "Where are you now?"

"Arizona. I gotta roll out, man. I see her."

"Make sure she doesn't see you," Werner instructed. "Just follow her to her house, then drive away. All I need is an address and your job is done."

"You need to make something right with this girl? You fucked up? That what this about?"

"You might say that," Werner replied cagily.

"Sometimes, you gotta cut your losses."

"Thank you for the advice." Werner sniffed. "Call me when you have that address."

He dropped the receiver back in its cradle and paced around the library for a few minutes, pondering his next move. Werner prided himself on being a patient man. He'd waited a long time for Rhianna to come to her senses and appreciate all she was being offered. But she had put him through hell, and it was time for her to see the error of her ways.

He had tried the romantic approach, but look where that got him. His mother was still infuriated and Werner could understand why. She had endured public humiliation and Rhianna's behavior had cost her a fortune. Werner could put up with a lot on his own account. He could forgive Rhianna for her foolishness toward him. But if there was one thing that made him really angry, that was having his mother upset. In that regard, his policy was zero tolerance. Rhianna would have one more chance to do the right thing, and if she decided to be difficult, the consequences would be upon her head.

Werner had hoped he would not have to resort to Plan B, but he no longer had any choice. A curious thrill made his pulse jump. The hour was upon him, and his reward was well-deserved. He felt a pang of regret that he would have to lock her away from the world until she understood her role. He had wanted her on his arm at the events he usually attended as Mommy's escort. He could almost feel the envious stares of other men. But he could wait a few more months.

Images crowded his mind, each one featuring Rhianna. He pictured her in the courtroom, taking the stand. How modest and frail she had looked, and how confused she was. He could tell from the way the prosecutor browbeat her that she had been coached in her testimony. They had used her. They had turned her against him. It would take time to win her over, he thought, but the task would be very stimulating.

He had created a comfortable prison for his reticent bride and had given serious thought to her re-education. She would have to earn her privileges. At first she would be in the basement room; then, when she showed sufficient gratitude and compliance, she would occupy the luxurious suite he had prepared. It had taken four months to complete the renovations on the home he'd purchased for this purpose. He had started the project the moment he discovered Rhianna had left Denver.

Werner stopped pacing and leaned against the edge of his desk, gratified by his foresight. The timing could not be better. Rhianna had been forced to confront the truth in the courtroom; he had Julia Valiant to thank for that. He disliked the woman intensely, and he could tell the acrimony was mutual. But he owed her a debt of gratitude all the same, and he was big enough to admit it.

One day, if he showed enough strength of purpose to bring his plan to fruition, Rhianna would be able to look back upon the trial as the most important turning point in her life. She would understand why Werner had to take the steps he was taking, and recognize that he had to be strong because she was weak. Finally she would grasp that he knew her better than she knew herself. He alone saw her potential. For that, she would love him.

At the sound of a knock, Rhianna wiped her face on her pillow and got up off the bed to open her door.

Bonnie stood in the hallway with two cups of herb tea, her

customary recourse when her nerves were shattered. "It's been three hours," she said. "I can't listen to you crying anymore."

"I'm sorry." Rhianna let her in. "With all the soundproofing, I didn't think anyone could hear."

"Okay, so I had my ear to the door."

She followed Rhianna into the small living room and they both sat on the sofa. For a few minutes they sipped their tea.

"I'm not stupid," Bonnie said, "You walk in the door looking like someone died, then you hide in your room as soon as Alice is asleep. Talk to me."

Rhianna had already decided to come clean with her good-natured employer. She had never felt okay living under the Mosses' roof without telling them her name. "Well, let me see. For starters, I'm not Kate Lambert. My real name is Rhianna Lamb."

Bonnie did not speak at first. Rhianna suspected she was coming to grips with the idea that Kate did not exist. "Rhianna. That's pretty." Bonnie studied her curiously. "And your hair. Is that your real color?"

"It's close," Rhianna said.

"I knew you were a platinum blonde."

"I used to wear it long." Rhianna set her tea down on the occasional table near the sofa and pulled her journal down from the bookcase. She extracted the photographs she'd tucked inside the cover and handed them to Bonnie. "This is me, two years ago."

Bonnie's mouth parted in astonishment. "That's incredible. I wouldn't have recognized you."

Rhianna looked down over her shoulder. "It seems like a long time ago. I don't feel like the same person."

Bonnie handed the photos back. "Why did you go to Denver?"

"The man I told you about…he was on trial for raping me."

"Oh, my God." Bonnie went pale and some of her tea spilled. She put the cup down and wiped her lap. "I don't know what to say. Oh, my Lord. You should have told us." She hesitated. "That came out wrong. Obviously, it's entirely up to you what you say about your private business." She stopped talking again. Her shoulders shook. "Oh, Kate…Rhianna."

"It's okay." Rhianna found a box of tissues and sat down again, giving Bonnie a hug.

"This is nuts." Bonnie blew her nose. "Here I am crying, and you're comforting me, and *you're* the one who had to deal with this. I'm sorry. Just give me a minute. Okay?"

"I apologize for not telling you the truth," Rhianna said. "I intended to. I just wasn't—"

"Don't even start down that track." Bonnie raised her hand in protest. "You did what you had to do. I know what it's like. I helped women change their identities and relocate when I was working at the refuge." She shivered. "These men don't know when to stop."

"He stalked me for nine months, then he raped me," Rhianna said. "And when they finally got around to arresting him, they let him out on bail. Now he's been found not guilty."

Bonnie's color changed from white to red. "There's something wrong with that picture."

"His family is rich. They hired a fancy defense team. That's the other thing." Rhianna tried to say the words evenly, but her voice fractured. "Jules…the woman who sent me the flowers. She was his defense attorney."

"No!" Bonnie gasped. "I don't understand. How could she—"

"It's a long story," Rhianna said. "I made a mistake."

"She represented the man who raped you?" Bonnie squeaked.

"She didn't know. At least I don't think she did. I'm not sure about anything, anymore."

"You need a stiff drink." Bonnie set aside the herbal tea in disgust. "Come on. I've got a new frozen-margarita recipe I want to try out." She dragged Rhianna into the kitchen and set up the blender.

"I don't know if this is a good idea," Rhianna said as Bonnie upended a bottle of Cointreau into a measuring cup.

"It's the best idea I've come up with all day, apart from blowing up old man Entwhistle's truck with him in it."

"He still hasn't covered that pit?" Rhianna perched on one of the high stools at the counter.

"Lloyd thinks he wants us to buy him out." Bonnie measured some triple sec and sloshed it into her mix. "The irony is, if he would make us a realistic offer, we'd be willing to negotiate. Instead he thinks he can force our hand by making a nuisance of himself."

"I saw the barricade," Rhianna said.

"It's the best we can do for now. I wanted something there since we'll be away next week. You shouldn't have to worry about Alice falling into a hole at the end of the yard. And there's Hadrian. He can't see three feet in front of him and his hearing's gone."

Rhianna glanced into the den where the mastiff was snoring on his dog bed. "He doesn't come when he's called."

She hated to see the big, noble dog bang into furniture and jump with fright when he was touched unexpectedly. But he still had quality of life and he was dearly loved. She knew Bonnie was going to have a terrible time when she had to let him go.

"I feel bad about us going, with what you've been through," Bonnie said. "You could come if you want. We can get another room."

Rhianna shook her head. She didn't want to be stuck in a hotel taking care of Alice for a week while Bonnie and Lloyd were at their convention. The little girl would be bored after a day, and they would both be miserable.

"We'll be fine," she said. "And besides, it's too hard on Hadrian being in an empty house. Percy can't be here all the time."

Bonnie turned on the blender and they both covered their ears, then she filled a pitcher and poured their cocktails. They tapped glasses but made no toast.

"Was it serious?" Bonnie asked after a few sips. "With Jules, I mean."

"We only saw each other a couple of times."

Bonnie swirled her cocktail. "I was serious about Lloyd after our first date."

Rhianna had the impression her face must be revealing the emotion she sought to hide. And her throat felt sore, which made her voice husky. She wished she could stop it from wavering. "I thought we might have something," she confessed. "I've never been with anyone quite like her."

"So you were—"

"Sleeping together. Yes." Rhianna tried for a dismissive laugh, but all that came out was a sob. "When it was all over she tried to give me money."

"Money!" Bonnie flared. "Guilty conscience, I suppose. I'd like to meet this woman and give her a piece of my mind."

"I slapped her face. We yelled at each other." Rhianna jammed another scrunched tissue to her eyes. "Now I'll never see her again."

"Drink your margarita," Bonnie advised.

Rhianna gulped down half the icy liquid without tasting it. Her teeth hurt and her nose ran. She wailed, "I'm a mess. Just look at me. What am I going to do?"

"That depends." Bonnie took her question at face value. "What I always say is don't get mad, get even."

"There's no getting even for any of this."

Rhianna could hear her own defeat in the weary sorrow of her voice. She was tired of fighting, she thought. But she was also tired of running away and having no life. She was tired of being afraid, of looking over her shoulder and lying paralyzed in her bed, listening to bumps in the night. She'd had enough. Maybe Bonnie was right. Maybe she wasn't looking at her options the right way.

Toying with that notion, she murmured, "Are you saying I'm thinking like a victim?"

Bonnie shook her head emphatically. "You're a strong, brave woman or you wouldn't be here. You are not a victim, you're a survivor. You should be proud of yourself."

"I keep thinking I'm weak," Rhianna admitted. "There are so many things I could have done differently."

"It's not too late. Let me tell you something. I believe in fighting back. Do you think this creep is going to come after you again?"

"I know he is."

"Then you can't just sit around like a basket case waiting for him. That's playing by his rules."

Rhianna drained her glass. She could feel the alcohol rocketing through her system, making her emboldened. Forcing herself to tap into her common sense, she demanded, "What am I supposed to do? I have a restraining order against him. I've changed my name. I testified, for God's sake. I put myself through that whole ordeal for nothing."

And then there was Jules. Perhaps she was fooling herself to think they might have been able to build something. If so, the delusion was mutual. Jules had begged her to come to L.A. and had promised to take care of her. Was the offer motivated only by guilt? Would a woman like Jules Valiant ask someone to live with her for no reason other than to right a wrong?

Rhianna could not convince herself of that possibility for a minute. Neither could she forget the distress and desperation on Jules's face. "You know what I hate?" she said, thinking out loud. "I hate that I care about that woman. I hate that I keep on making excuses for her."

Bonnie replenished their glasses. "We're talking about Jules again?" she inquired dryly.

Rhianna cradled her head in her hands. "You're right. I need to stop thinking about her. She betrayed me and I'll never forgive her for what she did."

"Can I get something clear?" Bonnie asked. "Did she know? I mean beforehand. Did she know you were the one he attacked?"

"No, we found out when I took the stand."

Bonnie swirled her cocktail thoughtfully. "Do you think she has feelings for you?"

"I don't know." *Liar.*

"Well, if she does, that guy Werner hurt her, too."

Rhianna was silent. She hadn't considered that angle at all. "I'm not a vigilante," she said.

"No, but you have a right to defend yourself. And if that means going on the offense, why rule it out?"

"Because we're both intoxicated?" Rhianna suggested.

"Doesn't mean we're wrong." Bonnie lifted her glass. "Bottoms up."

Feeling a little queasy, Rhianna asked, "What do you mean by going on the offense?"

"We have to turn the tables on him somehow." Bonnie frowned. "What's he like?"

"Physically, he's pretty nondescript. Sandy blonde and thinning a bit at the temples. He's tall and he's carrying an extra forty pounds. You wouldn't notice him in a crowd."

"What about the attitude. Is he belligerent?"

"He's polite. Egotistical. Very arrogant. He has this whole fantasy going on and I'm supposed to play a role in it. We get married and live happily ever after. He thinks he's offering the perfect life and I'm a fool for not accepting him. I don't even *know* him."

"So, he's genuinely crazy as well as dangerous," Bonnie noted succinctly.

"Yes, and cunning. I wasn't allowed to see him testify in the trial, but my parents were there. Mom said if they hadn't known what he was like, beforehand, they would have felt sorry for him."

"You're kidding."

"Apparently, he told the jury he didn't care if he was convicted. He said he'd made the most terrible mistake of his life and offended the woman he adored, so nothing else mattered."

"They fell for that crap!"

"Mom said several female jurors ended up crying. And it gets worse."

Bonnie groaned. "Of course it does, because they turned the trial into a soap opera."

She was right, Rhianna thought. Even her own testimony and cross-examination had felt like a stage show. Filled with helpless rage, she concluded her story. "Apparently, when Jules gave her closing statement, people were nodding all the way through and staring at her like she was a movie star. Dad said that's when he knew Brigham would walk."

"I guess he thinks he can get away with anything, now," Bonnie remarked.

Rhianna nodded. She had the same impression. "You know… I'm so sick of having to think about him. He walked into my life and hijacked it. Since then I haven't had a single day I can call my own. It's like having a disease. Even when you can't see it, you know it's there. You live in its shadow. He's eating away at me, Bonnie, and I can't stop him."

"You know where he lives, don't you?"

"Yes. I've been to his house." Rhianna grimaced. "All part of my brilliant plan. Did I tell you about the guide I'm writing?—*Twenty Ways to Lose Your Rape Trial.*"

Bonnie ignored her bitter self-mockery. "Remember those people I told you about before you left?"

"Lloyd's friends in low places?"

Bonnie nodded. "I think it's time I made a couple of calls."

Rhianna stared at her. "Are you going to put out a contract on him?"

Bonnie smiled slyly. "It's time he changed his attitude. Maybe some forceful persuasion would help."

"I don't want you getting in any trouble." Rhianna bit her lip. "He's the type who'll go to the police."

"These guys are professionals," Bonnie said. "They'll sort him out."

Rhianna thought about how it would feel to wake up and know Brigham had been expunged from her life. "Why not," she said. "What do I have to lose?"

CHAPTER FOURTEEN

Jules couldn't breathe. She could see nothing. When she tried to cry out only the tiniest croak bled past her frozen lips. She started clawing around her body and realized that she was buried alive. A thin wail careened from her throat and she bolted up in bed. Panting, she groped for her lamp and spilled a feeble yellow haze into her room. Her alarm clock showed three a.m.

Jules did what she always did when she pried herself free of this nightmare. She got out of bed and went to the kitchen to make hot chocolate. If she tried to go back to sleep immediately, she would drift into her bad dreams once more.

She knew what they were about, and over the years, she had paid shrinks to make them go away—with little success. When she was ten, she'd suffered a fall at a school camp in the canyons. A walking bridge had collapsed during a rock slide, sending her and six other children plummeting into a chasm. She had regained consciousness, buried in debris, a dying classmate on top of her. Hours passed before the rescue team arrived to dig them out. After someone heard her cries for help, an air tube was fed down and she was gradually unearthed with machinery and shovels.

A man had spoken to her throughout, urging her to stay awake. Eventually, all she'd wanted to do was close her eyes and surrender to the silent mercy of sleep. She was cold, she couldn't move for pain, and every breath was an effort. The time finally came when she let the air creep from her lungs and did not fight for her next breath. She released the limp hand of her dead schoolmate, letting go because she had no power to hold on. A fog closed over her and she fell into in a dark vortex, a whirling, mindless oblivion.

Jules was never sure if the loud voice she'd heard then belonged to God, or to the man who pulled her out, or to the woman she would one day become. *If you let go now you will die.*

With nothing left, she had reached for life and a big warm hand seized hers.

More than two decades had passed since that childhood trauma, and she still had trouble falling asleep. She still feared the dark and avoided the unknown. She also suffered from claustrophobia, a condition she kept in check by force of will, medication when she had to fly, and conscious choices about her surroundings.

Her survival, labeled "miraculous" in the press, had instilled confidence. Jules knew how strong she was and that she was incredibly lucky to be alive. She knew she could beat the odds. Of the children who fell to the bottom of the chasm that day, she was the sole survivor.

She made a point of understanding her own strengths and weaknesses. There were times when she felt she lived her life too cautiously, sticking to the well-lit paths she had carved out for herself. She liked to think she took risks, yet all she really did was gamble, and her gambles were carefully calculated. She avoided unpredictable outcomes.

To outsiders, her choice of career probably seemed absurd for a woman who needed certainty, but Jules found it the opposite. For her, knowledge was power. Case law provided precedent and interpretation. Jury consultants took care of a potential weak link in every trial process. Judges could be second-guessed. Statistical likelihood could be measured, and Jules left little to chance. That was one reason she worked for Sagelblum; her personal philosophy was a perfect match for the firm's business model. Carl sometimes joked that if he wasn't married to his job and she wasn't queer, they were made for each other. Her ruthless logic and his killer instincts made for a lethal combination they exploited to the max. She seldom questioned the choices they made, the cases they fought, or the clients they accepted. In the past, she had been guided by a single ethic she truly believed in—that everyone had a right to the best possible defense. No exceptions.

In a perfect world, the accused was perennially innocent and the lawyer defending him was a hero on a quest for the truth. But in reality, someone had to do the dirty work. Guilty, remorseless assholes stood in courtrooms every day of the week, and so far nobody had come up with a surefire means of identifying them. Such a litmus would be nice, a color code to flag the bad guys in every case.

Perhaps that would make it legitimate to dole out a different quality of defense for different people. Certain categories of undeserving offenders could be denied any defense at all. What did society owe those who betrayed it—the serial killers, child molesters, rapists? But where would the lines be drawn? Was a sliding scale possible in a justice system inherently flawed by its human component? Would gay people get defended?

Despite high-minded goals, an enviable constitution to uphold, the checks and balances of an appeal-court process, and the presumption of innocence, the playing field would never be level. Some people would always receive more "justice" than others, especially those with cash or celebrity. Attorneys stricken with occasional bouts of conscience because they sold their services to the highest bidders could do penance by working *pro bono* and donating to legal-defense funds for the deserving. Jules did not feel noble or self-righteous about her own forms of "giving back." She did not kid herself that making a few minor sacrifices would maintain karmic balance or score points with the man upstairs. Sometimes it was just easier to do the right thing than to know she hadn't.

She took her hot chocolate from the microwave, poked some marshmallows into it, and sat down at the small Shaker-style table in the windowed recess next to her kitchen. She did not turn on the floodlights in her garden, but stared out into the velvet darkness and thought about Rhianna.

Justice had served her poorly. In a case like Rhianna's, where hard physical evidence was virtually absent, the facts could not speak for themselves. The trial was little more than an adversarial contest between prosecution and defense played out in front of an audience who voted more on emotion than on reason. For her part, Jules could have backed out and faced the professional consequences. But she had only wounded Rhianna; Carl would have obliterated her.

Jules sipped her warm drink. She could justify her decisions any way she wanted, but she still felt like shit. Rhianna would never see her actions as the lesser of two evils, as an attempt to shield both of them as best she could. Rhianna had to live with the consequences. Her rapist was set free, and she knew, just as Jules did, that he had not seen the error of his ways.

Oatman was only three hundred miles from her bungalow in the Hollywood Hills. Maybe she would just get in her car and make the drive. If she showed up on Rhianna's doorstep and asked for ten minutes of her time, would she be turned away? She could be in Oatman by nine a.m. if she left soon.

The thought of seeing Rhianna made her quiver, and Jules felt demeaned by this involuntary response. Was the face slap not enough to quash her Pavlovian arousal? Did she need to subject herself to a further humiliating episode? Where was her pride? She vacillated, teetering at the periphery of a helplessness she found unacceptable. That this part of her psyche could exist, despite every accomplishment, every triumph, appalled her. She did not crawl for any woman, under any circumstances.

Feeling disgusted with herself, she considered a painting on the wall, an oil reproduction of Gustav Klimt's *Goldfish*. She saw just enough of Rhianna in the red-haired nymph provocatively displaying her rear to recognize how morose she had become since the episode in the parking garage. She was pining. Feeling sorry for herself. She felt diminished, uninspired by her work, depressed by a soul-shrinking vision of the future.

She had a terrible fear that she would turn forty, or fifty, and look back on a life shaped by a wrong decision she would regret forever. Cowardice was unbecoming in anyone. In herself, it was unforgivable. This is not over, she thought. Rhianna would probably refuse to hear her out. Maybe she did not believe, as Jules did, that they owed it to themselves to find out who they could be to each other. But Jules was not ready to give up. To live with herself, she would have to try again.

Go back to bed, she thought, but her feet carried her to her workstation and she logged into her e-mail to see whether anything urgent had arrived since the previous afternoon. The messages were routine. Various motions copied for her to vet. Tedious reports. Briefs. An indictment or two.

She clicked on a message from Gilbert Desjardines.

> *Word is your man Brigham put a tail on Ms. Lamb. Damonique knows the dude—Notorious Hard. He's got some juice in the neighborhood. Sounds like he gave out a name and address. Arizona. That's what she heard.*

Jules stared at the screen and listened to the labored hum of her computer, a desktop that had so far cheated its planned obsolescence. She kept meaning to replace it, but she never found the time to surf through computer sites, comparing alternatives.

She read the message again, this time without letting her thoughts wander. The full impact of the words hit her. Werner Brigham now knew Rhianna's new name and her location. It would only be a matter of time before he decided to renew their acquaintance.

Rhianna waved Bonnie and Lloyd farewell, hoisted Alice higher on her hip, and tugged at Hadrian's collar.

"Let's go see the lambs," she told her charge.

Percy waved as she approached the barn. "Howdy." He knew her real name now, but he hadn't tried it out yet.

Rhianna smiled. "Guess why we're here."

Chuckling, Percy opened the doors to the lamb pen. "Milk's warm," he said, dipping a ladle into a small heating vat.

Alice's chubby little legs wiggled, and Hadrian swung his head from side to side to dislodge the stalactites of drool weighing from his mouth.

Percy filled a plastic nursing bottle and pulled a rubber nipple over the top.

"That's not for you to drink," Rhianna said as Alice clutched the lamb feeder to her chest. They'd been through this routine a few times since the six orphaned lambs arrived.

Percy filled several more bottles and carried them over to the front of the pen, where he rigged them on a suspended frame for the lambs to enjoy. He lifted the smallest of the woolly creatures over the gate and sat down on a bench nearby, gently holding it on his knee so that Alice could offer the milk. As the lamb suckled and wagged its tail, Hadrian patrolled the area for droppings to sniff. When he'd snuffled all he wanted, he plodded to Rhianna's side and leaned against her, crooning with pleasure as she scratched his back.

"Got the new targets." Percy pointed at a bundle of male half-silhouettes propped against the barn wall. Each had a bull's-eye over the chest.

"Maybe I'll try the .38," Rhianna said.

She hoped there would be no need to become an expert at putting bullets into the heart zone of Percy's new targets. Two of Lloyd's shady acquaintances had gone to Denver to have a conversation with Werner Brigham.

Rhianna wished she could be there to see the expression on his face when a couple of menacing thugs told him it was time to act right. She could almost see him licking his thick lips. He would probably offer them money to go away. Bonnie said, if he did, they were going to rough him up and talk about what their boss wanted them to do if he wasn't cooperative.

Rhianna adjusted the angle of the bottle so that Alice could hold it more easily and bent down to kiss the little girl's soft hair. Earlier this morning, she'd been jumpy as the Mosses packed their Lexus SUV, preparing to leave, but she felt calm now. Percy was going to sleep in a room off the den, so she wouldn't be alone in the house, and she would have Hadrian on her bed. He couldn't hear and his sight was almost gone, but Bonnie was convinced the ageing mastiff would defend his family.

Lloyd had unlocked the gun safe and put Percy in charge of the weapons. Intellectually, Rhianna had accepted that the chances of Brigham finding her and breaking into the house were remote, but her emotions were still raw and her flesh still crawled every time she thought about him sitting in the courtroom ogling her like a hyena. She kept her borrowed .22 in a concealed cavity Lloyd had built in her headboard. All she had to do was slip a hand behind her mattress and the gun was sitting there, loaded and ready.

Percy touched her shoulder lightly. "Looks like she's done."

The lamb was snuggling back in his arms and Alice had dropped the empty bottle.

"I was daydreaming," Rhianna said. Knowing the wizened ranch hand would get a kick out of her anger, she added, "Actually I was thinking about blowing Werner Brigham's brains out."

"Now you're talking." His eyes glowed like the deep blue prairie sky.

"Thanks for teaching me how to shoot, Percy."

He got to his feet and lowered the lamb down into the pen. "You'll get there," he said.

Rhianna grinned over this fulsome praise. Percy seldom remarked on her efforts, probably because she hadn't been able to hit a target twenty feet away until the past two days. She bent to pick Alice up when she heard a car and took the toddler by the hand instead. The Mosses didn't get a lot of visitors, unless they were hosting a party. Parcel deliveries only occurred in the afternoons.

"You expecting company?" Percy's hand was on his holster. He sidled toward the barn door.

Rhianna stayed behind him, her heart beating hard. "No."

With infinite caution, they both peered out from the shadowed interior.

A dark gray Mercedes CLS550 idled in front of the house. The driver was slouched over the wheel.

"That him?" Percy asked, drawing his gun.

"No." Rhianna lifted Alice and said, "Would you please take her out back to the playground for a few minutes? I'll handle this."

Percy holstered his weapon, and Rhianna transferred Alice to his shoulders for a piggyback ride. As the two set off around the corner of the barn, she slid her hand under Hadrian's collar and crossed the yard to stand a few feet from the car.

Something was wrong, she thought as soon as she saw Jules's pale face. Her throat dried with apprehension. At the same time, her limbs quickened with hungry life and a red-hot current skittered upward from her core. She knew she was blushing and immediately looked away, but the telltale color invaded her cheeks regardless.

"Rhianna." Jules started toward her. "Thank God."

She looked exhausted and her unease was palpable. Rhianna could not summon the will to ask her to leave. At a loss, she asked, "What are you doing here? Did you drive from Denver?"

"No, I'm back in L.A.,now." Jules aimed a SmartKey at the Merc, locking it by remote. Her eyes glowed onyx against the weary pallor of her face. "Can we talk inside?"

Rhianna wanted to muster anger but she couldn't; in her heart, she was crazily happy to see Jules. "Okay," she agreed.

Jules's gaze swung back toward the road.

Rhianna felt painfully conscious of Jules behind her as she opened the door. She took several nerve-wracking steps into the hall, and the atmosphere in the room suddenly felt airless and oppressive. Her mouth got even drier. Her gaze was drawn to the blue-black sweep of Jules's eyelashes and the smooth translucence of her temples. She yearned to take a step forward and fall into her arms.

Gesturing lamely in the direction of the kitchen, she asked, "Would you like something to drink?"

Jules glanced around as though taking an inventory of her surroundings. "Thanks. I need to wash my hands. That was some drive."

"There's a half-bath this way," Rhianna said, embarrassed that she hadn't offered this small courtesy in the first place.

She led Jules past the formal living room and opened the bathroom door. They faced each other, but did not touch. A shiver played down Rhianna's spine. She thought about Bonnie's words. Werner Brigham had harmed Jules, too. The damage was plain in her shadowed, uncertain gaze.

Regret chewed at Rhianna. She tried to harden her heart,

reminding herself that this was the woman who had sold her out, who had tried to give her money, as if that could make things right between them. But she could not shut out the memory of Jules's touch, the sense that this woman already knew her better than almost anyone. Jules had invited her to be herself as no one had before. Rhianna wasn't even sure if she knew who that self was, entirely, yet Jules seemed to. Should they just throw that away on Brigham's account?

"Can I say something?" Jules touched Rhianna's arm only for a second, but the contact tripped nerves in a chain reaction that surged all the way to her center.

Short of breath, Rhianna managed a little nod. A dull ache compressed her throat, thwarting her attempt to swallow. Her gaze settled on Jules's mouth and she could not look away.

"That first day in court, I asked my boss to release me from the case."

"I didn't know that."

"I'm not making excuses for myself," Jules said. "But I want you to understand something. Brigham would probably have been acquitted, whether I defended him or not."

"What are you saying?"

"My boss, Carl Hagel, has never lost a case. He would have taken my place. And he's not the most sensitive guy."

Rhianna struggled to absorb the information. She had not entertained the possibility that Jules had tried to step down, or that Brigham would still have won even if Jules had declined to defend him. She felt dazed.

"None of us can ever be a hundred percent certain which way a jury will swing, but—"

"You don't think I had much of a chance."

"Sometimes you have to pick your fights." Jules's tone was resigned but there was also an edge of ferocity.

Disconcerted, Rhianna watched the muscles work in her cheeks. Her face was already lean, but the narrow indentations on either side seemed more defined. She'd lost weight. Unable to resist, Rhianna touched her, just the smallest brush of fingertips near her serious mouth. "I'm glad you came."

Something seemed to fracture in Jules's composure. Her pupils dilated, engulfing the indigo-etched slate of her eyes. With a soft groan, she reached for Rhianna. "I've missed you."

Rhianna could feel her defenses crumbling. "I've missed you, too."

They fell almost drunkenly against each other, surrendering to a kiss so desperate there was no room for doubt about where they were headed next. No one had ever kissed Rhianna the way Jules did. Her mouth staked an insistent erotic claim, making promises Rhianna knew she could fulfill. Their tongues stroked and coaxed, deeper and harder until Rhianna could not stay upright. She felt drugged. Her pulse slowed to a languorous rhythm and the blood felt hot and heavy in her veins.

Jules raised her lips just far enough from Rhianna's to ask huskily, "Where's your room?"

Rhianna drew back, knowing where this was headed. "We can't." She caressed Jules's nape beneath the compact ponytail. "Not yet."

Jules sighed with wry humor. "I knew it was too good to be true."

"I'm a nanny," Rhianna explained, "and the little girl I take care of is playing out back with our ranch hand."

Jules transformed right in front of her. The dazed craving left her expression and she was instantly businesslike. "Get them indoors."

"Why?" Rhianna asked.

Jules took her face gently between her palms. "Because Brigham is on his way here."

Werner wrapped his fingers over the linen-textured handle of his favorite dagger. Named the Reaper by its creator, Jay Fisher—custom knife-maker extraordinaire—the weapon was a sleek-bladed tactical punch/pull knife designed for a quick kill of painful disablement.

He would probably try it out on the dog, first, Werner decided.

The animal was well past its prime and of no use to anyone. He would be doing the owners a favor. People had trouble letting go of pets and Werner could understand their reservations. A dog offered loyalty and devotion for the whole of its life, and the owner did not want to betray that trust. But people were weak and selfish. Werner had seen the chubby housewife who employed Rhianna. Had she asked herself if her dog wanted to spend the rest of its days limping around half-blind? Werner had his doubts.

He slid the Reaper back into its black leather sheath and fastened the retainer. He would ensure the death was quick and merciful. It gave him no pleasure to kill an animal. He was not a sicko.

"Did you say ten thousand?" Mr. Entwhistle asked. "You want to rent my shed for ten thousand dollars?"

"I do," Werner confirmed. "The one nearest the road."

He pointed to a run-down structure on a rise west of the ranch house. Its filthy rear window offered an unmatched view of the property next door. Werner would be able to see who came and went, what that beanpole ranch hand was doing and when he retired for the night, and which lights were on in the main house.

He would choose his moment, and this time he would not fail.

Chapter Fifteen

"So, you see, I don't think we have anything to worry about," Rhianna said brightly. "Bonnie says they're professionals."

Jules frowned. "Let me get this straight. Your boss sent hired muscle to scare Brigham off?"

"They left two days ago," Rhianna said.

"Any word from them yet?"

Rhianna shook her head. "Not that I know of."

"He was already gone when they got there, maybe." Percy flipped the cap off another bottle of beer.

"We need to find out," Jules said. "Can you call your boss?"

"Sure can." Percy took a cell phone from the pocket of his plaid shirt.

As he made the call, Rhianna got to her feet and padded into the den to retrieve a Cabbage Patch Kid from Hadrian. He never chewed on Alice's toys; he just drowned them in slobber. She returned the doll and said, "This baby needs clean clothes now."

She suspected Alice had engineered the situation herself so that she would have a reason to choose new garments for her doll. Beaming, the toddler opened the trunk in one corner of her playpen and extracted a pair of sequined overalls and a marabou-trimmed sweater, a recent gift from one of the showgirls Bonnie knew.

As Rhianna helped change the doll's outfit, she heard Percy say, "Both of them?" His weathered features were screwed up like he was squinting into the sun. He said, "No one's getting hurt." After a gruff good-bye, he put the phone away.

"Well?" Rhianna asked.

"They're in the hospital."

Jules stared at him unflinchingly. "What happened?"

"They both took bullets. One guy had knife wounds, too. I bet they didn't think he'd be armed."

Rhianna returned to the table. "I said he had a knife, and no one believed me."

"When did they attack him?" Jules asked.

"The night they got there."

"Well, that's a felony, so he probably left immediately," Jules said. "Even if he drove instead of flying, he could be here by now."

"If he's in town, someone will know," Rhianna said. "Around here, people notice strangers."

In Denver, Brigham could blend in, but in Oatman, a tall, pasty-faced man slouching along the street in a high-priced suit would draw attention to himself.

"I could ride into town," Percy volunteered. "Ask around."

"That would be helpful," Jules said. "He drives a Lincoln Town Car with tinted windows. I printed copies of his picture before I came." She placed her briefcase on the table and took out a file. "Mug shots and publicity photos. Help yourself."

Percy pored over a couple of images. "That's a mummy's boy," he observed perceptively.

Flicking through the stack with obvious distaste, Jules said, "If he wasn't a blimp, he could look like John Wayne."

Rhianna said, "I didn't think he had it in him to shoot at a couple of tough guys. I thought he'd give up."

"He's escalated," Jules said. "Fantasy is a dangerous thing. We already know he makes plans. He probably gets excited thinking about what he's going to do. It makes him single-minded. That's why he couldn't stop sending flowers to you and why he tried to give you an engagement ring. That was his fantasy and it became a compulsion."

A chill enveloped Rhianna and she glanced toward the kitchen window. It was closed and the blind was still, and she realized the faint breeze she'd felt was trapped in her own memory, the rush of air as Brigham had opened and closed his bedroom door that night. She'd thought then, with her wrists bound behind her, that evil had just entered the room, and she felt the same presence now.

"I think he's here," she said.

Her two companions regarded her silently. Percy reached for his gun. Jules took a Taser from her briefcase.

"I don't mean right here, in the house." Rhianna laughed nervously. "I mean he's around. I can feel it."

No one laughed at her.

"Are you sure all the doors and windows are bolted?" Jules asked.

"I checked them when Percy and Alice came indoors."

Jules rose. Signaling Percy, she said, "It's time you showed me that gun safe." As they started toward Bonnie and Lloyd's wing of the house, she called back to Rhianna, "Go in the den with Alice and the dog."

Rhianna's heart galloped. She curled up on the sofa near Hadrian and wiggled around so he would know he was not alone. When he opened a bleary eye, she scratched his chunky head and scooted down next to him. Alice cooed happily to herself as she played. Occasionally she deliberated in half-sentences over important matters such as who liked ice cream and what color Mommy's shoes were. She was getting sleepy.

Rhianna lifted her from the playpen and rocked her close, stroking her soft, silky hair and singing a lullaby to her. A band of fear closed around her heart as she thought about Brigham sneaking onto the ranch, breaking into the house, hurting Alice. Shooting Hadrian. Filled with panic, she swayed gently back and forth until the small body grew heavy.

She carried Alice into the nursery off the den and lowered her into the pink four-poster toddler bed Bonnie had decked out a few months earlier. Rhianna knew her employer worried about spoiling Alice. She and Lloyd had attempted to have a baby for eight years and had almost given up when Alice was finally conceived. Bonnie tried to spend as much time at home as she could, but the years she had originally freed up for child rearing had been filled with the casino when no baby came along. Now, like most mothers with demanding careers, she struggled to find a balance.

Rhianna knew Bonnie would die if anything happened to her baby. She felt sick that she had unwittingly placed Alice in peril. She brushed a light brown curl away from the sweet little face and planted a kiss on Alice's rosy cheek. She was sound asleep, sucking her thumb, oblivious to the turmoil around her.

When Rhianna returned to the den, she found Jules and Percy sorting weapons and ammunition. Two rifles were propped against the sofa.

Uneasy, Rhianna asked, "Shall I call 911?"

"And tell them what?" Jules loaded a cartridge into a pistol. "That a bad man might be coming to get you, but he's not here and no one is hurt?"

She wasn't mocking. She was simply stating a bald fact: there was no point calling the police when they had nothing to report.

"Percy and I are going to take a walk around," she continued. "Then he'll head into town."

"I think we should pack up and leave before things get out of hand," Rhianna said. "Laughlin's only twenty minutes away."

Jules shook her head. "You want this man locked up, don't you?"

"Yes, but we don't need to get involved. He injured those two men. If he's in Oatman, we could just tell the police and let them deal with him."

How ironic, Rhianna thought. No one could pretend a shooting hadn't happened. There was evidence. And the victims bore gun and knife wounds anyone could see. Pictures of their wounds could be displayed in a courtroom, where her own had been invisible. Brigham would end up in prison because he'd shot someone, not because he'd raped her. Not that it mattered. All she cared about was seeing him behind bars where he belonged. But she didn't want anyone else hurt in the process.

"I don't know the full circumstances, but I don't think we can count on anything. I want to catch him violating the restraining order." Jules leaned her shoulder against the door frame, sanguine and in control.

Rhianna let her gaze linger on the firm, compact breasts that gave shape to her black T-shirt. She wore this tucked into loose khaki pants Rhianna's fingers itched to unbutton. Jules caught her staring and offered a hot, knowing smile. She tapped her breastbone and her mouth formed several silent words, their shape unmistakable.

Rhianna read, *I want to fuck you.* Flustered, her cheeks flaming, she looked away, hoping Percy was too caught up in his mission to notice her distraction. She heard the kitchen door open and close. He was on the patio, lighting a cigarette.

"I should get out there," Jules said, intent again on the task at hand. She crossed the room and came to a halt in front of the sofa. "Don't stress. You can always call me on my cell."

Unable to help herself, Rhianna leaned forward just enough so she could rest her head on Jules's belly. She was so wet her arousal would soon seep into her pale beige shorts. She didn't care. All she could think about was undoing Jules's belt and dragging her pants down, so she could see her and taste her. A distant voice reminded her that the household was in a state of alarm and this was not the time for graphic sexual fantasies.

Setting common sense aside, she curled her hands over the curve of Jules's hips and buried her face in the lumpy khaki fly. The muscles beneath her palms tightened and Jules tilted her pelvis, thrusting her crotch against Rhianna's mouth. A hand closed upon her head, the fingers digging in.

Jules said, "Hold that thought."

As she walked away, Rhianna stared down at the floor and flinched at the emptiness she felt. Panic knotted her chest. Her longing for Jules defeated common sense and self-respect. She still wanted to detest her, but the wish could find no traction. Her heart and body had rebelled against the edicts of her mind.

She got to her feet and explored the seam of her shorts. Soaking. This was what her life had come to. A crazy man was stalking her. She was traumatized and afraid. And what did she think about? Sex.

❖

Jules strolled onto the patio and stared up at the blotchy ochre hills that surrounded the Mosses' ranch. Immediately beyond them the Black Mountains rose jagged and purple, scraping roughly across a painted sky. The landscape in this part of Arizona contrasted sharply with the flat basalt expanses to the south. Rain fell up here, and the moisture supported a badlands scrub that attracted herds of bighorn sheep.

The area was pockmarked with relics of its boomtown heyday. Ramshackle cottages clung to ridges throughout the canyons. Long-forgotten mining equipment lay idle near disused shafts. In the glare of the afternoon sun, the deserted valleys shimmered as though the miners of yesteryear had traipsed gold dust along every narrow path.

Jules had been struck by the eerie atmosphere of Oatman and its environs when she pulled into town that morning. The place seemed haunted, and somehow sorrowful, a forsaken outpost on the lost highway of dreams. At least half of the buildings were unoccupied. Doors swung in the wind. Empty window frames flanked shelled-out structures no one would ever restore. The town's tourist-driven survival had produced an eclectic mix of stores, some of them obviously set up by refugees from California. A tattoo artist and head shop. A store selling political T-shirts.

Why stay here? Jules asked herself as she watched a bird of prey cruise above the ranch, closing in on a dove. She was torn between using Rhianna as bait and spiriting her away somewhere that Brigham would never find her. Perhaps they should pack up and make the slow drive to Laughlin. They could wait and see if Brigham broke cover, and if there was no sign of him after a few days, Jules could persuade Rhianna to come away with her.

How would she lure him, if Rhianna was no longer here? Jules wanted Brigham to reveal himself, to be caught red-handed breaking into a house, carrying weapons. She pictured him ambushed, handcuffed, marched away by the authorities. There would be charges waiting back in Denver. Perhaps attempted murder. She would not represent him this time, and she would convince Carl to leave him in the wind.

"UFOs," Percy remarked, staring at the sky with her. "Folks see them 'round here."

"Have you seen one?"

"Yeah. Got myself abducted a few years back." He stubbed out his cigarette. Jules could not tell if he was serious.

They crossed the internal courtyard and cut past the gazebo so they could skirt the house. Percy's truck was parked next to the barn. Jules moved her Mercedes into the gap between his pickup and the barn door.

"Well, there's only one way he can approach," Jules said, staring toward the road.

From the front of the house, passing traffic was easy to monitor, and there was no cover for someone on foot. Brigham would have to make his move at night. She considered the odds. Three of them versus one of him. But he was dangerous and he had proven he would use deadly force. She had no right to expose Rhianna to that possibility, to place her and a baby at risk. What was she thinking?

"Percy," she said. "I have an idea."

Rhianna sighed with relief when Percy and Jules came back indoors and told her to get Alice ready. They had decided to play it safe and go to Laughlin. If Brigham was in town, he would not be able to hide for long.

"I want you to call the Mosses and let them know what's happening," Jules said. "I'll contact the Mohave County Sheriff's office. If Brigham's here, he'll be easy to corner. All they'll need is a couple of roadblocks and a few deputies to keep this place under surveillance."

"We're doing the right thing," Rhianna said. "I was worried about keeping Alice safe. And Hadrian, but he'll be fine with Percy."

"I know. I was worried, too." Jules followed her to her apartment at the rear of the house and glanced around. "This is nice."

"They treat me like family." Rhianna pulled a small suitcase from beneath her bed. "I'm very lucky."

As she methodically packed some clothes, she tried to suppress her prickling awareness of the woman lingering inside the doorway. She'd already dropped one set of wet panties and shorts into the laundry; it would be nice if she could stay comfortable in the jeans she was now wearing. Besides, she had responsibilities; she could not indulge herself in fantasy every time she looked at Jules.

"You decided to stay blond," Jules remarked.

Rhianna nodded. "And I told the Mosses my real name."

As if by tacit accord, they indulged in meaningless chitchat for a few more minutes, then Rhianna zipped her suitcase and said, "I'll go organize Alice for the trip. That will take a little longer. There's a lot to remember when you travel with a small child."

Jules dragged the suitcase from the bed and stood it upright on its wheels. "Is there anything I can help with?"

Rhianna shook her head. She could read in Jules's warm stare all that was unspoken. If they were in a different place, at a different time, under different circumstances, they would be making love right now. The thought thrilled her, but for the first time in the brief history of their dalliance, the force of their attraction made her uneasy.

She wished they had some other context in which to relate. Were they only about sex? If Werner Brigham hadn't happened and they'd continued to see each other as planned, would their relationship have fizzled after a few months, once the novelty wore off and the chemistry started to wane? Sure, they could have a great time until the inevitable loss of interest, but Rhianna was not sure if she wanted to invest months of her life in a connection that would ultimately lead nowhere.

Frowning, she packed her hairbrush and cosmetics into a kit. People fell into relationships after falling into bed all the time. They had a honeymoon period then built something permanent. Maybe she and Jules could do that. She glanced up to find Jules regarding her with faint amusement.

When Rhianna raised her eyebrows, Jules said, "Chill. We

don't have to figure everything out right away. You told me that, yourself."

Her eyes shone with something other than desire. Happiness, Rhianna thought. Despite the stress of the situation, her face had relaxed. She seemed completely at ease. And, apparently, mind reading was another of her formidable talents. Or perhaps Rhianna was more transparent than she realized.

Impulsively, she said, "I know we've fallen in lust. I guess, I was just wondering if that's all it is. I mean, we don't know each other so we can't like each other."

"Are you saying you don't like me?" The tone was gentle and tinted with self-effacing humor. "In my defense, may I point out our inauspicious beginnings? It's not every day a woman discovers she's sleeping with the enemy."

Rhianna could not help but smile. "You're talking like a lawyer."

Jules cocked her head. "Perhaps I feel like you're putting me on trial."

"If it's any consolation, I hated you yesterday," Rhianna said. "But today, I don't."

"You really know how to make a woman feel good." Gravely, Jules added, "Indulge me. Where did I go right?"

"Well, it certainly helps that you're hot," Rhianna explained with the same mock-solemnity Jules had adopted. "When you look at me, I can't concentrate on feeling angry anymore."

"And when I'm around you, I become incompetent," Jules said. "Actually, you don't even need to be physically present. I'm perfectly capable of ramming into a parked car all by myself."

"Oh, God. You didn't, did you?" Rhianna giggled.

"It was actually a rear-ender. At maybe ten miles an hour. Not that I was paying attention. Why concentrate on driving when one can enjoy oral sex fantasies?"

"I walked into a tree after that night in your apartment." Rhianna thought it was only fair to disclose one of her own fantasy-driven mishaps. "It even had one of those spiked cages around it. I nearly impaled myself."

Jules's mouth twitched. With a heartfelt sigh, she said, "Language like that...it doesn't help. You describe a painful and embarrassing accident, and I think about strapping one on."

Rhianna caught her breath, as a spasm clutched at her core. Her muscles contracted, heightening a sense of emptiness that made her feel needy and weak. The thought of Jules sinking into her cast a spell she couldn't bear to break. She murmured, "I've never done that."

Jules added to her enchantment, closing the short distance between them to gather her into a sensual embrace. Her kiss was delicate and full of promise. When she drew back, a little of the humor drained from her tone, and another emotion stirred the night ocean of her eyes, casting a melancholy shadow.

"We should have stayed in bed," she said. "In Denver. For the whole two weeks."

"Yes." Rhianna rested her head against Jules's shoulder and drank in her scent. She felt warm and contented.

Jules kissed her hair, "When I said I would take good care of you, I meant it."

"Why?" Rhianna asked. "I mean why would you ask me to live with you? We're virtual strangers."

"I think that's relative. Some people live together for years without sharing what you and I share." She hesitated. "I know there's supposed to be someone for everybody, but I've never believed that. Then I met you and it made me wonder. I've never felt close to any woman the way I feel close to you. So the idea of us living together wasn't such a huge leap."

"I thought you offered out of guilt."

"No," she said with certainty. "I felt some responsibility, but the truth is I asked you for selfish reasons. I couldn't bear to walk away and never explore this...magic between us."

Rhianna let herself relax, nuzzling Jules's neck, holding her close. Magic—yes. "People talk about recognizing each other the first time they meet," she said. "Having a feeling that they belong together and always have, because they were lovers in a past life." She trailed off, thinking she probably sounded flaky.

To her surprise, Jules lifted a hand to her cheek and said, "No one can prove them right or wrong. The jury is out."

"What do you believe?"

"I believe in evidence. My feelings are real, whether or not I can explain them. I don't know why I think you and I have a role to play in each other's lives, but I do."

"I feel that, too."

They stared at each other, and Rhianna was strangely aware of cogs shifting inside. Her anxieties subsided. The unease that accompanied her frantic physical longings seemed to fade. She felt calm and self-possessed, and with her mind free of clutter, a knee-buckling thought surfaced. She could fall in love with Jules.

She gazed into eyes that seemed too wise for a face so young. Jules was looking at her, really looking. People seldom did that. A stare invited too much guesswork and implied too much familiarity. Lingering looks were the rightful domain of lovers, cats, and mothers with infants.

Jules said, "It's too soon for us to talk about love. But the *possibility* of love…" Her smile was intimate. "Why not lay claim to that?"

They held each other for a short while, then by unspoken agreement committed themselves to the task of getting to Laughlin. They assembled suitcases, toys, baby paraphernalia, and Hadrian in the rear courtyard where they could not be seen. Jules said they had to assume someone was watching.

She wanted Brigham to see Percy leaving in his truck, followed by the Mercedes. They would drive to Oatman, pick up some supplies, and Percy would return to the ranch. She wondered what Brigham would make of her presence. He had to know, after her threat, that she was not neutral and she was not on his side.

CHAPTER SIXTEEN

Had they been followed? Jules wondered. A blue-gray Chevy Trailblazer had gradually closed in on the Mercedes when they stopped a few miles out of town to let the stagecoach by. The car had tracked them down Route 66, through rugged yellow canyons and hairpin bends that slowed the pace of the drive to a crawl. Every vehicle on the narrow, twisting two-lane blacktop rode its brakes. Most stopped at the pullouts that dotted the route, their nervous drivers parking carelessly trying to avoid scary cliff edges, then wandering along the side of the road, cameras stuck to their faces as they recorded their Wild West adventure.

Between slowing to avoid running these city slickers over and swerving around crows pecking at roadkill, Jules had plenty of time to notice the Trailblazer maintaining a constant distance all the way to Bullshead City. She lost sight of the SUV there and had not seen it since. She had tried to get a look at the driver, but the Trailblazer never came close enough. She wasn't sure why her neck prickled at the sight of that vehicle and no other, but she paid attention to her instincts. They seldom let her down.

There was no sign of the vehicle as they drove through Laughlin, however, and she reasoned that there was nothing sinister about one car among many stuck in a single lane of traffic, with every motorist headed for the same destination. The driver was probably feeding quarters into a slot machine by now.

When they finally reached the Mosses' "small" casino, Jules understood why Rhianna's employers could count petty mobsters among their friends. The Enchanted Palace was situated on the banks of the Colorado River not far from Harrah's. Like every establishment of its ilk, it reeked of stale cigarette smoke, alcohol, and hopelessness. Not even the most dogged air-conditioning and chemical cleaning agents could lighten the atmospheric load.

As soon as the revolving doors disgorged her into the noisy lobby, Jules was walloped by the closeness of the air, the low ceiling, the jostling crowd, and the random cacophony of flashing lights and casino noise. She had not thought to take one of her mild relaxants; she usually reserved medication for the special torture of air travel.

"We get to use the owners' suite, thank goodness," Rhianna said as they proceeded toward the elevators. "The hotels along this strip are all dreadful and, whatever you do, don't eat the buffet."

Jules distracted herself from the din and the pervasive tinge of body odor by finding small denominations to tip the bellboy. She followed this mechanical task with one of her self-calming strategies, visualizing a tranquil pool with a waterfall spilling from it in an endless rainbow-hued cascade.

The elevator was a cramped steel prison but, thankfully, they were its sole occupants. As they rode up, Rhianna hummed to Alice and kept casting appreciative looks in Jules's direction. Evidently, she'd scored points with the location change.

The Mosses' apartment was a spacious suite of rooms with calming views of the river. Jules stood at the windows, slowing her breathing and waiting for her tension to dissipate.

"Beautiful, isn't it?" Rhianna sighed.

"Yes." Jules wanted to kiss her, and ruffle her fingers in the short blond hair she was still getting used to.

Rhianna leaned against the back of a sofa immediately behind her. Alice was draped over her shoulder, sound asleep. If all toddlers were so placid, Jules thought she wouldn't mind having several kids, assuming domestic bliss was in her future. The odds seemed better than they'd ever been.

She stretched out a hand and petted the slumbering child's back. "She's very sweet."

"She's a doll." Rhianna smiled a stunning, carefree smile.

"Excuse me a minute. I need to put her to bed. Take a look around if you want. Help yourself to drinks. There's a fridge in the bar."

Jules thanked her and found a bottle of Evian. She sat down on one of several ivory leather sofas arranged for the view, sipped some water, then took out her cell phone. After checking in with Percy, she called Gilbert Desjardines.

"What do we know about the two goons Brigham assaulted?" she asked. "Are they cooperating?"

"I got Damonique monitoring that situation," Gil said. "I think we're good."

"Excellent. What are they looking for?"

"Fifty each."

"I'm hearing things," Jules scoffed. "These tough guys are supposed to lean on Brigham. They screw up, and he puts them in the hospital. They want fifty apiece for a police statement?"

"Pain and suffering. That's their story."

"They don't know the meaning of pain." Jules wished Rhianna's bosses had been less scrupulous. Paying a couple of enforcers to talk sense into Brigham without beating him up was naïve. "Tell them for fifty they have to testify, and if I hear Audrey Brigham has bought them off, they're going down. I'll dig up every mistake they ever made."

"Mrs. Brigham. Phew. That's one pissed-off lady."

Intrigued, Jules asked, "What do you know about her?"

"Your boss damn near shit himself." Gil had to take a moment to quit snickering. He always loved it when Carl wasn't happy. "She asked him to hire some dude to ice the girl. Make it look like an accident."

Audrey Brigham was trying to have Rhianna killed? Jesus. "Carl's not planning to do anything about it, is he?"

"Hell, no. He asks me to go see her and act like I'm the man. So, I'm wired and sitting across from her after a fine pork chop, and she's telling me about her problem, and how it needs taking care of so her son can get on with his lame-ass life."

"You have Audrey Brigham on tape trying to arrange a hit?"

"I sure do."

Jules grinned. Carl was a master of leverage. What was poor

little Werner going to do when Mommy couldn't save his ass anymore. "That's good news," she conceded.

"Where you at, anyway?" Gil asked.

"Laughlin, Nevada," Jules said. "It sucks, and I need a blond wig. Any ideas?"

"They got showgirls there?"

"You're a genius."

"What you up to?" Gil's tone came fitted with a built-in warning. He was a man who had seen it all and spent his life investigating screwups.

"Bait and switch," Jules told him with a casual air. "If you don't hear from me by tomorrow morning, call the Mohave County Sheriff. Ask him to send a car to that address in Oatman I gave you."

The P.I. made a sound like a dog whining. "You high?"

Jules said. "No, just taking care of business."

"Okay. Hit me with your crazy-white-girl plan."

"Thanks for the support. It's very simple. Werner Brigham will sneak into the house and I'll be waiting for him."

Gil sighed loudly. "I'm not coming to any memorial service. You got that?"

"Loud and clear."

"Who's your backup?" he asked.

"A decrepit cowboy, a deaf dog, and a ton of hardware."

"I got a bad feeling."

"You always have a bad feeling. You're a pessimist. That's why they give you Prozac."

"Don't do this thing," Gil said dourly.

"I'll let you know how it pans out." Jules said good-bye over his protests and dropped her cell phone into her pants pocket.

She wandered around the huge suite and found her lover in a bedroom. With a finger to her kissable lips, Rhianna backed away from the bed and joined Jules in the hallway.

"She was a little carsick, so she's clingy."

"You're good with her." Something came over Jules then, and she sappily pictured herself and Rhianna peering into a bassinette several years into a rosy future. *Get a grip,* she thought, and asked the question uppermost on her mind. "Does your boss hire showgirls?"

Rhianna frowned like Jules had just suggested they take in a strip joint while they were in the big city. "Yes, why?"

"I need some help with a project I'm working on," Jules replied vaguely.

She had decided the less Rhianna knew, the better. She and Alice were safe, and Jules didn't want her sitting up all night, phoning every ten minutes to check in with her.

"Bonnie is friends with one of the women who does the early evening show here," Rhianna said. "She's probably in the dressing room by now. If you go backstage in the theater, it's on your left past all the props."

"I'll find her." Jules produced a nonchalant smile and started toward the door.

"Jules?" Rhianna's suspicion was transparent. "What are you doing?"

A good question and one Jules had hoped to avoid. "Come sit down with me for a minute," she requested gloomily. She would now lose the next hour trying to convince Rhianna that they would have to catch Brigham themselves, or he would evade the authorities and she would never be safe.

Rhianna was a jump ahead. "Please don't tell me you're going back there." Panic swept the serenity from her face.

Wondering when she had become so obvious that her lover could second-guess her every move, Jules took Rhianna's hand and led her to the sofa. "Baby, I'm working with a detective at the sheriff's office, and we're going to catch Brigham. The two men he assaulted in Denver will testify against him. He's going to prison."

"I'm happy about that," Rhianna said mildly. "So why do I feel like I'm missing something?"

"That would be the part about me putting on a blond wig and waiting in your bedroom." Jules winced.

"I see." Rhianna's gaze was steady. "Is this your version of taking a bullet for me? You think you owe me something?" Anger leaked into her expression. "So you're going to place yourself at risk for the sake of past regrets? You want to serve me Brigham's head on a plate?"

Unnerved by the accuracy of her perception, Jules said, "There's some truth in that. But I'm also acting out of self-interest. I want him out of your life so there's room for me. For us."

Rhianna's chest rose and fell unevenly. "Don't you understand, I've already forgiven you." Her voice caught on a sob. "The last thing I want is for you to take a risk like that! That man has cost me everything I cared about. I can't let him take you away. I just can't."

"That's not going to happen," Jules said. "I know how to take care of myself." She held Rhianna in her arms and stroked her hair. "You have to trust me. I wouldn't do this if I thought there was any chance I'd never see you again."

"I'm afraid. Please don't go," Rhianna begged. "I've been learning to shoot. I don't feel so vulnerable anymore. Let's just get on with our lives. They'll catch up with him. If not now, later."

Jules shook her head. "He's a time bomb. I talked to him in the parking garage at your friend Mimi's building."

Rhianna drew back. "He was there?"

"He'll always be there," Jules said grimly, "biding his time, waiting for his opportunity. Screw that."

She felt a shudder pass through Rhianna's body. "If you're doing this, I'm coming, too."

"No. Absolutely not."

"This isn't a negotiation," Rhianna said with cool vehemence. "Lisette can look after Alice. They adore each other."

"Who's Lisette?"

"The showgirl with the blond wig you don't need to borrow anymore. There are plenty of standby dancers. I'll get her up here right away."

Jules tried again with the common sense. "It's not a good idea for you to be around. You're safe here and I don't have to worry about you. Please. Let me and Percy handle this."

Rhianna got to her feet, her expression mutinous. "That creep thinks he can hunt me? Well, the boot is on the other foot now, and I want to know how that feels."

"I understand—"

"No, you don't," Rhianna said harshly. "You think you owe me something? This is what I want."

From the safe, anonymous confines of his rental Chevy Trailblazer, Werner contemplated his options. He had pulled off the road at Bullshead City just in case he was making himself look suspicious. He knew exactly where that interfering bitch, Julia Valiant, was going with Rhianna. He'd done his homework since arriving in Oatman.

Rhianna was employed by the owners of the Enchanted Palace casino. If she was accompanying their child on a road trip to Laughlin, there could only be one destination. He had seen the couple depart in the morning and assumed they were on their way to their workplace. Parents like them routinely left their children to be raised by someone else. For a wild moment, he considered seizing both Rhianna and the infant. He felt sure she loved that baby. Its presence would mean a lot to her, and Werner could turn the situation to his advantage. Rhianna was tenderhearted and unselfish. If she feared for the child's safety, she would be extremely compliant.

But as the idea took shape, Werner realized he would be making a huge mistake. Imagine the furor if he kidnapped the child of wealthy casino magnates. The FBI would be on his tail. He would be at the center of one of those vast manhunts. He wouldn't make it out of the state, let alone north to the remote wilds of Minnesota, where Rhianna's home was waiting. But if by some miracle, he slipped through the police dragnet, a worse fate would be in store.

Those two fat cretins who had broken his door down back in Denver were hired by the Mosses. He had squeezed the details out of them while they pleaded for their lives. They were amateurs, but the fact that they'd been sent in the first place meant the Mosses had friends in organized crime. Werner could imagine the strings they would pull to get their baby back. They would put out a contract on him. He would be dead meat.

Werner plucked another chicken nugget from the box on the

passenger seat and stared at the dark gray Mercedes parked in the roped-off V.I.P. area. He still couldn't decide on the smarter move. Sooner or later, now that she'd dropped Rhianna and the baby off, Valiant would leave and his path would be clear. He had no idea what she was doing here in the first place, but it occurred to him that Mommy must have sent her.

He had told her about the two criminals bleeding in his study, and she had agreed that his leaving town was a good idea. She had promised then that she would deal with Rhianna for his sake. Perhaps she had sent the attorney with a cash offer—compensation for any pain he had inadvertently caused. Valiant's powers of persuasion were impressive. He knew she didn't like him, but she'd taken care of his interests all the same. He felt sure she would talk Rhianna around and leave her with the right impression of the Brigham family's power and wealth.

Perhaps he would not have to remove Rhianna by force. If the lawyer had done her job, Rhianna might even receive him warmly. Las Vegas was just down the highway. They could get married in one of those tawdry chapels with a preacher who looked like Elvis. Later on, their real wedding service would be held in Denver.

Werner ate another nugget, then cleaned the oily debris from his gums with his toothpick. He wasn't sure how realistic these hopes were, but it didn't matter. He could adapt to a change in circumstances if he had to. That's exactly what he was doing now. He stared at the elevator and wondered if it was time to locate the Mosses' accommodations. The family could not stay in their rooms indefinitely. The parents had a business to run. They would soon leave Rhianna alone with the baby, or perhaps they would send her back home to the ranch. That was the optimum scenario.

Werner sharpened his gaze as one of the uniformed valets entered the parking area. Apparently he would not have to wait much longer. The boy aimed a remote at the Mercedes and its lights flashed. Julia Valiant was on the move.

CHAPTER SEVENTEEN

I know he's coming," Rhianna said, listening for the sound of a footfall that did not belong.

Every home had its own unique nocturnal personality. In the winter it creaked and whined a hymn of protest to the cold weather. Summer made its wood stairs and panels thirst, and took a harsh toll on its painted skin.

Rhianna had lived in the Mosses' ranch house since the previous October, and she knew the sounds it made as it settled from the heat of the day to the cool of the desert night. She recognized the protests of certain floorboards when Hadrian moved from his beanbag in the corner of her bedroom to the food station in her tiny kitchen. She knew the muted click and sigh of the air-conditioning.

Bonnie and Lloyd had made a big deal out of soundproofing. They wanted to be able to turn up the bass in their home theater without waking Alice. Lloyd liked to work out in the gym with Cher turned up loud. Bonnie thought Cher was a fine actress but hated her singing. Rhianna was thankful they had stuffed the walls of her apartment with insulation. She played the piano and preferred not to torture the household when she practiced her scales and arpeggios every night.

During the day, she barely noticed the subtle noises that seemed so loud at night. Her hearing was amazingly acute when she was lying in bed with all the lights out. She could make out the faint cries of night creatures, the wet plunk of insects landing in the swimming pool, the ghostly drone of passing cars, the occasional bleat or whinny coming from the barn.

She usually kept her blinds tightly closed after dark, but tonight Jules had arranged them with a couple of tiny gaps in strategic places. She said she wanted to invite Brigham to peep in so they could see him. There was more light outside than there was in the apartment, once all the lamps were extinguished. They would see Brigham if he came around the back of the house, and Jules was certain that he would. She and Percy had walked around the exterior and interior soon after they got back, planning which rooms would be lit and at what times. Jules wanted Werner to make faulty deductions about where people were.

"Are you saying he's coming right now?" Jules asked from the sofa near the sliding doors.

"Yes, I can feel him. It's not my imagination." A malevolent presence seemed to have entered the house. Rhianna didn't want to let her imagination run away with her, but she could swear that Werner had been inside her room. She detected the taint of evil, and her senses shrank from it. "I think he's been in here. Maybe he broke in while we were out."

"That's unlikely," Jules said. "He followed us to Laughlin."

"He did? How do you know?"

"Because I saw him. Remember when we stopped for gas in Needles? He was parked on the other side of the road."

Jules had almost had a heart attack when she recognized the gray-blue Chevy Trailblazer from earlier in the day. While she was filling the Mercedes, she'd paid close attention to the driver. Male, tall, light hair, droopy shoulders. She could not identify him with any certainty, but what were the odds of the same Trailblazer showing up twice in one day exactly where they happened to be? She had taken down the tag number and an accurate description of the make and model.

"Why didn't you call the police?" Rhianna said.

"I thought you wanted to go through with this."

"I did…I do." Rhianna dropped down onto the sofa, too far away for a hug. There was misery in her eyes. "What if everything goes wrong? Situations like this can get out of hand. We're not experts."

"Calm down," Jules said. "As soon as we know he's on the property, I'll put in a call to that detective I told you about."

Rhianna stood up again, clearly agitated. Her right hand wrapped itself tightly around her waist. "I'm going to close the blinds. What if he sees you in here and shoots you?"

"He's not going to risk it," Jules said. Without good light he can't be absolutely sure who he's shooting. That's why I still borrowed the wig in the end."

Rhianna looked up at Jules's head and humor soothed her puckered brow. "Blond is *so* not your color." Her gaze became slightly more intent. "But I could still go there."

Jules held out her arms. "Turn those lights down a little and come here."

"Oh, no. This is a stakeout. We can't get distracted."

Jules laughed. "We're not doing the staking out. He is."

"Are you sure about that?" Rhianna peeped out a narrow gap in the blinds. "We're playing chicken with him. Waiting for him to make his move."

"He's not going to do anything until two a.m.," Jules said. "He'll want to catch us sleeping. That gives you and me four hours to find new and interesting ways to keep ourselves awake."

"Are you seriously suggesting we make love?"

Jules wasn't, but her mildly flirtatious overtures were having the desired effect. Rhianna's shoulders were no longer rigid, and she was moving away from her paranoid vigil at the window.

"We could make out," Jules suggested. She was not in the mood, and she needed to keep her guard up, but they had a long night ahead of them and Rhianna's jitters were infectious. She patted her lap. "Just first base."

Rhianna smiled with endearing shyness. "I never thought you'd be here. In my room." She sidled over and positioned her butt daintily before settling. "I mean, I thought about it a lot. After Palm Springs."

"Tell me about that."

Rhianna tucked herself in a little closer. Her head came to rest on Jules's shoulder. "I used to imagine you were coming home from work and I was getting ready for you, and I had to hurry because when you got in the door you couldn't wait. I would put on a sundress and no panties. Then I would hear you and—"

"I'd walk in and have to fuck you immediately," Jules said huskily. "We don't get to the bedroom because I back you up against the wall."

"You bite my throat hard and I'm so wet there's no resistance. You slide into me and I hold you tight so I won't fall."

"You wrap you legs around my waist." Jules teased Rhianna's lips with her own. "And you're talking like a slut. 'Fuck me. Come on. I know what you want.' And it's making me crazy. I want to come in you. My legs get weak."

"We slither down the wall, and we're on the floor." Rhianna found a nipple and squeezed it between thumb and finger. "I try to crawl away."

"But you don't get far." Jules felt her squirm. "I come after you and haul you back against me. I throw your dress up over your pretty ass, and because you tried to get away I spank you, just a little, just because I want to leave a print."

"And then you're back inside me again, and this time you're fucking me so hard I want to collapse. And I put my head down on my hands."

"God." Jules fluttered inside.

She kissed Rhianna deeply, stroking inside, letting her tongue announce her desires. Rhianna consumed her, sucking and softly biting. She bore down, working herself against Jules's thigh. Weakly, Jules tried to arrest the urgent motions, knowing where they would lead and why that was a bad idea under the circumstances.

Rhianna broke away, flushed and panting. Her eyes were dreamy. She slid off and turned. Clamping her hands down on Jules's shoulders she kneeled astride her and lowered herself. Next to Jules's ear, she whispered, "Do me." She felt fearless. Greedy. Hot. She wanted to be naked.

Jules's eyes shone back at her like black diamonds in the semi-darkness. Her irises had almost disappeared, swallowed whole by pupils huge with desire. Rhianna loved that look. She wanted to drink from it every night. No one was going to steal that from her. A man had thought he could own her. She had news for him. No one could own her unless she gave herself.

"I'm yours," she said. "Take me, Jules."

❖

The palms of Werner's hands were slick with sweat. Rage forced his eyes wide open, making him see what he did not want to believe, and accept what he had never suspected for a moment. He gritted his teeth and tried to shut out the sight of the two women in the dimly lit room. His blade scythed helplessly at the darkness. He needed to carve something, to open the flesh undulating before him and pare away the vile witch who had stolen his Rhianna. But he could see only one person in the moving bodies. In his blurred vision, two had floated into one.

He wiped his free hand across his eyes and concentrated his thoughts. He had come prepared, after seeing the rangy cowboy with the gun slung under his arm and the old dog trailing after him. Werner wasn't sure which room these two feeble guards had chosen as their headquarters. He should take care of them first, he reasoned, but his legs refused to carry him away from Rhianna's window.

They were separated only by a quarter inch of glass. Nothing to a man with the right tools for the job. Werner crouched and opened the leather bag at his feet. He holstered the Reaper at the rear of his belt and took out his .9mm. Maybe he should blow them both away. Let them know how it felt.

The moon cast drifting shadows across the shuttered house. He stood tall and his senses jangled with the sounds and smells of the night. Blood pumped in his ears like a giant hand thumping against the stone walls of a prison. The gun jerked up as if he had no control over his own reflexes. Adrenalin, he supposed. It heightened everything. The trigger felt firm and cold against the ball of his finger, and the grip welded to his palm like part of his anatomy. In his other hand, the crowbar felt light. He swung it back. His dark-adapted gaze zeroed in again on the impossible, and he smashed the image away.

Like two insects caught in a blast of hot wind, the women fell back, their mating dance abandoned.

Werner aimed his gun at Rhianna's chest. "Whore. Traitor." The words welled from the deep red darkness within and rolled like thunder around them. "Move and she dies," he told the shivering woman next to her.

He had known she was bad from the start. The gun wavered in front of him, as he seized control over his tensing muscles. What to do. A lesser man would surrender to this insult and lash out in anger, depriving both these fallen women of their lives, and depriving himself of what could be redeemed and savored.

"I offered you a gift," Werner said. "But you were weak. Now, look at yourself. Corrupted by *this*." He shifted his aim to the lawyer.

"Don't." A feeble whisper. Rhianna was begging. He knew that whisper well, the nervous cry of a woman paralyzed by his strength.

"You want me to spare her?" he asked disdainfully.

"Yes. Please, Werner. I'm sorry if I hurt you."

The lawyer touched Rhianna on the shoulder.

Werner shoved the gun closer. "Take your hands off her."

Something brushed past the back of his legs and he spun around. The gun went off in the air and he jerked back, almost dropping it in surprise.

"Put it down." The lanky cowboy stood in the shadows a few feet away. He cocked his rifle. "This is private property."

Behind Werner a second voice commanded, "You heard him. Drop it."

Werner felt a hard muzzle between his shoulder blades. He craned his head slightly, trying to see Rhianna. "You can still come with me."

"I'm counting to three," the lawyer said. "Then it's all over and we'll drop you down a mining shaft and no one will ever know you were here. Put your weapon down. One. Two…"

Werner released his grip on the gun and only then did he see what had startled him. That useless dog. Bitter gall rushed up from his gut, and he swung a vicious kick hard into its ribs. The dog released a howl of pain and all around Werner movement erupted. Seizing his opportunity he ran.

❖

Rhianna plunged after him, groping for the handgun he'd dropped. Her fingers closed around the grip.

"No!" Jules cried.

But Rhianna's legs were propelling her through the courtyard and past the gazebo, driven by a barrage of pulses from an overloaded brain. She was screaming, "Don't you fucking kick my dog. Asshole! Pig!"

She fired the gun wildly at a form she saw ahead of her. The recoil altered her pace, making her run sideways for a moment. She clutched her shoulder. She could hear the drum of feet behind her.

"He's getting away!" she shrieked.

"Go back!" Jules yelled from behind her. "Rhianna, stop!"

He passed the pool. She gave chase, panting and gasping. He was gaining ground. Rhianna sprinted. She knew this yard and he didn't.

A loud report shattered the night, coming from her left. Percy, she thought. He had doubled back and was trying to cut Brigham off.

Fury drove her. She wanted to lay her hands on the man who had shattered her world. She wanted to pummel him and smash his teeth. He veered left and Rhianna was momentarily disoriented. She stumbled and picked herself up. As she found her stride again, she heard a creaking sound and knew exactly where he was. The barricade.

She bellowed, "Werner. Stop!" and then the night was filled with screams and grunts, and by the time she made it to the edge of the cactus pit, Werner was lying inert, pierced by a thousand needles.

CHAPTER EIGHTEEN

He's doped out with morphine, but he'll live." Bonnie closed her cell phone. "Sounds like prickly pear can be rather toxic. If the spines are deeply embedded they can cause arthritis."

Rhianna managed a weary smile. "I guess he won't be stalking anyone else in the near future."

"With all the long, shiny needles they'll be pulling out of him for the next week," Jules remarked grimly, "that toothpick will never look the same again."

No one spoke for a moment, then all three woman howled with laughter.

"Poetic justice." Rhianna mopped her eyes. She felt mildly hysterical. The events of the evening seemed unreal.

Bonnie rose and smoothed her black chiffon cocktail dress over her hips. She had been at a charity ball when Lisette phoned to explain the situation. "Are you sure you don't want me to hang around?"

"Leave now," Rhianna urged, "before they decide to ask you any more questions. Percy's still in there. I hope they're not holding him responsible."

They'd been at the Mohave County Sheriff's Office in Kingman for the past four hours. Bonnie had flown in by helicopter while Rhianna and Jules were giving their statements. She said this was one occasion when it helped to be a millionaire.

"I'll walk out with you," Jules volunteered.

She and Bonnie regarded each other with interest. They'd been exchanging brief looks for the past half hour. Sizing each other up, Rhianna surmised. She had half-expected Bonnie to march in and give Jules the piece of her mind she'd mentioned previously. But as time went by and Jules raved earnestly about what a remarkable and gifted child Alice was, Bonnie appeared to be charmed.

"Don't drive back to the ranch tonight," she advised both of them. "The road is too dangerous."

Rhianna yawned. "It'll be daylight before we get out of here, anyway."

"The Hampton Inn's a decent place to stay." Bonnie dragged her spangled purse out from beneath the chair she'd been using. "It's in the middle of nowhere, needless to say."

"I'm sorry about the convention." Rhianna felt terrible that Bonnie had been dragged away from an important business event because her nanny was a kook-magnet.

"Hell." A full-bodied laugh spilled from Bonnie's plum-tinted mouth. "If I never see another Elvis impersonator in this life, it'll be too soon." To Jules she said, "By the way, Lisette asked me to give you a message. You can keep the hair."

"That's a relief."

When Bonnie looked bemused, Rhianna explained, "We borrowed one of Lisette's wigs. Then, when the police got to the ranch, they found Hadrian slobbering all over it. They wanted it for evidence, so when we called Lisette—"

"Sweetie." Bonnie patted her hand and gave her a little farewell peck on the cheek. "It's been a long night. You can tell me the whole story another time."

Jules grinned. Dropping a kiss of her own, this one on Rhianna's mouth, she said, "I'll be back in a minute. If they ask you to come into the interview room again, tell them you can't speak without your attorney present."

As the pair strolled off along the bland corridor toward the exit, Rhianna heard Bonnie remark, "Now that we've met, I understand some things a whole lot better."

"I hope that's a plus," Jules replied carefully.

Bonnie stopped walking. "You're going to take her from us, aren't you?"

There was only the smallest pause. "I'm afraid so."

Rhianna hugged herself. Joy flowed through her veins.

"You know something. That's good news," Bonnie declared. "No, it's *fantastic* news."

She cast a big smile in Rhianna's direction, and from the sparkle in her eyes, Rhianna could tell her eavesdropping could have been more discreet. Impulsively, she got to her feet and hurried over to join the women who had been her fellow travelers on the most frightening, illuminating, emotional journey of her life.

"Why is that good news," she asked.

"Because I've told Lloyd this is the last straw. I'm going to be a full-time mom now. And it's good news because I have a wonderful friend who will give me the perfect excuse to get the hell out of this place whenever I want." She bundled Rhianna into a full-scale cuddle and said, "But wait. There's more. It's *fantastic* news because if anyone deserves to have the love of her life walk in the door when she least expects it, that woman is you."

Rhianna could feel her cheeks heating to lobster red as Bonnie sashayed away. "The love of my life?" she murmured.

Jules slipped an arm around her waist and said, "I like the sound of that."

❖

At some point in the afternoon, Rhianna had rolled onto her back, and she now slept with the abandon of a child, arms flung away from her body, one foot dangling over the side of the bed. The fickle light of dusk gave contour to the sheet that swathed her, revealing the limber form beneath. With each breath she drew, the pale fabric floated over her breasts, then settled once more to resume its teasing contact with her nipples.

Her mouth was moist and carelessly parted. Her bed-hair had formed a disorderly clump on one side of her head. Jules had waited a long time to be fascinated by a sleeping woman. She could not wrest her gaze from the tiny pulse at Rhianna's temple, the silky sheen of her eyelashes, the faint flutter of her lids. She stared, unfettered by convention or self-consciousness. She felt weak. Breathless. Frayed at the edges. She couldn't think of any other time in her life when she had been so conscious of another woman, and so at home.

The knowledge shook her. How had she found her way here to this unfamiliar terrain? How long did it take to fall in love? When was it appropriate to announce the feeling? Jules's feet carried her to the end of the bed and she idled there, prayerfully smitten. She recalled a similar moment—another day, another dusk—when she had stood transfixed in the presence of beauty. The priest had left her alone at the base of the pedestal, to offer thanks to the Virgin Mary for her grace and intercession. Jules alone had survived beneath the mountain of rubble. The reasons were a mystery she could only hope to solve by proving herself worthy of this divine blessing, and by following the Blessed Virgin's selfless example.

She stared up at the statue and saw a beguiling woman stifled in a marble shroud, the embodiment of womanhood held prisoner by men's fears. Jules did not think the mother of God had spared her so that she could emulate this captivity. Her promise to herself that day took some time to bear fruit, and Jules could see that for a long while she felt unworthy—survivor guilt, various shrinks had determined over the years.

Jules slid her hand beneath the sheet that veiled Rhianna. She could understand why a man like Werner Brigham would seek to place this woman on a pedestal, and build a shrine to her in his imagination. Like so many, he mistook his own needs for her purpose in life. He was completely blind to the person.

Warm skin claimed her attention and Jules began a leisurely exploration of the body she was still getting to know. It occurred to her that if there was a reason she had won life in the cosmic lottery of doom and disaster, perhaps it was simply that she had reached out for it. And here, years later, was the real prize.

Carefully, she lifted the sheet away. She bent and gathered her lover's scent then stroked her fingertips along Rhianna's inner thighs. Her right leg flopped open as if by reflex. There she was, pink and wet and waiting. Jules drifted closer until she could almost taste her.

Rhianna made a soft noise in her sleep, and wriggled a little. Her breathing changed and she gave the sheet a tug. When she met resistance, she mumbled something and woke up. Hazy-eyed, she stared at Jules. "Hello."

"Good evening."

"What are you doing?"

"I was just looking." Jules sat down on the edge of the bed.

The fog of sleep cleared, and Rhianna's eyes shone bright and inviting. "You were touching, too." Her voice was suddenly full of sexy threat. "Were you trying to have sex with me while I was asleep."

"Guilty as charged." Jules grinned.

Rhianna took her own nipples between her fingers and examined them suspiciously. "You've been sucking these," she declared with mock outrage. "What's your defense?"

"Desperate cravings and an inability to suck on my own?" Jules suggested.

Laughing, Rhianna scrambled onto her knees and crawled over to her. "You don't seem to appreciate the seriousness of the situation."

"On the contrary." Jules said. "I've never been more serious."

"Do you seriously want to come back to bed with me?"

Jules turned so they were face to face. "More than that." When Rhianna angled her head, she said. "Is it too soon to tell you I love you?"

Rhianna leaned forward until their foreheads rested together. "Better too soon than too late."

"That's what I thought, too."

They found their way into each other's arms and cradled each other as the dusk succumbed to darkness.

After a while, Rhianna said, "I love you. And now that I have my body back, I want to give it to you."

Jules kissed her slowly and sweetly. "Now?"

"Always," Rhianna promised.

Author's Note

Some years ago a stalker invaded my life, and his threat remained long after it ceased to be physically immediate. This story is not a fictionalized account of my own experience. Instead, it provided me with an opportunity to deliver the kind of poetic justice that seldom transpires in life.

In the United States, it is estimated that 1.4 million people are stalked annually; two thirds are women. 20% of the women affected are stalked by a stranger. 87% of stalkers are male. Around 80% of protection orders issued to victims are violated. Of the women ultimately murdered by their stalkers, half had reported the stalking to police. The average duration of a stalking is about two years; however, in a small number of cases the stalking continues for decades. Stalkers follow and spy constantly on their targets in around 75% of cases. In 30% of cases the stalker vandalizes property, and in 10% of cases he harms or kills a target's pet. 11% of women relocate and attempt to live under the radar to escape a stalker.

About the Author

New Zealand born, Jennifer Fulton lives in the West with her partner and daughter, and a menagerie of animals. She started writing stories almost as soon as she could read them, and never stopped. Under pen names Jennifer Fulton, Rose Beecham, and Grace Lennox she has published fifteen novels and a handful of short stories. She received a 2006 Alice B. award for her body of work and is a multiple GCLS "Goldie" Award recipient.

When she is not writing or reading, she loves to explore the mountains and prairies near her home, a landscape eternally and wonderfully foreign to her.

Jennifer can be contacted at: jennifer@jenniferfulton.com

Books Available From Bold Strokes Books

Red Light by JD Glass. Tori forges her path as an EMT in the New York City 911 system while discovering what matters most to herself and the woman she loves. (978-1-933110-81-3)

Honor Under Siege by Radclyffe. Secret Service agent Cameron Roberts struggles to protect her lover while searching for a traitor who just may be another woman with a claim on her heart. (978-1-933110-80-6)

Dark Valentine by Jennifer Fulton. Danger and desire fuel a high-stakes cat-and-mouse game when an attorney and an endangered witness team up to thwart a killer. (978-1-933110-79-0)

Sequestered Hearts by Erin Dutton. A popular artist suddenly goes into seclusion, a reluctant reporter wants to know why, and a heart locked away yearns to be set free. (978-1-933110-78-3)

Erotic Interludes 5: Road Games, ed. by Radclyffe and Stacia Seaman. Adventure, "sport," and sex on the road—hot stories of travel adventures and games of seduction. (978-1-933110-77-6)

The Spanish Pearl by Catherine Friend. On a trip to Spain, Kate Vincent is accidentally transported back in time—an epic saga spiced with humor, lust, and danger. (978-1-933110-76-9)

Lady Knight by L-J Baker. Loyalty and honor clash with love and ambition in a medieval world of magic when female knight Riannon meets Lady Eleanor. (978-1-933110-75-2)

Dark Dreamer by Jennifer Fulton. Best-selling horror author Rowe Devlin falls under the spell of psychic Phoebe Temple. A Dark Vista romance. (978-1-933110-74-5)

Come and Get Me by Julie Cannon. Elliott Foster isn't used to pursuing women, but alluring attorney Lauren Collier makes her change her mind. (978-1-933110-73-8)

Blind Curves by Diane and Jacob Anderson-Minshall. Private eye Yoshi Yakamota comes to the aid of her ex-lover Velvet Erickson in the first Blind Eye mystery. (978-1-933110-72-1)

Dynasty of Rogues by Jane Fletcher. It's hate at first sight for Ranger Riki Sadiq and her new patrol corporal, Tanya Coppelli—except for their undeniable attraction. (978-1-933110-71-4)

Running With the Wind by Nell Stark. Sailing instructor Corrie Marsten has signed off on love until she meets Quinn Davies—one woman she can't ignore. (978-1-933110-70-7)

More Than Paradise by Jennifer Fulton. Two women battle danger, risk all, and find in each other an unexpected ally and an unforgettable love. (978-1-933110-69-1)

Flight Risk by Kim Baldwin. For Blayne Keller, being in the wrong place at the wrong time just might turn out to be the best thing that ever happened to her. (978-1-933110-68-4)

Rebel's Quest: Supreme Constellations Book Two by Gun Brooke. On a world torn by war, two women discover a love that defies all boundaries. (978-1-933110-67-7)

Punk and Zen by JD Glass. Angst, sex, love, rock. Trace, Candace, Francesca…Samantha. Losing control—and finding the truth within. BSB Victory Editions. (1-933110-66-X)

When Dreams Tremble by Radclyffe. Two women whose lives turned out far differently than they'd once imagined discover that sometimes the shape of the future can only be found in the past. (1-933110-64-3)

Stellium in Scorpio by Andrews & Austin. The passionate reunion of two powerful women on the glitzy Las Vegas Strip, where everything is an illusion and love is a gamble. (1-933110-65-1)

The Devil Unleashed by Ali Vali. As the heat of violence rises, so does the passion. A Casey Clan crime saga. (1-933110-61-9)

Burning Dreams by Susan Smith. The chronicle of the challenges faced by a young drag king and an older woman who share a love "outside the bounds." (1-933110-62-7)

Fresh Tracks by Georgia Beers. Seven women, seven days. A lot can happen when old friends, lovers, and a new girl in town get together in the mountains. (1-933110-63-5)

The Empress and the Acolyte by Jane Fletcher. Jemeryl and Tevi fight to protect the very fabric of their world…time. Lyremouth Chronicles Book Three. (1-933110-60-0)

First Instinct by JLee Meyer. When high-stakes security fraud leads to murder, one woman flees for her life while another risks her heart to protect her. (1-933110-59-7)

Erotic Interludes 4: Extreme Passions, ed. by Radclyffe and Stacia Seaman. Thirty of today's hottest erotica writers set the pages aflame with love, lust, and steamy liaisons. (1-933110-58-9)

Unexpected Ties by Gina L. Dartt. With death before dessert, Kate Shannon and Nikki Harris are swept up in another tale of danger and romance. (1-933110-56-2)

Broken Wings by L-J Baker. When Rye Woods, a fairy, meets the beautiful dryad Flora Withe, her libido, as squashed and hidden as her wings, reawakens along with her heart. (1-933110-55-4)

Combust the Sun by Andrews & Austin. A Richfield and Rivers mystery set in L.A. Murder among the stars. (1-933110-52-X)

Sleep of Reason by Rose Beecham. Nothing is as it seems when Detective Jude Devine finds herself caught up in a small-town soap opera. And her rocky relationship with forensic pathologist Dr. Mercy Westmoreland just got a lot harder. (1-933110-53-8)

Grave Silence by Rose Beecham. Detective Jude Devine's investigation of a series of ritual murders is complicated by her torrid affair with the golden girl of Southwestern forensic pathology, Dr. Mercy Westmoreland. (1-933110-25-2)

Too Close to Touch by Georgia Beers. Kylie O'Brien believes in true love and is willing to wait for it. It doesn't matter one damn bit that Gretchen, her new and off-limits boss, has a voice as rich and smooth as melted chocolate. It absolutely doesn't… (1-933110-47-3)

Carly's Sound by Ali Vali. Poppy Valente and Julia Johnson form a bond of friendship that lays the foundation for something more, until Poppy's past comes back to haunt her—literally. A poignant romance about love and renewal. (1-933110-45-7)

Passion's Bright Fury by Radclyffe. When a trauma surgeon and a filmmaker become reluctant allies on the battleground between life and death, passion strikes without warning. (1-933110-54-6)

Tristaine Rises by Cate Culpepper. Brenna, Jesstin, and the Amazons of Tristaine face their greatest challenge for survival. (1-933110-50-3)

Of Drag Kings and the Wheel of Fate by Susan Smith. A blind date in a drag club leads to an unlikely romance. (1-933110-51-1)

100th Generation by Justine Saracen. Ancient curses, modern-day villains, and a most intriguing woman who keeps appearing when least expected lead archeologist Valerie Foret on the adventure of her life. (1-933110-48-1)

The Traitor and the Chalice by Jane Fletcher. Tevi and Jemeryl risk all in the race to uncover a traitor. The Lyremouth Chronicles Book Two. (1-933110-43-0)

Whitewater Rendezvous by Kim Baldwin. Two women on a wilderness kayak adventure—Chaz Herrick, a laid-back outdoorswoman, and Megan Maxwell, a workaholic news executive—discover that true love may be nothing at all like they imagined. (1-933110-38-4)

Erotic Interludes 3: Lessons in Love, ed. by Radclyffe and Stacia Seaman. Sign on for a class in love...the best lesbian erotica writers take us to "school." (1-9331100-39-2)

Punk Like Me by JD Glass. Twenty-one-year-old Nina writes lyrics and plays guitar in the rock band Adam's Rib, and she doesn't always play by the rules. And oh yeah—she has a way with the girls. (1-933110-40-6)

Forever Found by JLee Meyer. Can time, tragedy, and shattered trust destroy a love that seemed destined? When chance reunites two childhood friends separated by tragedy, the past resurfaces to determine the shape of their future. (1-933110-37-6)

Sword of the Guardian by Merry Shannon. Princess Shasta's bold new bodyguard has a secret that could change both of their lives. *He* is actually a *she*. A passionate romance filled with courtly intrigue, chivalry, and devotion. (1-933110-36-8)

Sweet Creek by Lee Lynch. A celebration of the enduring nature of love, friendship, and community in the quirky, heart-warming lesbian community of Waterfall Falls. (1-933110-29-5)

Wild Abandon by Ronica Black. From their first tumultuous meeting, Dr. Chandler Brogan and Officer Sarah Monroe are drawn together by their common obsessions—sex, speed, and danger. (1-933110-35-X)

The Devil Inside by Ali Vali. Derby Cain Casey, head of a New Orleans crime organization, runs the family business with guts and grit, and no one crosses her. No one, that is, until Emma Verde claims her heart and turns her world upside down. (1-933110-30-9)

Chance by Grace Lennox. At twenty-six, Chance Delaney decides her life isn't working, so she swaps it for a different one. What follows is the sexy, funny, touching story of two women who, in finding themselves, also find one another. (1-933110-31-7)

Turn Back Time by Radclyffe. Pearce Rifkin and Wynter Thompson have nothing in common but a shared passion for surgery. They clash at every opportunity, especially when matters of the heart are suddenly at stake. (1-933110-34-1)

Promising Hearts by Radclyffe. Dr. Vance Phelps lost everything in the War Between the States and arrives in New Hope, Montana, with no hope of happiness and no desire for anything except forgetting—until she meets Mae, a frontier madam. (1-933110-44-9)

Innocent Hearts by Radclyffe. In a wild and unforgiving land, two women learn about love, passion, and the wonders of the heart. (1-933110-21-X)

Protector of the Realm: Supreme Constellations Book One by Gun Brooke. A space adventure filled with suspense and a daring intergalactic romance featuring Commodore Rae Jacelon and a stunning, but decidedly lethal Kellen O'Dal. (1-933110-26-0)

Course of Action by Gun Brooke. Actress Carolyn Black desperately wants the starring role in an upcoming film produced by Annelie Peterson. Just how far will she go for the dream part of a lifetime? (1-933110-22-8)

Coffee Sonata by Gun Brooke. Four women whose lives unexpectedly intersect in a small town by the sea have one thing in common—they all have secrets. (1-933110-41-4)

The Temple at Landfall by Jane Fletcher. An imprinter, one of Celaeno's most revered servants of the Goddess, is also a prisoner to the faith—until a Ranger frees her by claiming her heart. (1-933110-27-9)

Rangers at Roadsend by Jane Fletcher. Sergeant Chip Coppelli has learned to spot trouble coming, and that is exactly what she sees in her new recruit, Katryn Nagata. The Celaeno series. (1-933110-28-7)

The Walls of Westernfort by Jane Fletcher. All Temple Guard Natasha Ionadis wants is to serve the Goddess—until she falls in love with one of the rebels she is sworn to destroy. The Celaeno series. (1-933110-24-4)

Erotic Interludes 2: Stolen Moments, ed. by Stacia Seaman and Radclyffe. Love on the run, in the office, in the shadows…Fast, furious, and almost too hot to handle. (1-933110-16-3)

The Exile and the Sorcerer by Jane Fletcher. First in the Lyremouth Chronicles. Tevi and a shy young sorcerer face monsters, magic, and the challenge of loving. (1-933110-32-5)

Force of Nature by Kim Baldwin. From tornados to forest fires, the forces of nature conspire to bring Gable McCoy and Erin Richards close to danger, and closer to each other. (1-933110-23-6)

In Too Deep by Ronica Black. Undercover homicide cop Erin McKenzie tracks a femme fatale who just might be a real killer…with love and danger hot on her heels. (1-933110-17-1)

Hunter's Pursuit by Kim Baldwin. A raging blizzard, a mountain hideaway, and a killer-for-hire set a scene for disaster—or desire—when Katarzyna Demetrious rescues a beautiful stranger. (1-933110-09-0)

Erotic Interludes: Change of Pace by Radclyffe. Twenty-five hot-wired encounters guaranteed to spark more than just your imagination. Erotica as you've always dreamed of it. (1-933110-07-4)

Justice Served by Radclyffe. Lieutenant Rebecca Frye and her lover, Dr. Catherine Rawlings, embark on a deadly game of hide-and-seek with an underworld kingpin who traffics in human souls. (1-933110-15-5)

Justice in the Shadows by Radclyffe. In a shadow world of secrets and lies, Detective Sergeant Rebecca Frye and her lover, Dr. Catherine Rawlings, join forces in the elusive search for justice. (1-933110-03-1)

A Matter of Trust by Radclyffe. JT Sloan is a cybersleuth who doesn't like attachments. Michael Lassiter is leaving her husband, and she needs Sloan's expertise to safeguard her company. It should just be business—but it turns into much more. (1-933110-33-3)

Fated Love by Radclyffe. Amidst the chaos and drama of a busy emergency room, two women must contend not only with the fragile nature of life, but also with the irresistible forces of fate. (1-933110-05-8)

Storms of Change by Radclyffe. In the continuing saga of the Provincetown Tales, duty and love are at odds as Reese and Tory face their greatest challenge. (1-933110-57-0)

Distant Shores, Silent Thunder by Radclyffe. Dr. Tory King—along with the women who love her—is forced to examine the boundaries of love, friendship, and the ties that transcend time. (1-933110-08-2)

Beyond the Breakwater by Radclyffe. One Provincetown summer, three women learn the true meaning of love, friendship, and family. (1-933110-06-6)

Safe Harbor by Radclyffe. A mysterious newcomer, a reclusive doctor, and a troubled gay teenager learn about love, friendship, and trust during one tumultuous summer in Provincetown. (1-933110-13-9)

shadowland by Radclyffe. In a world on the far edge of desire, two women are drawn together by power, passion, and dark pleasures. An erotic romance. (1-933110-11-2)

Love's Masquerade by Radclyffe. Plunged into the indistinguishable realms of fiction, fantasy, and hidden desires, Auden Frost is forced to question all she believes about the nature of love. (1-933110-14-7)

Honor Reclaimed by Radclyffe. In the aftermath of 9/11, Secret Service Agent Cameron Roberts and Blair Powell close ranks with a trusted few to find the would-be assassins who nearly claimed Blair's life. (1-933110-18-X)

Honor Guards by Radclyffe. In a wild flight for their lives, the president's daughter and those who are sworn to protect her wage a desperate struggle for survival. (1-933110-01-5)

Love & Honor by Radclyffe. The president's daughter and her lover are faced with difficult choices as they battle a tangled web of Washington intrigue for…love and honor. (1-933110-10-4)

Honor Bound by Radclyffe. Secret Service Agent Cameron Roberts and Blair Powell face political intrigue, a clandestine threat to Blair's safety, and the seemingly irreconcilable personal differences that force them ever farther apart. (1-933110-20-1)

Above All, Honor by Radclyffe. Secret Service Agent Cameron Roberts fights her desire for the one woman she can't have—Blair Powell, the daughter of the president of the United States. (1-933110-04-X)